PUBLISHER'S NOTE

L ate in 2012, I came up with a crazy idea to create a science ficti
already been working with Mike Resnick on a number of projects and he had become a mentor to me—I was akin to a Writer Child, but on the business side.

My budget was very limited and so I went to Mike who knew (and got along with) virtually everyone in the science fiction field to ask him if he knew of someone who would be willing to take on
the task as editor within the limited budget I had. It never even occurred to me to offer the job to
Mike, since I knew I could not pay him what he deserved.

Mike and I discussed it for awhile and then he stunned me with an offer. He told me he would do
it himself, with *one* condition: I could pay him whatever I could afford, but I had to let him publish
new writers and I would pay them a proper professional rate and pay them on time.

Back when Mike was a young writer, there were all sorts of science fiction magazines that gave new writers
their start. Nearly all the greats, including Heinlein and Asimov, started with short stories in magazines. But
over the years magazines died, less anthologies of short fiction were being produced, and so the writers of
today have more limited options—or at least options that pay anything that can be considered a decent rate.

Mike found this very distressing—that newer writers had fewer and fewer places to sell their stories—and he bemoaned the harm it was doing, both to the field and to young writers.

To him, *Galaxy's Edge* presented him an opportunity to make a difference.

Our scheme was simple; he would go to veteran authors (see the bit above about him getting along
with everyone) and get reprints of their stories on the cheap, and then buy new stories (around half
the magazine) from newer authors.

And he did it entirely on his own. He would get the submissions, he would select the stories and
work with writers to make the stories more readable, and then he would create a complete issue
of the magazine—all so that new writers could headline in an issue with the likes of Orson Scott
Card, Mercedes Lackey, Nancy Kress, George R.R. Martin, Robert Silverberg and so many other
outstanding writers in the field (who also willingly gave of their work to help).

He did this tirelessly, from early 2013 through his recent illnesses, until the very last few days,
when, finally, he was too sick to do any more.

He did this because he loved science fiction, and he loved his writers.

We have lost an icon in this field, and an icon that truly embodied Heinlein's oft-quoted principal,
"Pay it forward." I have lost my very close friend.

Goodbye, Mike Resnick. I miss you.

SHAHID MAHMUD, *Publisher*
January, 2020

PS. How much did I offer to pay him back in 2013?
Two hundred dollars per issue. He just laughed and
said, "That's fine."

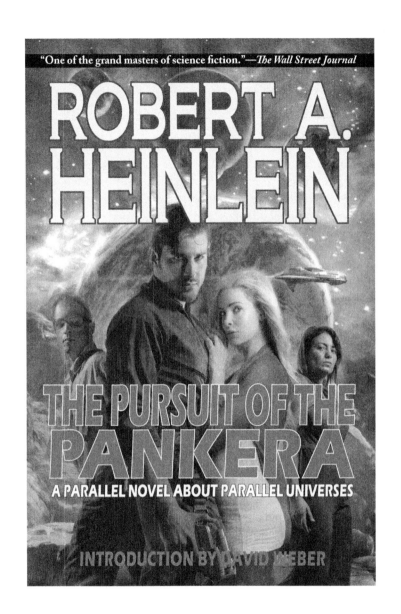

"One of the grand masters of science fiction."—*The Wall Street Journal*

ROBERT A. HEINLEIN

THE PURSUIT OF THE PANKERA

A PARALLEL NOVEL ABOUT PARALLEL UNIVERSES

INTRODUCTION BY DAVID WEBER

MARCH 24, 2020

GALAXY'S EDGE
CREATED BY MIKE RESNICK

ISSUE 43: March 2020

Mike Resnick & Lezli Robyn, Editors
Taylor Morris, Copyeditor
Shahid Mahmud, Publisher

Published by Arc Manor/Phoenix Pick
P.O. Box 10339
Rockville, MD 20849-0339

Galaxy's Edge is published in January, March, May, July, September, and November.

Please check our website for submission guidelines.

ISBN: 978-1-61242-491-0

SUBSCRIPTION INFORMATION:
Paper and digital subscriptions are available (including via Amazon.com) . Please visit our home page: www.GalaxysEdge.com

ADVERTISING:
Advertising is available in all editions of the magazine. Please contact advert@GalaxysEdge.com.

FOREIGN LANGUAGE RIGHTS:
Please refer all inquiries pertaining to foreign language rights to Shahid Mahmud, Arc Manor, P.O. Box 10339, Rockville, MD 20849-0339. Tel: 1-240-645-2214. Fax 1-310-388-8440. Email admin@ArcManor.com.

CONTENTS

EDITOR'S NOTE

by Lezli Robyn

These were not meant to be my words, but Mike Resnick's. This was his magazine. His editorial.

Mike's way of paying it forward.

But instead these words are written by one of his Writer Children. One of many who are grieving this great man's passing, along with the wife he loved so dearly, the daughter he was so proud of, and the friends, peers, readers and fans he so valued.

While I was assembling this issue, filled with so many words from people he loved or loved to publish, I could not help but feel the love he had for *Galaxy's Edge* in every page. When the magazine's publisher, Shahid Mahmud, showed me the cover that would grace this issue, I cried; it could not be a more perfect send off for a fan of science fiction.

For he was foremost a fan of the field, then a writer, then an editor, and—even more importantly for so many of us—then a Writer Dad.

I often joke on convention panels that I bought my collaborator off eBay, for that is where Mike and I first met. I was wanting to buy a signed limited-edition book by Anne McCaffrey and he was the one who was selling it. Sure, I was the one who gave him the money, but what I got in return cannot be measured by any monetary amount. He gave me my career in this field, introduced me to so many people who are now my dearest friends, and he showed me a way to put my heart on paper. That gift cannot be captured by any words I can write here.

What Mike also gave me was the confidence to find my true self. To follow my dreams, quite literally.

You see, I always wanted to be a writer. In fact, when I was sixteen I wrote to Anne McCaffrey asking what I had to do to become a published author. She responded to this wannabee writer's email, like so many famous authors do as their way of paying it forward to the next generation.

And no one paid it forward more than Mike. In the pages of this issue, you will read so many stories of how Mike Resnick inspired people or helped them in their careers. But with me, Mike actually *created* my career. I was not a writer before he came along. I had never written a story, despite my aspirations of doing so "one day."

But Mike was so determined to show me what he knew I could do that he convinced all his peers to gift me signed novels of theirs at my first Worldcon, then at the end of the convention he asked me, frankly, "Wouldn't you like to see your name alongside theirs on the shelf? Because you can do it—I *know* you can."

I had to ship a box filled with forty personally-inscribed books home to Australia, where I was still living at the time. And then, after Lee Modesitt convinced me to take Mike up on his offer to help me start my writing career, I penned my first fiction words, and a new Writer Child was born.

There are so many stories I could tell about Mike—the touching, the funny and the truly inspirational—but I will pick one that says so much about his character.

When our first collaborations were getting published in the pages of *Clarkesworld*, *Analog* and *Asimov's*, we were getting a lot of positive reviews. The buzz was great, and, in fact, we loved writing together so much, we wrote a collection worth of stories—something he had only ever done one other time with another author, his first Writer Child, Nick DiChario.

But a lot of the reviews about our collaborations would forget something. They often would omit my name or put me in parenthesis, like I was an afterthought. I was new to the field, and they were used to giving Mike Resnick the praise—not some random Australian girl.

Mike was furious. I told him it didn't matter, that I took it as a compliment when reviewers would say my new, fledgling words were "the best words Mike Resnick has ever written." It was a real amazing back-handed compliment, because I knew they were reading my words too, and their judgement was also on their quality. To me, being thought of as an author of Mike Resnick's caliber was the highest praise.

But Mike wouldn't have it. He never cared if he got bad reviews—he was never a bad sport—but he did care I wasn't getting what he saw as my due credit. For the first and only time in his forty-plus year career, he emailed all three of those reviewers (all from reputable reviewzines, I might add) to make a complaint—and he dressed them all down:

"There is a reason why there is two names on the byline of this story, and the only reason why Lezli's name is not first, as the primary writer, is because it is precedent for the bigger name to get first credit. Please amend your reviews accordingly."

And they all did. Every single one of them. Because not only was Mike my mentor, my friend, but he was also my number one fan and my fiercest protector as my Writer Dad.

I realize, in many ways, this issue is our last collaboration. One last publication with Mike Resnick & Lezli Robyn together on the same byline. And boy does it both break my heart and make me so incredibly proud. I know Mike was happy for me to become editor of this magazine after him—was "chuffed," even (a word I taught him that he so loved to use). I don't think it is possible to fill his shoes, for those are really big shoes to fill. But I do hope I can step most assuredly in his footsteps, follow his direction until I forge my own path with this magazine to bring it into the future.

This issue of the *Galaxy's Edge* is filled with the stories he bought as editor, and many appreciations and tributes to him as a writer, editor, friend, husband and father. You will read about how Mike Resnick was an incredible author and the best Writer Dad a fledgling author could wish for.

This magazine now belongs to his Writer Children, and their children after that. And I think that is exactly how he would have wanted it. For his legacy to go on. For new words from new writers to find a home. For a new generation of Writer Children to be born.

And what could be a better legacy than that?

THE MIKE AND NICK SHOW

by Nick DiChario

In the months and years to come, I'm sure many people will write about Mike Resnick, the author. As they well should. His multiple awards, books and writings, and impressive career accomplishments deserve to be acknowledged in the science fiction and fantasy community. What awards did he win? Which works were nominated and who published them? How many anthologies did he edit? At what conventions did he deliver his most legendary and hilarious Guest of Honor (GOH) speeches? I'll leave all that to the genre experts and trivia buffs. It's Mike, my friend and mentor, I'd like to talk about here. For those of you who knew him well, you might see your own stories somewhere within mine. For those who didn't, maybe you'll come to know Mike a little better and understand why so many of us loved him as much as we did.

The first time I spoke to Mike was by phone back around 1990 or so. I was struggling my way through a summer creative writing workshop at Brockport University with Nancy Kress. Mike called Nancy one evening after class and asked her if he could speak to me. At first, I thought she was joking. Mike and I didn't know each other. Why would a giant in the science fiction world want to talk to an unknown kid taking a creative writing seminar in upstate New York? It made no sense. Until I got on the phone, and Mike said, gruffly, "What did you think you were doing sending an unsolicited story to an invitation-only anthology?" Then it hit me. It was true that I'd submitted a story to Mike for his Alternate Kennedys *anthology. And it was true the anthology was by invitation only and I hadn't been invited. But Nancy had read the story and thought it was a good fit for the book. She'd encouraged me to send it and use her name in the cover letter. And yet here was Mike, one of the biggest names in the field, scolding me for it over the phone. I was sure my career was over before it began. But a few seconds later (it felt like an eon) he let me off the hook. As it turned out, it was Mike who was* joking. He loved the story and wanted to publish it. Ha ha. *Meet Resnick, the comedian.*

Mike's interest in the story launched my writing career. He bought "The Winterberry" even though it had been rejected everywhere else I'd sent it. He saw something in it, and he saw something in me, that he was willing to bet on. Not long after that, I met Mike for the first time at MagiCon in Orlando (1992), my first Worldcon. Mike took me on that year as his project, guiding me through "the hucksters room," introducing me to everyone he knew, dragging me to parties, and showing me how to get everything there was to get out of a convention, and then some. We became fast friends. Then collaborators. Then lifelong comrades.

Mike never stopped advocating for me. Every time he edited an anthology, he'd ask me to contribute to it. For a while, in the mid-90s, that was a lot of books and a lot of stories. By then he knew I was going to have a tough time publishing in the genre. I didn't write traditional science fiction or fantasy. My work tended to fall between the cracks. He knew I couldn't help it, and he didn't want me to change, so he asked me to collaborate with him, thinking his name would help me sell. He was right. I had a lot to learn back then and took advantage of his experience and professionalism. We loved writing together and eventually produced enough stories to publish a collection of our own titled Magic Feathers: The Mike and Nick Show (2000). Once you pen a book with someone, you have a special bond that will never be broken. Now, Magic Feathers, nearly forgotten by almost everyone else, holds some of my fondest memories of Mike and our time working together.

Our friendship would change not only my trajectory but Mike's too. He could never get over the fact that the Hugo and World Fantasy nominated story, "The Winterberry," could pile up so many rejections before it crossed his desk, a piece that would later be reprinted several times in several countries and end up in an anthology titled The Best Alternate History Stories of the 20th Century. This was a wakeup call for him. He hadn't realized how difficult it had become for new writers to break into the field. He decided he needed to do something about it, or we'd run the risk of losing

talented authors to other genres. In that spirit, he made it a point to publish beginning writers whenever he could. He started collaborating with more newbies, helping them jumpstart their careers, and he supported them as he'd once supported me. Whenever he went to a conference, he'd tell the tale of The Mike and Nick Show to anyone willing to listen. His mantra was, "Pay it Forward!" And he did. Every chance he got. His new discoveries would eventually number so many we'd come to be known collectively as "Mike's Writer Children," and he loved every one of us.

Once Mike got a taste for collaborating, he couldn't get enough. He'd soon expand from working with new authors to working with experienced ones. In addition to me, he'd go on to collaborate with Barry Malzberg, Catherine Asaro, Harry Turtledove, James Patrick Kelly, David Gerrold, Nancy Kress, Pat Cadigan, Eric Flint, and Janis Ian, among others. Enough to fill two volumes of work, With a Little Help from My Friends (2002), and With a Little More Help from My Friends (2012). He enjoyed every minute of it. All this while producing his own books and stories, selling options to Hollywood, winning Hugos, Nebulas, HOmers, American Dog Writers awards, and international honors from Spain, Japan, France, Poland, etc. Sixteen years after Magic Feathers, he'd publish his only other collaborative short story collection with someone not named DiChario: Soulmates, with Lezli Robyn, who is now my good friend and the new editor of Galaxy's Edge.

I came to love Mike for so many reasons I've lost count. One of the biggest was that he and his wife Carol loved my parents. When I brought Mom and Dad to Worldcons, which I often did, the Resnicks couldn't wait to see them. My folks (Nick and Josie) were not SF readers, writers, or fans, but Mike and Carol took time out of their busy conference schedules to share a meal with them or take them on a tour around town. This meant the world to me. Mike and Carol had almost nothing in common with my parents, other than me. Mike and my dad shared a birthday (March 5). Mike also loved my mom's cooking, which he experienced for the first time in 2009 when he visited my hometown of Rochester, NY, to be GOH at

Astronomicon. After that, he tried every gimmick in the book to get Josie to move to Cincinnati and take over the cooking duties at the Resnick household. Never mind what Carol and Nick might have to say about it. Mama's Sicilian spaghetti sauce had mesmerized him.

Of course, I was not naïve to the fact that Mike had much closer personal relationships with other people than he did with me. But I can honestly say it never felt that way. Whenever I produced a story, he insisted upon reading it. If I needed advice (writing or otherwise), he was always there for me. Always. If I needed a favor, he'd drop everything to do it. Always. He asked me to write the introduction to his special edition of Seven Views of Olduvai Gorge *(1994) when I was an absolute no-name. He could have asked any high-profile writer in SF to do it, and they would have jumped at the chance. When I asked him to write the intro to my first novel,* A Small and Remarkable Life *(2006), he couldn't have been more excited. Mike believed in me more than I believed in myself. He never gave up on me, even though there were times when I gave up, when I thought I was falling short of his expectations and mine, when I wasn't writing or publishing enough, or when I was simply feeling all the insecure things authors feel because we are who we are and we do what we do. But let me be clear. That was how I felt, not Mike. For the thirty years that I knew him, he never stopped praising my work or encouraging me to write. After he became the fiction editor of* Galaxy's Edge *in 2013, he kept asking me to send him stories. And he leveraged the magazine to continue publishing aspiring authors right alongside icons in the field. That's the kind of friend Mike was. Faithful to the end.*

But I'm not alone in my deep appreciation for Mike Resnick, am I? My experiences might be your experiences. The Mike I remember could very well be the Mike you remember. He touched the lives of so many people. Friends like Mike come along once in a lifetime. I was lucky, very lucky, to know him for as long as I did. I'm sorry I didn't stay closer to him these past few years when he was going through so many medical challenges. He kept saying he was fine, getting better every day, and

soon he'd be back to his old self again. I wanted to believe him. Maybe you wanted to believe him as much as I did. It didn't seem possible that this extraordinary man would one day not be here with us. And while I'll miss him far more than I can say, I know he lived the life he'd always wanted to live. At the heart of things, he was a SF guy, and he couldn't have been happier for it. He loved Carol and his daughter Laura more than anything in the world, but he considered the science fiction community his extended family.

I asked him once if he could pick between writing one book that would be remembered forever, or writing many books that would all be forgotten, what would he choose? He didn't even hesitate before saying that if writing many books meant he could live the life he was already living, and writing one book that would last forever meant he'd have to give it all up, the answer was obvious. He was living his dream. He didn't need anything more. Being remembered couldn't hold a candle to that.

But we will remember him. And we will hold the candle he has lit in us all.

EDITOR'S NOTE: This issue of the magazine is the last one filled completely with fiction Mike bought for the magazine. This story also one of the last pieces that Mike acquired for Galaxy's Edge, *and his email response to the author when he bought it was so indicative of his love for great writing and bolstering newer authors. I thought I would share his response with our readers: " 'Life is too Short to Drink Bad Wine' isn't really a science fiction story. It certainly isn't a typical* Galaxy's Edge *story. What it is is the best and most moving story that has been submitted here in years, and there is no way I'm not going to buy it and proudly run it. Beautiful job!"*

Gerri Leen lives in Northern Virginia and originally hails from Seattle. In addition to being an avid reader, she's passionate about horse racing, tea, and creating weird one-pan meals. She has work appearing in Nature, Escape Pod, Daily Science Fiction, Cast of Wonders, *and others. See more at gerrileen.com.*

LIFE IS TOO SHORT TO DRINK BAD WINE

by Gerri Leen

The water is beating on the sand as the sky starts to change: the last sunset of the world. The last night for the soft slurp of water hitting the dock she's sitting on. For the snap pop of fish jumping and the soft, sweet flash of a firefly.

Her phone buzzes with an alert: someone has come in the side gate. She's left it unlocked, ever since the newscasters could no longer sugarcoat what was happening. She didn't call him, didn't send him a text or an email or some old-fashioned romantic piece of paper with scrawled sentences full of love. She didn't reach out to him at all, but he's been the first thing she thinks of when she wakes up and the last thing she sees before she closes her eyes. Impending doom has made her memory of him clearer; when she tried to remember his face before, all she got was a cloudy image.

She hears him coming down the dock. His stride is not as assured as it once was. He limps a little, but when she turns to look at him, his smile is no less bright than when they were young. And his face—his beloved face—even older, it still moves her so.

He holds up a bottle of wine and two glasses. "I come bearing gifts."

In the dim light, she sees etched lines on the glasses. He had them made on a trip to Italy. Back when things were easy and uncomplicated and life consisted of drinking coffee in plaza cafes, exploring new restaurants in an attempt to try every kind of pasta, seeking out the best negronis at bars littering the tourist areas, and making love in every way they could think of.

She smiles, and it's not her normal sour smile that those who know her now probably think is the only smile she's capable of. It's the smile of her youth, of the time she spent with this man, when love was new and a revelation and not something that happened to others. "Our glasses. You kept them."

"They resisted being given away. I tried, several times, but I could never quite bring myself to put them into the bag for the charity shop."

She nods, understanding. The glasses don't have their names on them. Nothing so sappy. The etching is an age-old pattern, or so they were told at the time. One that would bring good fortune, healthy children, and a strong union. It brought none of those things but despite everything, she still loves this beautiful crystal.

"I can't believe you came," she says as she takes the bottle and glasses from him. "After all these years."

"I can't believe you didn't think to invite me," he says with just enough pepper in his voice to let her know that the past isn't forgotten—just forgiven. "It's the end of the world. Who else would I spend it with?"

"I imagine there are plenty of women who might have liked to breathe their last with you. But I'll admit it: I hoped you'd come."

"That's why the gate was unlocked? Dangerous, you know. Not everyone believes it'll all be over. They're stockpiling."

"Then they're fools." But isn't that what she's doing in some ways? Those others want water and food and probably guns. She wants this man, all to herself, a surplus of her own kind, the thing that will get her through this.

She waits until he has plopped himself down next to her, till he swings his legs over the water the way she's done, before handing him the bottle of wine.

He takes out a corkscrew, the basic "waiter's friend" kind—it looks like the one he used to carry in his pocket just in case. The wine's a simple red they loved when they were young, before their palates grew up and moved on.

She knows they both have bottles in their cellars that cost ten times more, but they drank this on their first date. They drank it the night they first made love. They drank it when his father died and when her mother, lonely and wasted, drove the wrong way into traffic.

She drank it the night she lost his baby. She quit drinking it the night he left her.

Or did she leave him? Depends on who you ask, she supposes. He did the actual leaving, but the break happened so much earlier, the subtle drawing back, until there was nothing left of them.

"I've missed you," he says as he hands her a glass.

She sips the wine and tries not to make a face. This isn't good wine, and yet, for tonight, it tastes right.

"The normal response would be 'I missed you too,'" he says, not turning to look at her, simply staring out to sea, his hair lit by the last rays of the sun.

"I never let myself miss you. We were done." She plays with the glass, swirling the wine as if to check its legs before finally putting it down. "I couldn't afford to miss you."

He waits, and she thinks he'll have to break the silence because she doesn't plan to say more, to share more, not after they've been apart so long.

But he's so quiet, and he drinks their wine so easily, that she finally whispers, "I had to move on. I had to pretend you were gone forever. My heart was broken. You—we broke it."

"I know." His voice is soft and sad and partly guilty and partly accusing. They did this to each other. Neither of them solely the bad guy.

But he'd moved on. A new wife. A new city. A job that took him all over the world. No room for her. No need for her.

No desire for her.

"I never stopped loving you." He pours them both more wine.

'No, you just stopped liking me."

He has no comeback for that.

"I tried to find someone else," she says. "Someone who made me feel even half as alive as I felt with you. I failed. It was easier to be alone. Just be myself with our dog on this beach. To paint pictures of places I'd dreamed of going with you. To make collages of things that broke my heart because no matter how I tried not to, I always managed to put something of us in it." She stops to breathe—the words have come out in a rush, as if they've lived for years waiting to erupt.

"I came to an art show you were at. The outdoor one in Atlanta?"

She nods. She was only there once. It was expensive to get a space and the weather had been bad. Sales were horrible, and then her booth had collapsed. That had seemed like the end of the world at the time—now she wishes such simple miseries were all there were to worry about. "I didn't see you there. Was this before or after the wind knocked down my booth?"

He laughs softly. "It was when you were setting up. I was...in the area. I had a hunch you'd be there, so I went."

He used to do that all the time. Find her places she hadn't even known she was going to go. Showing up around corners or smiling at her in doorways like: "There you are."

"You didn't say hi."

"It didn't seem right to. You had a guy helping you."

Mark. The wrong guy for her. Too nice maybe. Willing to be used, to be stepped on. The worst possible thing to give to someone like her. "He wasn't anyone important."

"Good." He meets her eyes. "Should I take that back?"

"What difference does it make now?" She points up, in the direction of the sky, but the asteroid will hit them on the opposite side of the planet. Will the Earth blow apart? Will she and he still be on the same little piece of terra choking for air?

"Did Caesar like him?"

She laughs. "Hated him. Growled at him every time he came in the house." Her throat tightens when she thinks of their dog. He lived to be thirteen and he never stopped looking out the window around five o'clock, tennis ball held securely, as if someday everything would go back to normal and his master would come home. "I buried him in the yard."

"I'm sorry. I loved that dog."

"I should have let you take him. He might have been happier with you."

"No, he was our dog, but I think if he couldn't be with us both, then I felt better knowing he was here with you—that you weren't alone."

Talk of poor dead Caesar is making her sadder than she ever gets thinking about the asteroid that will soon obliterate the planet. How will it start, this death from outer space? Will they be swept out to sea by a tsunami—should they get off the dock? But she doesn't want to. It feels right here.

"I thought you might apply for the ark program. With your computer skills..."

She'd thought about it. Briefly. Art had never paid the bills and coding came easily. "There were others. More eager to survive. Cramming in as much knowledge as they could." She laughs softly. "It just seemed like so much work, and for what? To maybe survive?"

"Yeah. To maybe survive."

She doesn't ask why he didn't. He's older than she is and with less fungible skills. And maybe, like her, he's just the slightest bit sick of life.

A problem that will soon be solved.

"Hold my hand," she murmurs.

He reaches for her.

"Not now. When it happens. Hold my hand when it happens. I want to die with you."

"It'd be a sweeter thing if you wanted to live with me." He lifts his glass. "This is horrible wine."

"I know. But it's our wine."

"Yes, full of memories I can't think of without getting angry or hurt."

She feels stupidly wounded by his words. "Go get something else, then. There are plenty of others in the cellar. Ones not so cheap."

"No, this *is* our wine. And it isn't cheap, not with this much heartache, this many memories. This is dear wine. Precious beyond measure."

She swirls her glass again. "A pearl beyond price?"

"Don't mock. I hate when you mock."

"I know. It's probably why I do it." She leans back onto her elbows, kicking her feet through the water, trying to shove away the sadness she feels, going

for breezy, and it comes out all wrong as she says, "Should we have sex?"

He shrugs and doesn't meet her eyes.

"We used to not be able to keep our hands off each other."

"That was lust, not love."

She feels a pang that he remembers it that way, that all they had was a momentary slaking of carnal appetites. Because as good as the sex with him was, he was always more than just that to her.

"I've said something wrong," he murmurs.

She knows he's fully aware of how he's hurt her. It's their gift: the ability to hone in on the most tender spots. "It may not have been love, but it was more than just lust. It was chemistry." She moves so she can rest her head on his shoulder, trying to let go of the hurt, not wanting it to be the last thing she feels.

Especially not now, when she can feel it, the chemistry, the simple thrum-snap of an energy that has always been between them, no matter what they put each other through. "I still love you."

"I love you too." He slips his arm around her waist and pulls her closer. "I always will."

She can't help it; she laughs. How long is "always" anymore? "Do you think everything's really going to end?"

"It ended when we did. This is just a formality. Taking the world off life support."

She smiles. "Poetic."

"I was always more for words than pictures."

"And more for doing than saying." She pulls away so she can see his face. "There's something you should do now."

"Right now?" At her nod, he smiles and leans in, pulling her closer with his hand soft on her neck. "This?" And then he kisses her. The same way he did when they were young and newly in love and nothing terrible had happened to them yet.

Or rather, they hadn't visited such terrible things on each other.

But it's all just semantics and at the end of the world, who cares?

Especially when kissing him is coming home, the smell of his soap—the same after all these years—and the taste of him. Every man tastes different, his skin, his mouth, his breath. And this man tastes like all the things she gave up, all the things she regrets, all the things she wants back.

All the things she has back, even if it's just for a little while.

At least neither of them will have to make the first move, to be the first to walk away. The mighty cataclysm waiting to bring down the planet will end the act in a bigger firestorm than either of them could manufacture. And that's saying quite a lot given they both can be ridiculous drama queens.

He eases away from the edge of the dock, drawing her with him. He makes short work of their clothing—he always was efficient—and then they are together. Risking splinters and the neighbors seeing them.

On this last night of the world, she doesn't give a damn.

"This. No one could ever come close." She kisses him and it's a kiss worn golden by time and pain and soul-deep knowledge. It's the feeling of forever—and of just a few more minutes.

"No, no one ever came close." He smiles and it's a sad but trusting smile.

This is their moment. Their final moment. And there is no one in the entire world she'd rather spend it with.

They finish, nearly clawing at each other, gasping out their pleasure, and then they lie quietly, nuzzling each other, giving each other soft, sweet kisses that each seem like a benediction, like forgiveness in touch, sanctification in the face of mortal danger. She runs her fingers across his cheeks, learning the feel of his skin, now that he is older—as old as he will get.

Of all the things she's ever hungered for over the years, this is her favorite. His touch. His kiss. His body joined with hers. And the lovely moments afterward, before real life intrudes again, forcing them into roles that make them...ugly.

"You're still so beautiful," he says, and he pours the wine out onto the dock like it's an offering to the gods, his smile one of forgiveness and grace.

"I think I'm beautiful when I'm with you. I'm not sure I am otherwise."

"You are. But being it and feeling it may be two different things." He closes his eyes and murmurs something that sounds like "Thank you."

She wonders who he's saying it to.

Suddenly there's a lurch, and the water slaps as violently against the dock as they used to shoot words at each other. So much pain, and for what?

"You're the love of my life," he says, as the world starts to come apart. He takes her hand. "I'll love you to the end of the world and back." His eyes are sweet and calm and generous. "I used to say that and had no idea what it meant. Now—now it seems too little too late."

"It's the right thing at just the right time." She blinks and realizes she's crying because he's more generous than she deserves. "I'll love you until my last breath." Then she laughs.

He laughs too. That's part of their chemistry. That they can speak truth and make a joke at the same time. Their black humor has saved them more than a few times.

"I hope they make it. Up there somewhere."

"I do too." He rolls so they're on their sides, facing each other. Tracing her lips, as the world they know slowly comes apart, he says, "Look at me. Just at me."

There's nothing else she'd rather see.

Copyright © 2020 by Gerri Leen.

SPARKLING MIKE

by Robert J. Sawyer

Here's something most people don't know about my dear friend, the late, great Mike Resnick. His middle name—I kid you not—was Diamond.

Now, as a writer myself (one of the legions who learned much of their craft by reading Resnick and being mentored by him), I know how important the symbolism of names is, and Diamond really was the perfect name for Mike.

First, of course, the guy was brilliant. All you have to do is read any of his dozens of books to know that.

Second, he was multifaceted. Mike wrote some of the most socially relevant fiction in the history of SF (see the "Kirinyaga" stories, for instance), but he also wrote lots of laugh-out-loud funny stuff. And, of course, he wasn't just an award-winning novelist and an award-winning short-story writer, but also a screenwriter, a magnificent essayist, a wonderful fan writer, and an indefatigable anthology editor.

Third, he was transparent. There was absolutely no guile in our Mr. Resnick. He spoke plainly—even bluntly; wrote with Asimovian clarity; and made no secret of his ambitions.

Fourth, as the Diamond Merchants Association's slogan has it, "a diamond is forever." Most twentieth and twenty-first century SF writers will be quickly forgotten. Not Mike. Because his work was often parable, it goes beyond being mere entertainment (although it most assuredly is entertaining); Mike wrote passionately about things that matter to him and will matter to us, as a species, far into the future.

Fifth, like a diamond, our man Mike was known by his statistics: he won five Hugo awards, a Nebula award, the Skylark Award, a Locus award, the Prix Eiffel, two Ignotus awards, two Ictineu awards, the Seiun award, China's Galaxy Award for Most Popular Foreign Writer, the Universitat Politècnica de Catalunya's SF award, six Science Fiction Chronicle awards, four Asimov's readers' polls, a Hayakawa SF Magazine readers' poll, and ten—count 'em, ten—HOMer Awards voted on by the members of the SF Literature forums on CompuServe.

Sixth, Michael Diamond Resnick was the very symbol of generosity. No writer in recent history had done more to encourage beginning talent. He bought lots of first stories for his anthologies and this magazine (and got jaded fools like me back into writing short fiction after having given it up), he freely dispensed advice on all aspects of the writing game, he was an enthusiastic judge and mentor for the Writers of the Future contest, and he constantly took time to promote other writers.

(I'll give you an example: for years at the SF convention Eeriecon in Niagara Falls, New York, I did a panel on Friday evening called "The Late Night Talk Show," where I pretend to be Jay Leno and interviewed the other convention guests about whatever they want to promote. Mike was Guest of Honor at Eeriecon one year, and when it came time for me to interview him, he said, "You'll all hear enough about me over the weekend. I'd rather talk about another writer who excites me," and he spent his whole time in the spotlight promoting William Sanders instead. That's class.)

Seventh, as the saying goes, a diamond is a girl's best friend. There was no better marriage in the SF industry than that between Mike and his lovely, charming, witty wife Carol. Mike always referred to Carol as his "uncredited collaborator," and he dedicated every single book to her first, and then, secondarily, to somebody else.

Eighth, diamonds are associated with Africa, the continent with the world's best mines. Mike's affinity with Africa is well known, and his nickname throughout the SF world was Bwana. Not only did he edit the Resnick Library of African Adventure, and frequently visit that continent, but his African-tinged tales—from short works like "Seven Views of Olduvai Gorge" and "The Manamouki" to novels like Ivory, Paradise, Inferno, and Purgatory—were the sort of thoughtful, important writing that let the rest of us hold our heads high when we say we're science fiction writers.

And now, sadly, too soon, he's gone. Rest in peace, my dear friend: you were and evermore shall be a true gem of a man.

Andrew Peery lives in Durham, NC, with his wife and two children. His fiction has appeared in Writers of the Future *and* Orson Scott Card's InterGalactic Medicine Show.

THANK YOU FOR YOUR SERVICE

by Andrew Peery

It was just like Dad to fuck up the gas. Four miles from Chimney Rock, our Datsun sputtered dead on a narrow road with no pull offs. Tall pines grew like a wall beside the pavement, and with the traffic bad in both directions the drivers behind us laid on their horns. I guess every waiting car carried someone who was dying. A scrawny burnout in the Buick behind us screamed out the window about his wife's melanoma, his voice even louder than the mountain's deep machine rattle. I was sixteen and pretty, and I thought he should go rot in whatever shithole town he came from.

Tommy heard the mountain miles before Dad and I had noticed. His ragged breathing slowed, and the wheezing movements of his chest finally smoothed under his Chewbacca T-shirt. He was using less oxygen, needing only one liter to keep his cracked lips from turning blue. It was my job to adjust the flow so we didn't drain the last tank, and it was my job to give him water. We were almost out of time, so I never told Dad that he had stopped drinking water. Eight months of leukemia, and my four-year-old brother was a skin bag of bones.

I should have stayed in the Datsun, but without air conditioning everything smelled too much like Tommy. Dad was standing in the narrow space between cars coming and cars going, the Buick guy so close to him that the man's spit was on his glasses. The dirt bag held a pocket knife, the kind that comes with pliers and a bottle opener and a small useless saw, and he kept tapping the rounded blade on Dad's plaid shirt like it could hurt him. "Not everybody makes it," the guy said. "Some don't even make it through the machine."

"One in forty-nine," my dad said, as though statistics would calm things down.

The guy spat tobacco on the road and made another jabbing motion with his knife. "You push your

car between two trees and get out of my way." I smiled at the idea of my Dad pushing a car. Then I felt guilty, because Mom had laughed at him changing a tire on the day she finally left.

"Put your Swiss Army away before you hurt yourself," I told the loser. I did teen martial arts at the Y, and I knew he would cut his own hand if he tried to stab my father. He was a scrawny five feet tall, shorter even than me, and he wore a cigarette T-shirt with actual cigarette holes in it.

"You bring your daughter to all your fights?" he asked. I stepped forward and kicked him in the balls, taking the greasy knife as he bent forward.

"Just the ones he wants to win," I said. I kicked him again in the stomach and again in the ribs. The big-haired wife with melanoma was healthy enough to scream, but I gave her a look that made sure she stayed in her car.

Dad shook his head, then cleaned his glasses with his shirt. He had the long hair all the English professors liked, and the back pocket of his jeans bulged with a .22 that was more likely to hurt him than anyone else. "I could have handled that, Stace," he said. I nodded politely, as though he could have.

I was wearing cheap pink flip-flops that cut between my toes, and the hum in the earth made my feet itch. The rattle felt like my skeleton wanted to step out of my body, which made me want to get in the Datsun and put big round tires between me and the ground. Three cars behind us I saw an army jeep, and I walked back to tap on the window. "This thing got a gas can?" I asked.

The soldier inside was huge, with an Afro cut to stubble and a uniform covered with ribbons and medals. I spent enough time with base kids to know that the bars made him a lieutenant and the tan hat made him a ranger. He blinked a few times, surprised that I was there. Then he lifted enormous hands off the wheel and smiled. "I don't want trouble, young miss," he chuckled.

"Yeah, yeah," I said. "Help us out so we can keep traffic moving."

"Of course." He nodded toward the guy crawling away from my Dad. "Us fighters have to stick together." The metal jeep creaked and groaned as the giant twisted out from behind the wheel, arms the size of my waist pushing the rest of him out of the door. I should have known what he was even then, but I couldn't stop looking past him. A woman was almost asleep in the passenger seat, her brown face gaunt and haunted like Tommy's. She watched me for a moment, like she was thinking of what to do with me, then closed her eyes from the effort. I was going to ask the ranger what cancer she had when I noticed the silver circle on his uniform.

"You're a glow soldier." I freaked and took two steps back, squinting to look for a halo of radiation around him. The base kids said you could see it, even years after a soldier had been altered, but the base kids were usually wrong. The lieutenant held up his giant-sized hands, trying to calm me down.

"Nothing happens fast," he told me, walking around to the back of the jeep. "You won't get hurt standing there, and all these people are safe in their cars." He unfastened the can on the back bumper, lifting twenty gallons with one hand. Dad watched him without blinking, wanting to trust a black man but uncomfortable with the massive soldier.

I looked back at the woman. She would have been pretty when she was well, with a long neck and high cheekbones. At the scoop of her tank top I saw a bandage with dried brown blood. I wondered how she could stay with him, always knowing what was going to happen. "How long does it take before she gets sick?" I asked.

"Weeks," he said, walking toward our car. "It takes about eight weeks before I give my wife a new cancer."

☼

Dad drove another two hours to the staging area, the traffic winding past abandoned tobacco fields and boarded-up farm houses. I would have moved away too. The alien machine sounded like a bag of hammers dropped through a glass table, all of it shaking the pennies in our cupholder. Volunteers stood along the road, handing out foam ear plugs to anyone who wanted them, and billboards spelled out warnings in English and Spanish:

US ARMY NOTICE

No human knows how the Chimney Rock machine works.

The machine cures cancer in most people who pass through.

One in forty-nine people do not come out the other side.

We do not know what happens to the disappeared.

So of course Dad waited too long. Only I was certain that Tommy wouldn't vanish.

The Army had clear cut the forest for parking, and privates barely older than me directed cars into rows along the muddy, torn-up ground. We weren't allowed to drive the rest of the way, but medics helped patients and their families into buses or the gated backs of cattle trucks. I saw a Chinese man weeping as they took his dead wife out of a green Chevette. She was stiff, and it took the men a few tries to angle her body out the door. I turned around in my seat to make sure Tommy was still breathing.

The ranger's jeep was waved out of line toward a road with no civilians. At sixteen I was pissed about everything, but I figured the lieutenant had earned a faster trip up the mountain. The soldier who checked his ID stood so far away I doubted the kid could see his picture. The other guards stayed behind, gripping the rifles on their chests and looking down at their feet. At this distance, I realized a silver circle was painted on each side of the jeep, making it obvious who the vehicle was carrying.

"Sir, you're going to park over there," a private shouted at my Dad, and at the sound of his voice Tommy stirred and opened his eyes.

"Stacy," he said, "I remember my code word." It was hard to hear him, so I unbuckled and climbed in back.

"Don't worry," I said, trying to sound confident.

"I won't forget," he said. Then his eyes rolled back into his head and his whole body started shaking.

Dad shouted for a medic while Tommy's lips turned a deep blue. Two boys in camo opened our back doors and pulled my brother away from me, laying him onto the dirt. One uncapped a syringe and injected him in the shoulder. The other checked his pupils with a flashlight. They both had peach fuzz mustaches like the boys who asked me out, and in the headlights of cars around us their pimples looked enormous.

"Sir," the injection one said, "I don't think he'll make it to the top. It's a slow ride, and once you get up there you'd have to wait in line."

I knew the ranger was behind me without even turning around. "Put them into my jeep," he said.

The private frowned. "Standing orders, sir. No civilians on the back road."

The lieutenant looked down at the medals on his uniform, most of them for planets I couldn't name. "We should talk about those orders. Perhaps you and I could sit in the barracks and discuss them. How many hours do you think that would take?"

The medics both shook their heads and carried Tommy to the jeep. The thin woman stood beside it, waving them toward her.

"It's not that we aren't grateful," the private said, backing slowly away.

"I know you are, son," the ranger said, stepping even closer to him. "You probably want to shake my hand." The kid took off running, sprinting away into the long rows of cars.

The inside of the jeep was quiet, with insulation that would let me curse at the ranger when he drove off the side of a cliff. I had been in beater Mustangs with stupid boys who raced, but the soldier hurled his boxy machine up the road like he wanted to kill himself. My Dad was pale white and sweaty. The jeep threw him against the seat belt and the door, one collision starting a trickle of blood down his forehead, but he still kept a tight grip on Tommy.

"Why does your brother have a code word?" he asked me.

"Some kid told Tommy the machine replaces people with aliens. Tommy was scared, so I gave him a code word that only we know. When he comes out the other side, he'll tell me to prove that it's him."

I knew my idea was stupid, but Tommy had calmed down once I came up with a plan. I thought Dad might ask for the actual word, and there was no way I would tell him. He just nodded, though, ducking his head when a bump threw him against the roof.

The lieutenant's wife seemed pleased to have us, and she laid a thin, delicate hand against the cheek of her husband. He gave her a quick wink, then turned back to the road. She watched him for a while, smiling and then not smiling. It reminded me of my mom watching Tommy asleep in his bed. I don't think he was sick when she left, but she didn't come back when Dad told her.

Through the trees, I saw the machine ring lit from skeletal towers the army had built. As the road straightened out the full entrance came into view, a sparkling black circle set in the face of the mountain. Images rippled over the surface, thousands of moving sculptures that ran and fought on the stone. Glow soldiers battled beside squishies the size of small dogs, their hands lightning bright with radiation. The aliens looked like they did in our textbooks, eyeless tubes with wispy tentacles. I could see why squishies died so easily, even with all their technology. Watching them slither forward left me feeling sick.

"Why did you agree to fight for them?" I asked.

The ranger looked at his wife, who nodded to give him permission. "Anne had her first cancer before I went through the process. The army docs said she didn't have long, and I knew what the squishies were promising. When soldiers signed up they cured our family members before the machines were even built." On the mountain, something like a dragon with three heads attacked, vomiting burning acid onto the soldiers. The lieutenant tightened his grip on the wheel, and I knew better than to ask him more questions.

There was no line for us. The entrance to the machine was thirty feet above the ground, a polished spit of black rock that stopped in the air. Privates waved us past a long maze of chain link filled with the dying, people on stretchers and in wheelchairs pushed by exhausted family members. "It's like a shitty amusement park," I muttered. Then we started up stone steps carved into the mountain, Dad carrying Tommy and leaving me to lug the oxygen tank.

Once we reached the spit there were no more soldiers. We were high above a valley, with the slick water of a lake in the distance below us. The tunnel was barely high enough for people, and the inner walls were the same glittering black as the surface of the mountain. The soldier's wife walked forward, and her face appeared in the crystals. She was almost inside when she took a wheelchair from beside the entrance and brought it back to us, helping my father put Tommy down. "Well come on," she screamed in my ear, pointing in case I couldn't hear her. "You have to bring your brother."

My dad shook his head and tried to take the chair himself. The ranger put one hand on his shoulder, then pointed to the side of the mountain. My face was there beside Tommy's, and I wondered if I might have cancer too. The ranger shouted some sort of explanation that none of us could hear. I grabbed the wheelchair and ran into the gloom before I could change my mind.

Inside everything was quiet. My dad was saying something behind us, but I couldn't hear him. "My husband always finds someone to walk with me," the woman said. She put her hand to my head, the same gentle touch she had given the lieutenant. "We should hurry," she said, "because there is something I will need you to do."

☼

The tunnel was always turning, sometimes in long curves and sometimes with sharp angles. We went so deep into the mountain that water seeped from the walls, pooling darkly around our ankles and sloshing around the wheels of Tommy's chair. I knew there were people near us but I could never hear or see them. The woman and I walked by ourselves in the soft light of the crystals, a faint glow that let us see each other and the area just ahead. When I took off my shoes the floor felt like sand at the beach, soft and warm beneath my feet.

"Can you smell it?" the woman asked. "It's like a field of lavender." I couldn't smell anything but Tommy, who seemed to be barely breathing, but I nodded in the way that grownups expect.

I kept waiting for the woman to tell me what she needed. She stayed quiet, though, sometimes running her fingers through the grit of the walls. The flesh on her legs thickened, and twice I saw muscles ripple underneath the thin fabric of her shirt. At one point she sighed so pleasurably it was embarrassing to be near her. I kept the wheelchair between us while Tommy made his own groans and grunts, mostly hidden under the dirty fabric of his blanket. I was scared to look down at him, afraid he might be dying. Every time I looked behind me there was no light at all.

After an hour a small breeze from ahead smelled of pine trees and diesel. The woman turned around to face me, and I could finally see her for the beauty she was, wide brown eyes and round cheeks like a sculpture, all carried by the thin, muscular body of a runner. She ran her hands over her arms and shoulders, enjoying the feeling of her own skin, but her face was utterly somber.

"I always wanted a daughter with Cal," she said, then looked down at the ground and sighed. "Do you know what happens now?"

I nodded sadly.

☼

My Dad and the lieutenant waited at the end of the tunnel, scuffing their feet on the ramp and trying not to look at each other. In the mud-wet chair Tommy kicked off his blanket, a healthy four-year-old who still smelled like gym socks and shit. He took a deep breath and cried out for me, and I lifted him onto my chest. He was incredibly heavy, back to the kid he had been. I pushed his sweaty hair out of his face and laid his head against my shoulder.

The lieutenant stepped to the side to see if his wife was behind me. I was afraid he would approach me immediately, but he only sat on the ground and covered his face with his hands. I could finally see the radiation, a sad blue glow around his fingers. None of it was fair, and I didn't know what I would tell him.

"Just say the machine took me," she had said. "Tell him that I walked around a corner and then I was gone." She was backing up a second tunnel, a dark granite passage much older than the alien machine. Trees rustled in the night air above her, and once she reached the top she would disappear into the forest.

"Cal has suffered so much," she said, so quiet I could barely hear her. "I can't stand getting sick again, but it would break his heart to know." She gave me an unconvincing smile, doing everything she could not to cry.

"You could just fucking stay!" I shouted. Instead she turned and started to run, quick upward strides into the world above us.

Outside of the tunnel, Tommy nuzzled into my neck in the way that only little kids do. "Han Solo," he said happily. "It's still me! It's still me! It's still me!"

"I know it's you, buddy." I hurried him past the ranger and into the arms of my dad. The steps beyond them went down to the waiting line of buses, and I took them two at a time. I was only sixteen, and I let my dad turn back to comfort the lieutenant. It was best, I decided, if I told the man nothing at all.

APPRECIATION

by Harry Turtledove

I'm not going to spend much time talking about Mike Resnick the writer. Unlike—dammit!—the man himself, his work is still there. It speaks for itself. Suffice it to say that he wrote a lot, and just about all of it was mighty good. He won five Hugos and a Nebula, among other awards, and he was nominated for more rocket ships than a medium-sized country owns. He was a Worldcon Guest of Honor. He deserved all the acclaim he got for his work, and more besides.

No, I want to talk about Mike Resnick the Mike Resnick. We were friends for somewhere between twenty and thirty years, which was about half his time in science fiction. He knew or had known everybody in the racket. He was a student and historian of science fiction, of science-fiction publishing, and of science-fiction publishers. He could tell stories about them, and he did. Oy, did he ever! Some of them showed up in the SFWA Bulletin columns he did for so long with Barry Malzberg. Some were oral only, told at cons or over dinner. Those were the good ones.

We collaborated on a short story. The process was easy and enjoyable, which collaboration isn't always. I sold him a few things, originals and reprints for Galaxy's Edge. *Yes, he edited, too, of course, and did that well. But the other thing Galaxy's Edge is about is being a forum for new writers to get their words in print. Mike always wanted to see that happen and cooked up a way to make it so. Mike was a mensch, and Mike was a makher.*

A mensch is an all-around good person. "Gentleman," in the older sense of the word, comes fairly close, but mensch is more down-to earth. Mike was always that. If somebody was down on his or her luck, he would find a way to help that did the most good. And he was a makher, a fixer, a doer. If he couldn't find a way to help, he'd make a way, and get other people to give him a hand in the doing.

He introduced me to Janis Ian, which still blow my mind after close to twenty years. He put up with my bad puns (I put up with his, too). He and I talked baseball. He and my wife Laura talked

Broadway while his wife Carol and I talked birding. I'm going to miss him like hell. A big piece of my world, a big piece of the SF world, left with him. We're better because that piece was there as long as it was.

A FRENCH TRIBUTE TO MIKE RESNICK

by Jean-Claude Dunyach

More than twenty years ago, when the French SF magazine Galaxies *was created, it was decided to organize each issue around a major writer, alternatively French and foreign. Mike was the key figure of issue #8, but appeared in issue #2 with one of the Kirinyaga stories. And in half a dozen issues after that.*

The impact of his work was huge (the full Kirinyaga collection was published shortly after, along with large handful of novels).... Mike was the Guest of Honor of the French festival les Galaxiales in 1998; he was again invited in the literary festival Étonnants Voyageurs in 2000 and appeared in the festival's yearly anthology. He also won the prestigious "Grand Prix de la Tour Eiffel" that year—we celebrated on the restaurant at the top of the Eiffel tower. He came back for the festival Utopiales in 2001, then to the Imaginales in 2016 (we even co-signed a story in the festival's yearly anthology, "Queen's robot sacrifice"). And he should have been the Guest of Honor in Utopiales 2019....

More importantly, Mike was one of us. When he first came to a French literary festival, he asked for samples of the local production. He met with our most preeminent authors and offered advice on how to be published in the Anglo-Saxon world. And he really helped us, he welcomed foreign authors in Galaxy's Edge, he always made himself available for those of us seeking advice. I remember his intense curiosity, his dry humor ("What kind of science fiction can we expect from people eating amphibians on a regular basis?") and, above all, his kindness. We miss you, Mike.

Kristine Kathryn Rusch is the only person in the field's history to win a Hugo for her fiction and another one as Best Editor. We're thrilled to have her back in the pages of Galaxy's Edge *again.*

PETRA AND THE BLUE GOO

by Kristine Kathryn Rusch

They squooshed. That's what Petra first thought when she heard them approach. They squooshed.

Worse, they left not-so-little blobs of wet blue goo wherever they went.

Petra stood behind the desk at the Nuovo Italiano Rare Books Library and thanked every god she'd ever heard about that the actual books were behind clear walls. Because these creatures had no respect for anything.

She folded her hands together so that she wouldn't hit the security button below the desk. She'd hit it too many times in the early days of her career here, and she'd become known as Petra the Panicker. Quintavas, one of the guards, even called her Pee-Pee, and winked whenever he did it, as if she appreciated the joke as much as he did.

Maybe she was folding her hands together so she didn't have to call him.

The Bathybobles bounced their way past security, holding their gold passes in their cilia. The gold was striking against their bright blue bodies which made her think of nothing more than ugly pulsing balloons with hair stuck randomly to the exterior.

She tried not to shudder as she watched them bobble inside. That bright blue splotchy trail they left smelled of rotting fish tacos, and made her think of the night she got the job, when she and her then-boyfriend celebrated at a campus food cart, and followed everything with tequila.

She hadn't had fish tacos or tequila since.

The Bathybobles did not speak any human languages. In fact, they did not speak in the way that humans understood speech. Instead, a pale little balloon floated about the group and then broke into pieces, spelling:

We Have Come For Our Book.

The fifth group today. Damn the organizers and their lack of specificity.

The first four times, she'd been polite. But the idea of these squooshy damp things near her precious books made her want to heave. (Okay, to be fair, it was the stench that made her want to heave. But the sentiment remained the same.)

"No, you haven't come for your book," she said, not caring that she sounded both annoyed and rude. She had no idea that Bathybobles could even hear, and she doubted they understood tone.

We Need A Book.

"Read your—" she almost said "damn" and caught herself just in time. "—instructions. You're not entitled to a book. You need some kind of image of yourself—" *Yourselves?* she wondered, and that sent her down the thicket of nouns, proper nouns, and aliens.

If the chair of the museum headquarters had wanted her to deal with aliens, then that chair should have trained her in alien communications. But nooooo, she'd been promised a humans-only job, in a humans-only environment, in the humans-only section of *Nuovo Italiano's Roma Principa.*

She wasn't supposed to interact with aliens if she didn't want to.

Well, she didn't want to, and yet here she was, staring at the fifth group of them today.

They were all looking at her expectantly, with beady black eyes that popped up along the front of their balloony selves. A dozen beady black eyes each.

Oh, these creatures gave her the creeps, worse than the last ones had.

"You need some kind of image of yourselves with a book," she said as firmly as she could. "That's all we can provide here. If you want to *purchase* a book, then you can go to Delia's Old Earth Treasures, which is six neighborhoods from here, in Antique Village. I can give you a map—"

No Map! the broken-up pale bubble read. *Book!*

Oh, great. Their translation program was weak. Who the hell designed this stuff anyway?

She leaned over the desk, raised her voice, and spoke slowly. "I am not authorized to give you a book. I am only—"

Not Give. We Buy.

"Not here," she said. "This is a library. We don't sell anything."

Yes. The stupid balloon was forming to read. *Library. Book Home Base. We Understand.*

"You don't understand," she said, raising her voice even more. Then she realized what she was doing. She was yelling at smelly things that had no ears.

Good job, Petra. Very mature.

But she didn't know what to do. She obviously didn't speak Bathyboble either.

"We. Do. *Not.* Sell. Books," she said, deciding to keep it simple.

The stupid translation balloon thing formed a question mark. Well, that, at least, was clear.

"Go. To. Delia's Old Earth Treasures," she said, just as slowly. "They. Sell. Books."

Not here? the balloon read.

"Not here," she said.

Then there was hissing and burbling. The Bathybobles piled on top of each other, forming some kind of blob. Their cilia merged into hairy tentacles. Two tentacles gripped the desk, pulling it back. Two more reached for her.

She managed to push the security button before she got swept up in a mound of cold blue goo.

✿

Rotted fish tacos really didn't come close to describing the smell. Maybe gigantic mound of rotted fish combined with gallons of cat urine and an undercoating of stale beer came closer. But not much closer.

Petra had never smelled anything like it, and she had never smelled anything like it *on her,* and the only thing that kept her from vomiting was the feeling that she was already covered in vomit—and not her vomit either. Cold vomit, collected from the back of some restaurant that had given all of its patrons food poisoning.

She shook her hands, trying to get the blue goo off them, and then realized it was hopeless. *She* was hopeless. And the white linen dress—*historical* white linen dress that vaguely suggested something one of her heroines, Jane Austen, would wear—was completely and forever ruined.

Petra had donned that dress early in the morning, when she had thought the promotion that the library had signed up for would be decorous, and she needed to be part of that decoration.

She considered wearing something that suggested Earth's New York of the 1930s, where the scavenger hunt rose in popularity among the wealthy. An homage, she thought, to the current scavenger hunt, which had been designed to serve as adventure travel and local promotion.

Of course, it had evolved beyond that—various wealthy alien groups trying to outdo one another by winning the hunt the fastest—but she had never imagined this.

She had imagined herself, leading scores of new tourists through the displays, explaining how, even though books and reading had gone digital five centuries before, collectors still liked the feel of actual paper books, so much that when those collectors first traveled into space, they used up some of their weight allowance to bring a beloved *physical* book.

So many beloved physical books made it into space that the Nuovo Italiano Rare Books Library was actually a branch of rare books libraries all over the human-inhabited system. And each branch, each and every one, had at least one book by Jane Austen.

Only a handful of other authors writing in English could claim that distinction—and only a few of that subset, a very few, were women.

Oh, Petra had imagined her little talk, and then maybe a promotion because her clear love of the written (emphasis on *written*) word would make her invaluable to the library, and her boss would realize what a treasure he had in her, and she would become the head librarian, someone allowed not only to touch the books, but to actually read one without a guard in place to make sure she didn't rip a page out of the book or try to slip it into a pocket.

On some level, she had known that the dream wouldn't become reality, but she hadn't expected it to explode in a geeble of blue goo as Bathybobles ran roughshod over her library.

She wanted to cry.

Instead, she wiped goo out of her eyes as Quintavas the security guard touched the edge of the overturned desk as though it might burn him.

"Where'd they go?" he asked her.

She looked at him incredulously. "Follow the trail," she said, and somehow did not add *you idiot.* "And hurry."

Suddenly, alarms went off throughout the section. She closed her eyes to gather herself, and instead, her eyelids stuck together. She wiped her hands on her dress, then wished she hadn't. All she could do was shake off her hands, and then shove her fingers in her eyes, ignoring the sting, and hoping that nothing bad was happening to her eyeballs.

When she finally got her eyes open, she saw Quintavas slowly picking his way around the bright blue slime trail.

"Oh, for God's sake," she said and pushed past him, deliberately bumping into him along the way.

"Hey!" he said.

"They're getting that crap on the books," she said, "and if the books are ruined, you'll lose your job!"

Somehow, that didn't galvanize him into action. Maybe he thought the books were already ruined. Maybe he didn't like the job.

She didn't care. She loved her job (except on days like today) so she sprinted down what was usually one of her favorite corridors in the entire building.

It was built of real wood from Earth, and if she had given the tourists their imaginary tour, she would have pointed out each type of grain, and which wood was made from extinct trees, and maybe even mentioned how difficult it was to import those woods to this place.

Instead, she could see the slime eating away at the wood's surface, and as she ran, she thanked her lucky stars that she hadn't been the one who suggested the scavenger hunt to promote the library. In fact, she had argued against it.

You like the quiet a bit too much, Ms. Relling, her boss had said. *We need a bit of excitement around here.*

Well, they had excitement, in spades, as the wealthy set in Old New York used to say. The alarms were screeching, and she was running (running!) and that made her breathe in the occasional drop of goo, stinging her tongue and hoping to hell that the goo wasn't peeling the enamel off her teeth the way it peeled the varnish off the floors.

She reached the first T intersection where the main corridor branched into two before a wall of floor-to-ceiling books encased in a clear box that protected them against the light.

And apparently, against Bathyboble tentacles, since goo dripped off the display.

She paused for only a moment, trying to decide which way to go. The screeching alarm seemed to come from everywhere and nowhere, so she couldn't use that as a way of determining where the Bathybobles were and what they had done.

She had to go by the layers of goo. And there was more goo heading off to the right than there was to the left.

She glanced over her shoulder. No Quintavas. He was probably still daintily picking his way past the goo trail, trying to keep his stupid shoes pristine.

Normally, she would hope that the other security guards would hurry to the crisis, but she'd never been in the library during a crisis, and Quintavas's behavior made her doubt the initiative of his colleagues.

So she stopped long enough to do something that was completely forbidden for someone of her level: she broke a tiny seal on one of the walls, activating emergency protocols. Now the security guards in the facility had to respond, as did the guards within thirty minutes of the library.

Anyone who failed would lose their jobs.

On any other day, she would have felt guilty about putting their jobs at risk, but today, she didn't care. She wasn't going to be able to stop the Bathybobles alone.

She rounded the corner, and saw a long bulging line of blue pressed up against a wall display. It took her a moment to realize that all of the Bathybobles had become one long Bathyboble, which was trying to squeeze itself (themselves?) into the cracks between the floor and the protective covering.

Tentacles were forming, and heading for the bookshelves.

If the blue goo destroyed wood floors, it would definitely destroy books—which were, after all, made of wood.

"Stop!" she screeched.

They didn't. The tentacles waved, blue and out of control.

"*Stop!*" she screeched again.

They couldn't hear her. Dear God, she had forgotten that. They probably weren't taking time to read their translation program either.

She had to get their attention.

"*Stop!*" she screeched one final time. "You're violating your participation agreement! If you touch those books, you'll forfeit!"

The tentacles froze as if a hard frost had hit the shelves.

What? the stupid little word bubble appeared over the thick blue line.

"You heard me," she said, although she knew that technically wasn't true. They hadn't heard anything at all. "If you touch those books, you'll forfeit, and you'll never be able to participate in a sanctioned scavenger hunt again."

She had no idea if that was true, but by God, she'd make it true if she had to fight the league to her dying breath.

(Which might be Real Soon Now, considering the way her lungs felt after she'd swallowed even more blue goo.)

You cannot make us forfeit, the pale blue bubble read. *We are district champions.*

"I wouldn't make you forfeit. Any violation of the rules automatically disqualifies you," she said. Or, at least, she prayed it was so, because if it wasn't, she had no leverage at all.

Where were those stupid security guys?

The tentacles waved, and her breath caught, forcing her to inhale even more goo. She cleared her throat so she wouldn't cough.

And then the tentacles slid out of the cracks and back into the long line of blueness. The blueness separated into its various blobs and bounced toward her.

She resisted the urge to kick them.

We need a book! the stupid bubble read.

"No," she said. "You need an image of you with a book, and we can get that from our security feeds."

The bubble's message remained the same, and she was about to repeat herself when the message reformed.

Acceptable.

She let out a tiny huh of satisfaction. Two birds, one little image. A sign that the Bathybobles had found the book for their scavenger hunt, and a sign

that the stupid creatures nearly destroyed thousand-year-old artifacts.

Then she realized that she had killed three birds here. She would have definitive proof for her boss that scavenger hunts involving non-humans were a stupid idea to promote a library in the human section of a human neighborhood of a primarily human city.

She almost told the Bathybobles to stay put, but she doubted they would.

She looked around. No security guards yet. And the alarm sounded far away.

She peered at the clear wall in front of the books. Technically, that wall had not been breached.

The alarm was coming from another part of the library.

Oh, joy.

✿

She corralled the Bathybobles and led them outside the library. She told them if they didn't wait on the sanctioned floor material that could absorb their slime (and yes, she said slime, and yes, it felt good), then she would personally disqualify them.

The Bathybobles vibrated, sending a hum through the area. It took her a moment to realize that her words actually scared them, and that was the Bathyboble equivalent of shaking in fear.

Before she went back inside the library, she stopped in the public restroom and washed off as much goo as she possibly could. Her dress (which was fortunately not dissolving—apparently linen was not composed of wood fiber) was plastered against her body, but there was nothing she could do about that.

She squeezed out the linen so it wouldn't drip, rinsed off her hair and face, and took off her ruined shoes. She rinsed off her legs and feet, then walked barefoot back to the library, carefully avoiding the trail of blue goo she and the Bathybobles had left.

As she stepped back inside, the alarm shut off mid-thrum. A group of Aenrosids huddled near the desk, shifting from foot to foot to foot to foot in unison, as if they were practicing some kind of dance. She had no idea that square four-footed creatures could be so coordinated.

EXCUSE ME, one of them said, BUT CAN YOU POINT US TO THE LIBRARIAN?

"I'm the librarian," she snapped, "and I'm dealing with an emergency. You stand still. If you so much as move a muscle, I swear, I will break you into little pieces."

Then she stomped off, not even berating herself for her unprofessional behavior.

She could just hear them. *Where are the books? We need a book. We'll buy a book. What's a book, by the way?*

She wanted to punch something. She wondered if she punched a Bathyboble, would it squoosh or explode?

She kinda hoped she would find out.

She stomped back to the security room, expecting to find the lazy guards sitting on their butts and laughing at her predicament. Instead, she found the room full of Hairy Maglefesians. She had no idea how they even got in.

They were the size of small dogs. They had probably snuck in when she wasn't looking. She'd heard that Hairy Maglefesians practiced the art of stealth; she just hadn't believed it until now.

She didn't see any of the guards. The Hairy Maglefesians looked at her as if she were going to kill them with long and slow torture.

She was tempted.

As she reached for the comm, the door opened, and Quintavas pushed a young human male into the room. He had a collector's bag, perfectly designed to handle the most fragile items.

"Look what I found on the way to the goo fest," Quintavas said. "The son of one of our sponsors."

The young man raised his hands and said to Petra, "I didn't do anything. Please, help me before this man ruins my reputation."

The young man's fingers glimmered in the light. Petra did something she wouldn't have done two hours before.

She slapped her palm against his.

His skin exploded in light and color.

Bastard.

"If you didn't do anything," she said, "why do you have a collector's bag and protective skin seal?"

Only people who handled fragile collectables even knew what that stuff was.

"I—I never come to the library without them," he said.

"I'm sure that's probably true," Petra said. "It makes theft of valuable artifacts so much easier."

The Hairy Maglefesians chuffed behind her.

"We're not stealing anything," one of them said to her.

"Oh, I know," she said. "You're participating in the scavenger hunt."

"Yes!" it said, its tail wagging. "All we need is a book."

She sighed in exasperation. "All you need is an image of you *with* a book."

"Actually, no," the young man said. "They need a book. It's in the rules."

Her gaze met his. "Give me a copy of the rules," she said.

He called the rules up on a small device, and she realized he could give her anything he wanted to.

"No." She whirled, and spoke to the Hairy Maglefesians. "You give me the rules. And the map."

One of the Maglefesians handed her a device that felt like someone had drooled on it.

She understood the map, but she couldn't read the words, if indeed the scratchings on the screen were words.

She extended the device back to its owner. "Call up the English version, would you?"

The Maglefesian tapped the device with its wet nose. She felt her gorge move again, and she swallowed hard.

If this day ended without vomit, she would be very, very happy.

The English version of the rules came up, in six-point type, sixty-five pages long. But she'd read more complicated documents in her day, and it didn't take her long to find the pertinent section.

The young man was indeed right. Participants had to have the physical artifacts.

Then she leaned over security's internal systems, and found the documents that her boss had agreed to. She had been right too: Images only. Participants were not allowed to touch any physical objects.

She looked at the young man. All of this was designed to protect someone from accusations of theft.

"Quintavas, get your colleagues and shut the library down. No one comes in or goes out."

"You can't—"

She raised her eyebrows at him—the Librarian Glare of Death—and, bless him, he got the message.

"Yes, of course. Yes."

And he backed out of the security room.

"It stinks in here, you know," the young man said. "I have to leave. I have allergies."

She was the one who smelled bad. (Although she knew that Hairy Maglefesians weren't exactly the most sweetly scented creatures either.)

"Too damn bad," she said. "You're staying with me. And you'll be here as long as it takes."

"As long as it takes to what?" he asked.

She raised her head, and looked down her nose at him. "As long as it takes to figure out why you people wanted to destroy my library."

☼

They didn't want to destroy it. They simply wanted one of the most expensive items in the collection, a first-edition *Harry Potter and the Philosopher's Stone* from late twentieth century Earth. On the open market, that book could raise enough money to fund a small country—or a spectacular library.

All in all, sixteen different groups reached the library before the authorities stopped the scavenger hunt and forced everyone to return the items—and/or pay for damages.

The Bathyboble paid the most, at least to the library itself, although Petra believed that when the suits and countersuits were done, the amount the Bathybobles paid would pale in comparison to the fines and fees the organizers of the hunt would pay.

After all, they were claiming a simple proofing error in the regulations was to blame. And that would probably have worked, if the error wasn't repeated in all languages—and if the founder's son hadn't been caught with a collector's bag and skin seals.

Petra followed the proceedings, partly because she had to testify several times and partly because she was feeling vindictive. She couldn't get a new dress to replace that linen one—she couldn't afford it. Not even with her promotion.

She now ran the library. Her boss, who wanted the scavenger hunt to come to the library as a promotional tool, had been fired, and so had his boss and his boss's boss.

Petra didn't have the qualifications to rise higher in the library food chain—yet—and she wasn't sure she wanted to when the time came.

She loved being among the books.

She could touch them now without guards watching her, and better yet, she could read the books whenever she wanted.

It only took her three months to get enough nerve to read the Harry Potter book that started all of this. Her hands shook the entire time.

The archaic language made her struggle. The references to things she did not understand, like drills and cupboards and traffic jams, slowed her down. But she worked her way through it all without using an Archaic English translation guide, and felt as accomplished as she had when she caught the Bathybobles.

Oh, hell. She felt more accomplished.

Because books stayed with you forever. Deeds remained only if they were recorded in story and song—and even then, such accomplishments were hard to understand without their proper context.

She didn't want to give anyone the context, although she had. Nor did she want to revisit that day, although the smell of a fish taco always made her slightly faint.

That, and a glance at the front desk.

She didn't ever want to work the front desk again. She simply couldn't be polite any more.

People came here wanting to gawk at her books. And she would do everything she could to prevent it.

Even if it meant telling her story, and thinking about slime, rotted fish tacos, and displaying her ruined dress.

Even if it meant a bit of notoriety.

A good librarian did what she could do to protect her books.

And Petra was a very good librarian indeed.

Copyright © 2016 by Kristine Kathryn Rusch.

APPRECIATION

by George R.R. Martin

I was deeply saddened to read of the death of Mike Resnick, one of the true giants of contemporary science fiction. Mike has been battling serious illness for some time, so the news did not come as a complete surprise...but it came too soon, too soon, and our field and our community will be the poorer for his absence.

I don't recall when I first met Mike, but it was a long, long time ago, back in the 1970s when both of us were still living in Chicago. I was a young writer and he was a somewhat older, somewhat more established writer. There were a lot of young writers in the Chicago area in those days, along with three more seasoned pros, Gene Wolfe, Algis Budrys, and Mike. What impressed me at the time...and still impresses me, all these years later...was how willing all three of them were to offer their advice, encouragements, and help to aspiring neo-pros like me. Each of them in his own way epitomized what this genre and this community were all about back then. Paying forward, in Heinlein's phrase. And no one paid it forward more than Mike Resnick.

He was fine writer, and a prolific one, as all his Hugo and Nebula nods will testify. After they started giving out those little rocket pins for Hugo nominations, Resnick would wear them on his shirt like medals: pointed up for a story that won, down for a story that lost. That always charmed me. Mike won the Hugo five times; once for novella, once for novelette, thrice for short story (like me, he never won the big one, best novel). He lost a lot more (we had that in common as well). He took that in stride, with a shrug and a smile, in the true spirit of a Hugo Loser.

He never won for best editor either, and as best I recall he was nominated only once, under unfortunate circumstances. That was a pity. He deserved more recognition for his editing. He edited something like forty anthologies, I believe, and he always made a point to fill them with a lot of young aspiring writers, new names and no-names making their first or second or fifth professional sale. I can't say how many careers he helped launch, but it was a lot. In modern times, only Gardner Dozois was more assiduous in searching out new talent.

Mike called his discoveries his "writer babies" and they called him their "writer daddy," and many a time I would see him in the lobby of a con hotel, with a dozen of his literary children sitting around his feet as he shared his wisdom with them...along with a funny story and ribald anecdote or two.

His last great act as an editor was the founding of Galaxy's Edge, a new SF magazine that he launched... in an act of madness that was all Mike...at the time when the old magazines were struggling to survive. Galaxy's Edge always featured a lot of new writers too, and Mike paid them decent rates...a feat he accomplished by twisting the arms of old coots like me to give him reprints for pennies, to free up more money for the newcomers. (Lots of us old coots were glad to do it. Like Mike, we believe in paying forward). I hope and trust that Galaxy's Edge will keep going strong, as a lasting testament to his legacy.

These days, all too often, I meet writers who come to conventions only to promote themselves and their books. They do their panels, and you bump into them at the SFWA Suite, but nowhere else. Not Mike. Mike Resnick was fannish to the bone. You'd find him at publisher's parties and the SFWA suite, sure, but he'd also pop up at bid parties, in the bar, in the con suite. He made more than one Hugo Loser party, both before and after the days I was running it. You'd see him in the dealer's room, at the art show, at the masquerade...his Chun the Unavoidable costume, from Jack Vance's Dying Earth, was a classic. When he appeared on panels, he was funny, sharp, irascible, irreverent, always entertaining... and he would do entire panels without once plugging his own new book, a trick more program participants should learn. The place you'd find him most often at Worldcon was the CFG suite, the redoubt of the Cincinnati Fan Group. He was the professional's professional, sure, but Mike was also the fan's fan. For some writers, conventions are for selling, selling, selling...for Mike, they were more about giving, giving, giving. And having fun. That too. Mike always seemed to be smiling or laughing. He loved science fiction, fantasy, fandom, writing, reading, cons...and he shared his passion with everyone around him.

Science fiction has lost a fine writer, a unique voice, a magnificent mentor...and a profoundly good and decent man.

Morgan Welch is a British writer of science fiction and fantasy, and a Writers of the Future finalist. He lives with his fiancée and dog in Shropshire—the fact no one knows where that is suits him just fine. This is his first appearance in Galaxy's Edge.

THE OPPOSITE OF GHOSTS

by Morgan Welch

The pressure equalized and the airlock door opened with a shriek. Gray dust covered the floor—particles of it hung in the air like dull stars in the cold void of space. But Raine knew the atmosphere was breathable, so she pulled off her mask.

The smell was no better than she'd expected—musty and vaguely metallic.

"You said this thing had been gone three days?" Neiman said, following her inside, his torch-beam sweeping through the darkness. "Looks like it's been abandoned for years. Doesn't feel right."

Raine glanced back at the pilot. He'd flown hundreds of sorties for the Union before she'd brought him into her service—a veteran of countless missions in enemy territory. And yet he was scared of an abandoned cruiser, floating in the black. Strange. He'd kept his flight mask on too. Couldn't blame him, but it was out of character.

She studied what she could see of his face, dark brown skin deeply lined and with a scar that left the side of his head shiny where hair should have been. His eyes shifted as he tried to make out passageways and gantries in the gloom.

He was right though, something about that place *was* unsettling. What could make a Union of Planetary States' cruiser disappear for days, only to reappear light years from where it started? The situation reeked of forbidden tech. Honouria Raine was the only investigator in the area. She'd been sent to get some answers.

"However it feels, we should get this done," she said. "Stay close—the readout doesn't show any signs of life, but we should still watch our step."

"Yes, ma'am." Neiman drew his pistol, braced it against his torch hand, and aimed it just ahead of him on the floor. Ready, but safe. Raine had no weapon but her mind. She touched a hand to the side of her head to check her curls were still in place. A coil of brown hair had worked its way free; she pushed it back behind her ear.

As they walked down the corridors, their boots kicked up clouds of fine dust that would take days to settle again. They passed the bodies of scores of navy personnel, mechanics, and crew. Dry husks of skin. Remnants of clothing and bone.

One room they entered was filled with charred documents and soot from a fire, long extinguished. There were more bodies amongst the debris—flesh scorched by intense heat.

"This wasn't an accident," Raine said. "They were desperate men if they were willing to start a fire on-board ship. But what happened? I can't see any enemies."

"Secessionists? Terrorists?" Neiman suggested. "They would look like all the rest, the bodies are so far gone."

"No, I don't think so. I think these people turned on each other—I'm just not sure why."

They kept going down a featureless corridor. A shiver crept up Raine's back. She knew her feelings must be showing on her face, because Neiman said, "Raine? You OK?"

Dizziness took hold. The investigator stumbled against the bulkhead and clutched at some exposed pipework to keep herself upright. Pain burned in her brain. A voice spoke from the gloom behind them.

"Honouria Raine, Investigator First Class. Yours is the first new face I have seen in centuries."

She looked up, still holding onto the pipes. Three men in navy jumpsuits and tactical gear stood a little way off, their body armor grimy and dull, lights shining from their guns. Behind them, a fourth figure stood. He wore no mask and held nothing in his hands. He was thin and medium-height, with brown hair spiked messily in the middle. Neiman's torch reflected from the man's small gold-rimmed glasses.

"I am Sebastien Tarot, Commander of the Persephone. *De facto* commander, you might say. I've been waiting for a long time, Investigator Raine. I found a way to keep myself and some select individuals alive, but I'm not fond of waiting. Not at all."

It was then Raine realized what was wrong. She could see Tarot and his men with her eyes, but not her mind. When she reached out into the ether, there was nothing. Her second sight slid off them like they didn't exist.

"What have you done?" she found herself saying.

"After the crew realized we were trapped in a rift and set about killing one another for control of the supplies, someone had to take charge. I conducted a little research. I don't imagine the Union would be too pleased, so I'll have to take care of you and your friend." Tarot's voice was flat and calm. "Nothing personal, you understand. I don't want to be the subject of experiments—I prefer to run them myself."

The distortion in the ether tugged at Raine's mind. She could feel psychic energy pouring out of her into a black hole of nothingness. She remained conscious just long enough to hear the crack of gunfire and feel a spray of warm blood on her face.

Then, there was nothing.

✺

Raine woke on a Union transport. Her eyes were blurry, her thoughts nebulous and strange. She mentally checked herself over—apart from a headache, she was unharmed. She rolled her head to the side. Neiman was talking to a medical officer in hushed tones. Raine could see tension in his face; she could feel his concern. She must have reached out somehow with her thoughts, because he turned and saw she was awake.

"What happened?" Raine's voice was barely a whisper.

Neiman poured some water and took it to her. The medic checked some instruments by the bed. She was a plump young woman, with expressive eyes and red hair. "You gave us quite a scare, Investigator Raine. It's good to see your vitals returning to normal." She smiled with white, straight teeth. "How do you feel?"

"Tired," Raine said, tilting her head forward to sip some water. "You seem to have the advantage of me."

"My apologies, ma'am." The medic straightened and saluted. "Lieutenant Corpsman Reid, assigned by Naval Command to accompany you while we're on route to the spire cities on Helios V."

Reid relaxed back into an easy pose. She leaned a little closer: "After your encounter with Tarot and his men, electrical activity in your brain fell to dangerously low levels. We thought you might not make it, but you're recovering well. You're safe. There's nothing to worry about."

Neiman sat on the edge of the bed, his frame obscuring some of the bulkhead lights and saving Raine's eyes from the glare. To Reid he said, "I'll fill her in."

"Of course," said Reid. "But don't tire her—she needs to rest. I'll be back to check on you both later."

Neiman nodded and turned back to Raine as the medic left the room. For a moment there was quiet; the only sounds were bleeps from the equipment and a distant rumble of engines.

"What do you remember?" Neiman asked.

"We were exploring the Persephone, and then…. Those men—they weren't really there. They were just bodies, not people. There was nothing inside. Even psychopaths don't feel like that. Psychopaths have no morals or conscience, but they still exist in the ether. Those men were just empty shells. I could feel my mind pouring out of me, trying to find them, but there was nothing to find. I couldn't stop it."

"You blacked out." Neiman's voice was a low rasp. It was then Raine noticed a dull ache in his mind—the awkward way he was sitting. "What is it?"

"They hit me in the shoulder—it's nothing. I managed to drop two of them and drag you away. Tarot escaped. He didn't care about killing us after all. The cruiser was dead in space, so the remaining operator covered his escape while he made for the ship. I don't know how he got around all the fail-safes and lockouts, but…"

Raine propped herself up on her elbows and wiped a damp straggle of hair away from her face. "He took the *Constellation*?"

Neiman's eyes shifted down and away.

"Vincent Neiman, look at me. You're telling me he took the *Constellation*?"

He met her gaze, face grim. "Yes ma'am. I killed the last of his men, but yes."

She collapsed back onto the bed. "He's taken my damned ship. Well, I suppose we should be thankful we're alive at all."

"We're tracking it, of course. I managed to get a message out and we were picked up by the *Diligence*, but it's just a supply vessel diverted for us by command—not what you'd call fast. He got a good lead on us. It looks like he's headed for the under-city of one of the spire worlds in the Helios system. Maybe to continue his work."

A feeling of dread returned to Raine's stomach. The too-clean smell of the room was making her feel sick. "What do you mean, 'work'?"

"Teams have arrived on the *Persephone* now. Analysis of compounds in the superstructure indicate the ship is *hundreds of years old*. Their best guess, it got caught in some kind of anomaly or rift in space-time. Tarot is probably the oldest human ever to have lived. He may have started off with bionic implants when pieces wore out, but in the end it looks like he resorted to some combination of chemicals that keep brain functions, cell division and mitochondria functioning when the host body should be dead."

"The human part of him *is* dead," Raine said. "So by 'work,' you mean experiments with eternal life? He's turned himself into an abomination."

"Well, his men were killed. Or at least, it looked like it. If they aren't, we'll probably never know. Command will be running some experiments of their own."

They looked at each other for a moment, then he asked, "What do you want to do when we find him?"

"I'm not sure yet. Update me on the planet he's heading for."

"The locals call it Pyrois. It's almost dead, with some spire cities in the northern hemisphere and not much else. A provisional government's been in charge since a civil war three years ago. The spires are mainly home to party members, scientists, elite types. Everyone else lives below and intel says that's where Tarot's gone. He may be looking to charter another ship, but we've forwarded his biometrics to the local authorities. It won't be easy for him."

"That's probably the only advantage we have right now," Raine said. "I can't even get near him."

She felt the beginnings of a plan forming in her mind. It seemed insane, but the more she considered, the more it seemed their only option. It would mean leaving some parts of their activity on Pyrois out of the final report to command, but if it meant completing the mission successfully…

"We have to kill Tarot," she said. "He can't be allowed to live."

"Agreed, but how?"

"We have to inhibit my abilities. With Myalorasadyne."

Neiman gaped at her. "You're going to take *slate*. With all due respect, ma'am, that's… You'd be completely disconnected from the ether. It's dangerous for regular people—who knows what it would do to you. You could become another mindless blank lying in the gutter. You could die!"

She pushed her empathy deep down inside. "I've made my decision."

"There must be another option."

"It's the only way to get close. Any psychic attack would leave me exposed—I'd have to get close to him in the ether, if nothing else. I'd love to just stop his heart, but I can't. All I can do is cut myself off, walk up and shoot him in the head."

Neiman looked as if he might try to argue the case some more, but he didn't. "Let me do it," he said.

"You're going to get me the slate. You're going to help me find Tarot. And then you're going to keep out of my way."

Neiman clenched his teeth together.

"Yes, ma'am," he replied.

✿

Pyrois was precisely as Raine expected. From far out it was a dark gray sphere, roiling with cloud and atmospheric storms. Only in the north were the skies clearer. Only there could life exist, and even then, just barely.

As they got closer, they could see spires of composite glass and steel jutting into the sky, light glinting from their surfaces. Those huge buildings were virtually cities in their own right, but home only to a privileged elite. Tarot would not be there. He would be in the dank undercity—choked alleyways and shanties that littered the planet surface, wreathed in smoke, noxious gases and despair.

Raine again found herself with the straps of a mask crushing her hair to her head. This time it wasn't safe to remove it, save for inside the buildings that happened to have working air recyc systems.

Most of the undercity buildings were made from little more than scrap. Blanks and wasters slept in doorways. They saw one man who'd vomited into his breather in the night and choked to death. Someone had stolen his boots, or he didn't have any to begin with. His naked feet were ashen in the dim light.

Squares and alleyways—at least those that were wide enough—were filled with market stalls, selling everything from food rations and salvaged machine parts to second-hand clothing, household goods, and tools. The enforcers stood by and did next to nothing to exert control. They simply didn't care.

The first part of Raine's plan went well. Neiman visited some of the less scrupulous stall-holders, asked a few questions, and had soon obtained a small amount of slate. It was a transparent gray-black crystal—quite beautiful in its way. When ground and inhaled, it would sever Raine's connection to the ether. The thought terrified her.

Before she could take the drug though, they had to find Tarot. Ordinarily, that would have been impossible—there had been no sightings for some time—but Raine's mind was far from ordinary. She would be able to feel Tarot as a disturbing presence in etherspace. Or a disturbing *lack* of presence.

It would be something like searching for a maelstrom in the ocean. If her ether body got too close, she would be dragged down. It was a risk she had no choice but to take.

"Counterpoint, this is Novaheart." Neiman's voice came through to her headset. "I'm in position. Over."

Raine was in a shabby room they'd rented to use as a safe-house of sorts. She didn't need the comm unit to respond. Not yet, anyway. Neiman heard her voice in his mind: *OK, Novaheart. I'm going to get a fix on the target's location now. You're to gain visual and stay on him while I take the product and move on your position. How copy?*

"Good copy, Counterpoint." said Neiman. "Good luck. Out."

Raine sat on the bed, trying to ignore the filthy sheets. She closed her eyes, rolled her head a few times from side to side, and settled into an easy pose. A veil fell over her physical senses as she plunged into the depths of the ether. She felt filaments and swirls of it as she moved through the shadows of the physical world. She drifted through the walls of her room, passing crowds of people who were like ghosts to her. She rose above the miasma of the undercity and accelerated to dizzying speed, her ether-form streaking between the spires like a shooting star, searching, searching for that spot of nothingness below.

She usually shut out the emotions of those around her to some extent. Now, she opened herself to the throng. The bitterness and loneliness and abject misery of the undercity were almost overwhelming, but she let it all in. And there, amongst all that humanity, was a fractured scrap of *absence*.

Tarot wasn't far from the spaceport, as they'd suspected. She swung around to the other side of the city, looking back from a different vantage point to check his position. Yes, there he was.

Raine snapped back into her physical body with a jolt.

Novaheart, come in. Over.

"This is Novaheart. Over."

The target's on your six, just a few streets back. Crossing a market square. The one with the pink and blue neons. How copy?

"Good copy, Counterpoint. On my way. Out."

Raine waited, trying not to see the room she was in. She breathed deeply through her mask to slow her heart rate, but it didn't do much good. That was the worst part—the waiting. She imagined Neiman working his way through the crowd, going back the way he had come. He would have his gun in his hand by now, hidden under his jacket. But his orders were to find Tarot and watch him, nothing more.

She began to count, slowly. One, two, three. By the time she'd reached twenty-six, the comm unit crackled backed into life. "I have visual. He's heading west."

Copy that. I'm taking the goods now. Stay on him. Out.

Raine picked up the vial of crushed slate and looked at it for a moment. Then she slotted it into an aperture on one side of her mask. She inhaled once, twice. Her vision swam. The world swirled into a million colors, all competing for her attention, then became dark and lifeless. She could feel everything and then nothing in an instant. Or perhaps both at the same time.

It was a few moments before she realized she was screaming. She clawed at her mask and nearly removed it before she caught herself and forced her hands to her sides, remembering that the room wasn't sealed. There was a strange pressure in her brain that left her feeling stupefied and blind. She got to her feet, stumbled, and staggered to the wall. She felt her way along it. She made her way outside.

There were people out there and every one of them was a soulless corpse—or so they seemed to Raine. They were moving about as if everything was normal. She felt groggy and sick, but she knew she was in no immediate danger. Her psychic energy was still there, hidden deep inside. It was trapped in a box so it couldn't escape. Latent. Untapped.

She touched her headset, "I'm on my way to your position. Over."

There was a pause, then: "He's still heading west, away from the port, where it's quieter. This could work to our advantage. Over."

"Copy that. On my way. Over." Raine checked the map on her ocular display. Neiman wasn't that far from the safe-house. Raine moved unsteadily in his direction. The people she passed were gray and indistinct one minute, grotesque and twisted the next. She ignored them and pressed on.

Neiman hadn't responded to her last message. "Novaheart, come in. What's your status?"

There was nothing but white noise in her ear.

"Novaheart. Do you copy?"

Nothing. She felt her heart lurch with fear, simultaneously heightened and dulled by the slate. She started to run, or at least move her legs in something resembling a run. She drew her pistol. She clicked off the safety.

Her shoulder struck a youth and knocked him into the wall of the alleyway. "Watch it!" he said, his voice muffled by his breather, but she was already loping onward. She crossed the market, her face lit pink and blue in the lights of advertising signs overhead. She headed west, down narrow gaps between buildings, bumping into cables strung in her path and tripping over her own feet.

"Novaheart. Novaheart, come in." She noticed a slightly hysterical tone in her voice. Was it the slate?

She rounded a corner, crashing into the opposite wall. The alley was empty, apart from Tarot and Neiman. They were both facing her. Tarot was virtually obscured by the pilot, but she could see the side of his face, part of the gold rim of his glasses. And his arm, holding a jet injector to Neiman's neck.

"Turn around and leave," Tarot said. "No one needs to get hurt. You arrived on a shuttle, yes? Walk away.

I'll take your ship and you'll never see me again. It's almost poetic, isn't it? This is exactly what happened on the *Persephone*. You can't win. I can't be killed, don't you understand?"

Raine thought it was probably best not to mention that the *Diligence*—the transport that had dropped them off—had already left. Or that the *Constellation* had been towed to one of the spires for repairs.

No one moved for a moment, then Raine took a slow step forward.

"No one needs to get hurt, Tarot," Raine said, realizing that he'd said the same thing only moments before. She held her gun out to one side; she didn't have a shot anyway.

"That's quite far enough," said Tarot. "One more step and I'll pump your friend full of a very special mix of chemicals. He'll live forever, but you might not be happy with the outcome. Put the gun down."

"Shoot him," said Neiman. "Shoot *me*."

She didn't need her powers to see the anguish in his eyes. He held one hand in front of his body, where Tarot couldn't see. He stuck out his index finger.

"Let him go," said Raine, knowing it was impossible to negotiate with this man.

Neiman stuck out a second finger and Raine realized it was a count. She nodded almost imperceptibly, then Neiman held up a third finger, twisted suddenly, and smashed his elbow into Tarot's face.

Neiman dropped to the ground; Raine leveled her gun and fired. She hit Tarot twice in the side and chest. He fell. She rushed forward, ready to grab Neiman's arm and drag him away, but he was strangely still in the dirt. Something pulled her gaze toward the jet injector, discarded to one side.

It was empty.

Raine roared into her mask as she rolled Neiman's unmoving face to the sky and tugged off his goggles. His eyes were glassy, dilated. He was alive, but she knew the serum was coursing through his veins, destroying every part of him. She knew that, if her abilities hadn't been dulled, she would have seen his ether form disappearing.

"Vincent. Vincent. Wake up. Wake up."

She took a second to check Tarot's body. He seemed dead, but what did that mean? He'd said he couldn't be killed. Maybe he was right.

She went back to Neiman and touched his face, touched his scarred head. "No. No. No." She repeated the word, over and over. She pulled the man's upper body and head to her chest and wished she could remove her mask. She wanted to touch her lips against his skin.

When she looked at him again, the pilot's eyes were moving. Soon they would settle on her, maybe recognize who she was. She couldn't bear it. She rested his head on the ground, got up and forced her body away.

"Honouria—"

She didn't turn back. She staggered down the alley.

Raine knew she would never see him again; he was already gone. Neiman was like Tarot now—the opposite of ghosts.

"Lieutenant Corpsman Reid. Come in. Come…" She could hardly breathe. "Come in… Please…"

There was a delay at the other end, then Reid's voice came through, steady and clear: "Investigator Raine? What's your status? Over."

She didn't respond.

"Investigator Raine? Sit tight. We're coming to get you. We're on our way back to you now. Over."

Raine couldn't speak. She made it to the market square. Tears seeped along the lower edge of her mask and she wondered if she would drown, but she didn't. She just stood there, under lights of pink and blue, waiting for someone—anyone—to come.

Copyright © 2020 by Morgan Welch.

APPRECIATION

by David Brin

One of the greats of all science fiction—the most-nominated author of all time—Mike Resnick explored many bold topics like multi-ethnicity and the price of human arrogance, in new and amazing ways, often challenging stereotypes long before that was fashionable. As Roger Zelazny did for Hindu and Buddhist cultures, he exposed many previously insular western readers to legends and beliefs of a wide variety of African peoples, sometimes stirring controversy but always empathy. He was also unlimited in his range, serving up irony, tragedy or comedy, almost on-demand. Mike even contributed a weird-gonzo chapter to my own new SF comedy novel, winning him a place in the dedication! A peerless bon vivant *at conventions, he would occasionally mis-speak with the over-eager carelessness that sometimes merits correction in us well-meaning boomer males, a trait that's far less morally fraught and more readily corrected than (for example) gossip. As editor of many anthologies and ultimately* Galaxy's Edge, *he fostered countless new talents. A true prodigy-polymath and friend, Mike Resnick showed us how to grab and shake tomorrow with gusto.*

Robert J. Sawyer's 24th novel, The Oppenheimer Alternative, *will be published in June 2020 by CAEZIK Books, the new imprint of the company that also publishes this magazine. Rob holds two honorary doctorates and is a Member of the Order of Canada, the highest civilian honor bestowed by the Canadian government. Find him online at sfwriter.com.*

BIDING TIME

by Robert J. Sawyer

Ernie Gargalian was fat—"Gargantuan Gargalian," some called him. Fortunately, like me, he lived on Mars; it was a lot easier to carry extra weight here. He must have massed a hundred and fifty kilos, but it felt like a third of what it would have on Earth.

Ironically, Gargalian was one of the few people on Mars wealthy enough to fly back to Earth as often as he wanted to, but he never did; I don't think he planned to ever set foot on the mother planet again, even though it was where all his rich clients were. Gargalian was a dealer in Martian fossils: he brokered the transactions between those lucky prospectors who found good specimens and wealthy collectors back on Earth, taking the same oversize slice of the financial pie as he would have of a real one.

His shop was in the innermost circle—appropriately; he knew *everyone.* The main door was transparent alloquartz with his business name and trading hours laser-etched into it; not quite carved in stone, but still a degree of permanence suitable to a dealer in prehistoric relics. The business's name was Ye Olde Fossil Shoppe—as if there were any other kind.

The shoppe's ye olde door slid aside as I approached—somewhat noisily, I thought. Well, Martian dust gets everywhere, even inside our protective dome; some of it was probably gumming up the works.

Gargalian, seated by a long worktable covered with hunks of rock, was in the middle of a transaction. A prospector—grizzled, with a deeply lined face; he could have been sent over from Central Casting—was standing next to Gargantuan (okay, I was one of those who called him that too). Both of them were looking at a monitor, showing a close-up of a rhizomorph fossil. "*Aresthera weingartenii,*" Gargalian said, with satisfaction; he had a clipped Lebanese accent and a deep, booming voice. "A juvenile too—we don't see many at this particular stage of development. And see that rainbow sheen? Lovely. It's been permineralized with silicates. This will fetch a nice price—a nice price indeed."

The prospector's voice was rough. Those of us who passed most of our time under the dome had enough troubles with dry air; those who spent half their lives in surface suits, breathing bottled atmosphere, sounded particularly raspy. "How nice?" he said, his eyes narrowing.

Gargantuan frowned while he considered. "I can sell this quickly for perhaps eleven million...or, if you give me longer, I can probably get thirteen. I have some clients who specialize in *A. weingartenii* who will pay top coin, but they are slow in making up their minds."

"I want the money fast," said the prospector. "This old body of mine might not hold out much longer."

Gargalian turned his gaze from the monitor to appraise the prospector, and he caught sight of me as he did so. He nodded in my direction, and raised a single finger—the finger that indicated "one minute," not the other finger, although I got that often enough when I entered places too. He nodded at the prospector, apparently agreeing that the guy wasn't long for this or any other world, and said, "A speedy resolution, then. Let me give you a receipt for the fossil..."

I waited for Gargalian to finish his business, and then he came over to where I was standing. "Hey, Ernie," I said.

"Mr. Double-X himself!" declared Gargalian, bushy eyebrows rising above his round, flabby face. He liked to call me that because both my first and last names—Alex Lomax—ended in that letter.

I pulled my datapad out of my pocket and showed him a picture of a seventy-year-old woman, with gray hair cut in sensible bangs above a crabapple visage. "Recognize her?"

Gargantuan nodded, and his jowls shook as he did so. "Sure. Megan Delacourt, Delany, something like that, right?"

"Delahunt," I said.

"Right. What's up? She your client?"

"She's *nobody's* client," I said. "The old dear is pushing up daisies."

I saw Gargalian narrow his eyes for a second. Knowing him, he was trying to calculate whether he'd owed her money or she'd owed him money. "Sorry to hear that," he said with the kind of regret that was merely polite, presumably meaning that at least he hadn't lost anything. "She was pretty old."

"'Was' is the operative word," I said. "She'd transferred."

He nodded, not surprised. "Just like that old guy wants to." He indicated the door the prospector had now exited through. It was a common-enough scenario. People come to Mars in their youth, looking to make their fortunes by finding fossils here. The lucky ones stumble across a valuable specimen early on; the unlucky ones keep on searching and searching, getting older in the process. If they ever do find a decent specimen, first thing they do is transfer before it's too late. "So, what is it?" asked Gargalian. "A product-liability case? Next of kin suing NewYou?"

I shook my head. "Nah, the transfer went fine. But somebody killed the uploaded version shortly after the transfer was completed."

Gargalian's bushy eyebrows went up. "Can you do that? I thought transfers were immortal."

I knew from bitter recent experience that a transfer could be killed with equipment specifically designed for that purpose, but the only broadband disrupter here on Mars was safely in the hands of the New Klondike constabulary. Still, I'd seen the most amazing suicide a while ago, committed by a transfer.

But this time the death had been simple. "She was lured down to the shipyards, or so it appears, and ended up standing between the engine cone of a big rocketship, which was lying on its belly, and a brick wall. Someone fired the engine, and she did a Margaret Hamilton."

Gargalian shared my fondness for old films; he got the reference and winced. "Still, there's your answer,

no? It must have been one of the rocket's crew—someone who had access to the engine controls."

I shook my head. "No. The cockpit was broken into."

Ernie frowned. "Well, maybe it was one of the crew, trying to make it look like it *wasn't* one of the crew."

God save me from amateur detectives. "I checked. They all had alibis—and none of them had a motive, of course."

Gargantuan made a harrumphing sound. "What about the original version of Megan?" he asked.

"Already gone. They normally euthanize the biological original immediately after making the copy; can't have two versions of the same person running around, after all."

"Why would anyone kill someone after they transferred?" asked Gargalian. "I mean, if you wanted the person dead, it's got to be easier to off them while they're still biological, no?"

"I imagine so."

"And it's still murder, killing a transfer, right? I mean, I can't recall it ever happening, but that's the way the law reads, isn't it?"

"Yeah, it's still murder," I said. "The penalty is life imprisonment—down on Earth, of course." With any sentence longer than two mears—two Mars years—it was cheaper to ship the criminal down to Earth, where air is free, than to incarcerate him or her here.

Gargantuan shook his head, and his jowls, again. "She seemed a nice old lady," he said. "Can't imagine why someone would want her dead."

"The 'why' is bugging me too," I said. "I know she came in here a couple of weeks ago with some fossil specimens to sell; I found a receipt recorded in her datapad."

Gargalian motioned toward his desktop computer, and we walked over to it. He spoke to the machine, and some pictures of fossils appeared on the same monitor he'd been looking at earlier. "She brought me three pentapeds. One was junk, but the other two were very nice specimens."

"You sold them?"

"That's what I do."

"And gave her her share of the proceeds?"

"Yes."

"How much did it come to?"

He spoke to the computer again, and pointed at the displayed figure. "Total, nine million solars."

I frowned. "NewYou charges 7.5 million for their basic service. There can't have been enough cash left over after she transferred to be worth killing her for, unless..." I peered at the images of the fossils she'd brought in, but I was hardly a great judge of quality. "You said two of the specimens were really nice." 'Nice' was Gargantuan's favorite adjective; he'd apparently never taken a creative-writing course.

He nodded.

"*How* nice?"

He laughed, getting my point at once. "You think she'd found the alpha?"

I lifted my shoulders a bit. "Why not? If she knew where it was, that'd be worth killing her for."

The alpha deposit was where Simon Weingarten and Denny O'Reilly—the two private explorers who first found fossils on Mars—had collected their original specimens. That discovery had brought all the other fortune-seekers from Earth. Weingarten and O'Reilly had died twenty mears ago—their heat shield had torn off while re-entering Earth's atmosphere after their third trip here—and the location of the alpha died with them. All anyone knew was that it was somewhere here in the Isidis Planitia basin; whoever found it would be rich beyond even Gargantuan Gargalian's dreams.

"I told you, one of the specimens was junk," said Ernie. "No way it came from the alpha. The rocks of the alpha are extremely fine-grained—the preservation quality is as good as that from Earth's Burgess Shale."

"And the other two?" I said.

He frowned, then replied almost grudgingly, "They were good."

"Alpha good?"

His eyes narrowed. "Maybe."

"She could have thrown in the junk piece just to disguise where the others had come from," I said.

"Well, even junk fossils are hard to come by."

That much was true. In my own desultory collecting days, I'd never found so much as a fragment. Still, there had to be a reason why someone would kill an old woman just after she'd transferred her consciousness into an artificial body.

And if I could find that reason, I'd be able to find her killer.

✿

My client was Megan Delahunt's ex-husband—and he'd been ex for a dozen mears, not just since Megan had died. Jersey Delahunt had come into my little office at about half-past ten that morning. He was shrunken with age, but looked as though he'd been broad-shouldered in his day. A few wisps of white hair were all that was left on his liver-spotted head. "Megan struck it rich," he'd told me.

I'd regarded him from my swivel chair, hands interlocked behind my head, feet up on my battered desk. "And you couldn't be happier for her."

"You're being sarcastic, Mr. Lomax," he said, but his tone wasn't bitter. "I don't blame you. Sure, I'd been hunting fossils for thirty-six Earth years too. Megan and me, we'd come here to Mars together, right at the beginning of the rush, hoping to make our fortunes. It hadn't lasted though—our marriage, I mean; the dream of getting rich lasted, of course."

"Of course," I said. "Are you still named in her will?"

Jersey's old, rheumy eyes regarded me. "Suspicious too, aren't you?"

"That's what they pay me the medium-sized bucks for."

He had a small mouth, surrounded by wrinkles; it did the best it could to work up a smile. "The answer is no, I'm not in her will. She left everything to our son, Ralph. Not that there was much left over after she spent the money to upload, but whatever there was, he got—or will get, once her will is probated."

"And how old is Ralph?"

"Thirty-four." Age was always expressed in Earth years.

"So he was born after you came to Mars? Does he still live here?"

"Yes. Always has."

"Is he a prospector too?"

"No. He's an engineer. Works for the water-recycling authority."

I nodded. Not rich, then. "And Megan's money is still there, in her bank account?"

"So says the lawyer, yes."

"If all the money is going to Ralph, what's your interest in the matter?"

"My interest, Mr. Lomax, is that I once loved this woman very much. I left Earth to come here to Mars because it's what she wanted to do. We lived together for ten mears, had children together, and—"

"Children," I repeated. "But you said all the money was left to your *child*, singular, this Ralph."

"My daughter is dead," Jersey said, his voice soft.

It was hard to sound contrite in my current posture—I was still leaning back with feet up on the desk. But I tried. "Oh. Um. I'm...ah..."

"You're sorry, Mr. Lomax. Everybody is. I've heard it a million times. But it wasn't your fault. It wasn't anyone's fault, although..."

"Yes?"

"Although Megan blamed herself, of course. What mother wouldn't?"

"I'm not following."

"Our daughter JoBeth died thirty years ago, when she was two months old." Jersey was staring out my office's single window, at one of the arches supporting the habitat dome. "She smothered in her sleep." He turned to look at me, and his eyes were red as Martian sand. "The doctor said that sort of thing happens sometimes—not often, but from time to time." His face was almost unbearably sad. "Right up till the end, Megan would cry whenever she thought of JoBeth. It was heartbreaking. She couldn't get over it."

I nodded, because that was all I could think of to do. Jersey didn't seem inclined to say anything else so, after a moment, I went on. "Surely the police have investigated your ex-wife's death."

"Yes, of course," Jersey replied. "But I'm not satisfied that they tried hard enough."

This was a story I'd heard often. I nodded again, and he continued to speak: "I mean, the detective I talked to said the killer was probably off-planet now, headed to Earth."

"That *is* possible, you know," I replied. "Well, at least it is if a ship has left here in the interim."

"Two have," said Jersey, "or so the detective told me."

"Including the one whose firing engine, ah, did the deed?"

"No, that one's still there. *Lennick's Folly*, it's called. It was supposed to head back to Earth, but it's been impounded."

"Because of Megan's death?"

"No. Something to do with unpaid taxes."

I nodded. With NewYou's consciousness-uploading technology, not even death was certain anymore—but taxes were. "Which detective were you dealing with?"

"Some Scottish guy."

"Dougal McCrae," I said. Mac wasn't the laziest man I'd ever met—and he'd saved my life recently when another case had gone bad, so I tried not to think uncharitable thoughts about him. But if there was a poster boy for complacent policing, well, Mac wouldn't be it; he wouldn't bother to get out from behind his desk to show up for the photo shoot. "All right," I said. "I'll take the case."

"Thank you," said Jersey. "I brought along Megan's datapad; the police gave it back to me after copying its contents." He handed me the little tablet. "It's got her appointment schedule and her address book. I thought maybe it would help you find the killer."

I motioned for him to put the device on my desk. "It probably will, at that. Now, about my fee..."

✧

Since Mars no longer had seas, it was all one landmass: you could literally walk anywhere on the planet. Still, on this whole rotten globe, there was only one settlement—our domed city of New Klondike, three kilometers in diameter. The city had a circular layout: nine concentric rings of buildings, cut into blocks by twelve radial roadways. The NewYou franchise—the only place you could go for uploading on Mars—was just off Third Avenue in the Fifth Ring. According to her datapad, Megan Delahunt's last appointment at NewYou had been three days ago, when her transfer had actually been done. I headed there after leaving Ye Olde Fossil Shoppe.

The NewYou franchise was under new management since the last time I'd visited. The rather tacky showroom was at ground level; the brain-scanning equipment was on the second floor. The basement—quite rare on Mars, since the permafrost was so hard to dig through—was mostly used for storage.

"Mr. Lomax!" declared Horatio Fernandez, the new owner; I'd met him previously when he'd just been an employee here. I'd forgotten what a beefy guy he was—arms as big around as Gargalian's, but his bulk was all muscle.

"Hello," I said. "Sorry to bother you, but—"

"Let me guess," said Fernandez. "The Megan Delahunt murder."

"Bingo."

He shook his head. "She was really pleasant."

"So people keep telling me."

"It's true. She was a real lady, that one. Cultured, you know? Lots of people here, spending their lives splitting rocks, they get a rough edge. But not her; she was all 'please' and 'thank you.' Of course, she was pretty long in the tooth…"

"Did she have any special transfer requests?" I asked.

"Nah. Just wanted her new body to look the way she had fifty Earth years ago, when she was twenty—which was easy enough."

"What about mods for outside work?" Lots of transfers had special equipment installed in their new bodies so that they could operate more easily on the surface of Mars.

"Nah, nothing. She said her fossil-hunting days were over. She was looking forward to a nice long future, reading all the great books she'd never had time for before."

If she'd found the alpha, she'd probably have wanted to work it herself, at least for a while—if you're planning on living forever, and you had a way to become super-rich, you'd take advantage of it. "Hmmph," I said. "Did she mention any titles?"

"Yeah," said Fernandez. "She said she was going to start with *Remembrance of Things Past*."

I nodded, impressed at her ambition. "Anybody else come by to ask about her since she was killed?"

"Well, Detective McCrae called."

"Mac came here?"

"No, he *called*. On the phone."

I smiled. "That's Mac."

I headed over to Gully's Gym, since it was on the way to my next stop, and did my daily workout—treadmill, bench press, and so on. I worked up quite a sweat, but a sonic shower cleaned me up. Then it was off to the shipyards. Mostly, this dingy area between Eighth and Ninth Avenue was a grave for abandoned ships, left over from the early fossil-rush days when people were coming to Mars in droves. Now only a small amount of maintenance work was done here. My last visit to the shipyards had been quite unpleasant—but I suppose it hadn't been as bad as Megan Delahunt's last visit.

I found *Lennick's Folly* easily enough. It was a tapered spindle, maybe a hundred meters long, lying on its side. The bow had a couple of square windows, and the stern had a giant engine cone attached. There was a gap of only a few meters between the cone and a brick firewall, which was now covered with soot. Whatever had been left of Megan's shiny new body had already been removed.

The lock on the cockpit door hadn't been repaired, so I had no trouble getting in. Once inside the cramped space, I got to work.

There were times when a private detective could accomplish things a public one couldn't. Mac had to worry about privacy laws, which were as tight here on Mars as they were back down on Earth—and a good thing too, for those, like me, who had come here to escape our pasts. Oh, Mac doubtless had collected DNA samples here—gathering them at a crime scene was legal—but he couldn't take DNA from a suspect to match against specimens from here without a court order, and to get that, he'd have to show good reason up front for why the suspect might be guilty—which, of course, was a catch-22. Fortunately, the only catch-22 I had to deal with was the safety on my trusty old Smith & Wesson .22.

I used a GeneSeq 109, about the size of a hockey puck. It collected even small fragments of DNA in a nanotrap, and could easily compare sequences from any number of sources. I did a particularly thorough collecting job on the control panel that operated the engine. Of course, I looked for fingerprints too, but there weren't any recent ones, and the older ones had been smudged either by someone operating the controls with gloved hands, which is what I suspected, or, I suppose, by artificial hands—a transfer offing a transfer; that'd be a first.

Of course, Mac knew as well as I did that family members commit most murders. I'd surreptitiously taken a sample from Jersey Delahunt when he'd visited my office; I sample everyone who comes there. But my GeneSeq reported that the DNA collected here didn't match Jersey's. That wasn't too surprising: I'd been hired by guilty parties before, but it was hardly the norm—or, at least, the kind of people who hired me usually weren't guilty of the particular crime they wanted me to investigate.

And so I headed off to find the one surviving child of Megan and Jersey Delahunt.

✿

Jersey had said his son Ralph had been born shortly after he and Megan had come to Mars thirty-six Earth years ago. Ralph certainly showed all the signs of having been born here: he was 210 centimeters if he was an inch; growing up in Mars's low gravity had that effect. And he was a skinny thing, with rubbery, tubular limbs—Gumby in an olive-green business suit. Most of us here had been born on Earth, and it still showed in our musculature, but Ralph was Martian, through and through.

His office at the water works was much bigger than mine, but then, he didn't personally pay the rent on it. I had a DNA collector in my palm when I shook his hand, and while he was getting us both coffee from a maker on his credenza, I transferred the sample to the GeneSeq, and set it to comparing his genetic code to the samples from the rocket's cockpit.

"I want to thank you, Mr. Lomax," Ralph said, handing me a steaming mug. "My father called to say he'd hired you. I'm delighted. Absolutely delighted." He had a thin, reedy voice, matching his thin, reedy body. "How anyone could do such a thing to my mother..."

I smiled, sat down, and took a sip. "I understand she was a sweet old lady."

"That she was," said Ralph, taking his own seat on the other side of a glass-and-steel desk. "That she was."

The GeneSeq bleeped softly three times, each bleep higher pitched than the one before—the signal for a match. "Then why did you kill her?" I said.

He had his coffee cup halfway to his lips, but suddenly he slammed it down, splashing double-double, which fell to the glass desktop in Martian slo-mo. "Mr. Lomax, if that's your idea of a joke, it's in very poor taste. The funeral service for my mother is tomorrow, and—"

"And you'll be there, putting on an act, just like the one you're putting on now."

"Have you no decency, sir? My mother..."

"Was killed. By someone she trusted—someone who she would follow to the shipyards, someone who told her to wait in a specific spot while he—what? Nipped off to have a private word with a ship's pilot?

Went into the shadows to take a leak? Of course, a professional engineer could get the manual for a spaceship's controls easily enough, and understand it well enough to figure out how to fire the engine."

Ralph's flimsy form was quaking with rage, or a good simulation of it. "Get out. Get out now. I think I speak for my father when I say, you're fired."

I didn't get up. "It was damn-near a perfect crime," I said my voice rock-steady. "*Lennick's Folly* should have headed back to Earth, taking any evidence of who'd been in its cockpit with her; indeed, you probably hoped it'd be gone long before the melted lump that once was your mother was found. But you can't fire engines under the dome without consuming a lot of oxygen—and somebody has to pay for that. It doesn't grow on trees, you know—well, down on Earth it does, sort of. But not here. And so the ship is hanging around, like the tell-tale heart, like an albatross, like"—I sought a third allusion, just for style's sake, and one came to me: "like the sword of Damocles."

Ralph looked left and right. There was no way out, of course; I was seated between him and the door, and my Smith & Wesson was now in my hand. He might have done a sloppy job, but I never do. "I...I don't know what you're talking about," he said.

I made what I hoped was an ironic smile. "Guess that's another advantage of uploading, no? No more DNA being left behind. It's almost impossible to tell if a specific transfer has been in a specific room, but it's child's play to determine what biologicals have gone in and out of somewhere. Did you know that cells slough off the alveoli of your lungs and are exhaled with each breath? Oh, only two or three—but today's scanners have no trouble finding them, and reading the DNA in them. No, it's open-and-shut that you were the murderer: you were in the cockpit of *Lennick's Folly*, you touched the engine controls. Yeah, you were bright enough to wear gloves—but not bright enough to hold your breath."

He got to his feet and started to come around from behind his funky desk. I undid the safety on my gun, and he froze.

"I frown on murder," I said, "but I'm all for killing in self-defense—so I'd advise you to stand perfectly still." I waited to make sure he was doing just that, then went on. "I know *that* you did it, but I still don't know why. And I'm an old-fashioned guy—grew up reading Agatha Christie and Peter Robinson. In the good old days, before DNA and all that, detectives wanted three things to make a case: method, motive, and opportunity. The method is obvious, and you clearly had opportunity. But I'm still in the dark on the motive and, for my own interest, I'd like to know what it was."

"You can't prove any of this," sneered Ralph. "Even if you have a DNA match, it's inadmissible."

"Dougal McCrae is lazy but he's not stupid. If I tip him off that you definitely did it, he'll find a way to get the warrant. Your only chance now is to tell me *why* you did it. Hell, I'm a reasonable man. If your justification was good enough, well, I've turned a blind eye before. So, tell me: why wait until your mother uploaded to kill her? If you had some beef with her, why didn't you off her earlier?" I narrowed my eyes. "Or had she done something recently? She'd struck it rich, and that sometimes changes people—but..." I paused, and after a few moments, I found myself nodding. "Ah, of course. She struck it rich, and she was old. You'd thought, hey, she's going to drop off soon, and you'll inherit her newfound fortune. But when she squandered it on herself, spending most of it on uploading, you were furious." I shook my head in disgust. "Greed. Oldest motivation there is."

"You really are a smug bastard, Lomax," said Ralph. "And you don't know *anything* about me. Do you think I care about money?" He snorted. "I've never wanted money—as long as I've got enough to pay my life-support tax, I'm content."

"People who are indifferent to thousands often change their ways when millions are at stake."

"Oh, now you're a philosopher too, eh? I was born here on Mars, Lomax. My whole life I've been surrounded by people who spend all their time looking for paleontological pay dirt. My parents both did that. It was bad enough that I had to compete with things that have been dead for billions of years, but..."

I narrowed my eyes. "But what?"

He shook his head. "Nothing. You wouldn't understand."

"No? Why not?"

He paused, then: "You got brothers? Sisters?"

"A sister," I said. "Back on Earth."

"Older or younger?"

"Older, by two years."

"No," he said. "You couldn't possibly understand."

"Why not? What's that got—" And then it hit me. I'd encountered lots of scum in my life: crooks, swindlers, people who'd killed for a twenty-solar coin. But nothing like this. That Ralph had a scarecrow's form was obvious but, unlike the one from Oz, he clearly *did* have a brain. And although his mother had been the tin man, so to speak, after she'd uploaded, I now knew it was Ralph who'd been lacking a heart.

"JoBeth," I said softly.

Ralph staggered backward as if I'd hit him. His eyes, defiant till now, could no longer meet my own.

"Christ," I said. "How could you? How could anyone...?"

"It's not like that," he said, spreading his arms like a praying mantis. "I was four years old, for God's sake. I—I didn't mean—"

"You killed your own baby sister."

He looked at the carpeted office floor. "My parents had little enough time for me as it was, what with spending twelve hours a day looking for the goddamned alpha."

I nodded. "And when JoBeth came along, suddenly you were getting no attention at all. And so you smothered her in her sleep."

"You can't prove that. Nobody can."

"Maybe. Maybe not."

"She was cremated, and her ashes were scattered outside the dome thirty years ago. The doctor said she died of natural causes, and you can't prove otherwise."

I shook my head, still trying to fathom it all. "You didn't count on how much it would hurt your mother—or that the hurt would go on and on, mear after mear."

He said nothing, and that was as damning as any words could be.

"She couldn't get over it, of course," I said. "But you thought, you know, eventually..."

He nodded, almost imperceptibly—perhaps he wasn't even aware that he'd done so. I went on, "You thought eventually she would die, and then you wouldn't have to face her anymore. At some point, she'd be gone, and her pain would be over, and you could finally be free of the guilt. You were biding your time, waiting for her to pass on."

He was still looking at the carpet, so I couldn't see his face. But his narrow shoulders were quivering. I continued. "You're still young—thirty four, isn't it? Oh, sure, your mother might have been good for another ten or twenty years, but *eventually*..."

Acid was crawling its way up my throat. I swallowed hard, fighting it down. "Eventually," I continued, "you would be free—or so you thought. But then your mother struck it rich, and uploaded her consciousness, and was going to live for centuries if not forever, and you couldn't take that, could you? You couldn't take her always being around, always crying over something that you had done so long ago." I lifted my eyebrows, and made no effort to keep the contempt out of my voice. "Well, they say the first murder is the hardest."

"You can't prove any of this. Even if you have DNA specimens from the cockpit, the police still don't have any probable cause to justify taking a specimen from me."

"They'll find it. Dougal McCrae is lazy—but he's also a father, with a baby girl of his own. He'll dig into this like a bulldog, and won't let go until he's got what he needs to nail you, you—"

I stopped. I wanted to call him a son of a bitch—but he wasn't; he was the son of a gentle, loving woman who had deserved so much better. "One way or another, you're going down," I said. And then it hit me, and I started to feel that maybe there was a little justice in the universe after all. "And that's exactly right: you're going down, to Earth."

Ralph at last did look up, and his thin face was ashen. *"What?"*

"That's what they do with anyone whose jail sentence is longer than two mears. It's too expensive in terms of life-support costs to house criminals here for years on end."

"I—I can't go to Earth."

"You won't have any choice."

"But—but I was *born* here. I'm Martian, born and raised. On Earth, I'd weigh...what? Twice what I'm used to..."

"Three times, actually. A stick-insect like you, you'll hardly be able to walk there. You should have been doing what I do. Every morning, I work out at Gully's Gym, over by the shipyards. But you..."

"My...my heart..."

"Yeah, it'll be quite a strain, won't it? Too bad..."

His voice was soft and small. "It'll kill me, all that gravity."

"It might at that," I said, smiling mirthlessly. "At the very least, you'll be bed-ridden until the end of your sorry days—helpless as a baby in a crib."

Copyright © 2006 by Robert J. Sawyer.

APPRECIATION

by Robert Silverberg

Mike Resnick was a warm-hearted, exuberant guy who enlivened any room he walked into. While he was enduring the cascade of medical problems that eventually took us from him after an ordeal lasting several years, he was unfailingly cheerful and optimistic, always talking about the projects he would get to as soon as all this hospital stuff was behind him. He loved science fiction, with a deep knowledge of it going back many decades, and he loved being a science fiction writer. He was a good one, too, nominated many times for Hugo awards. Hugo nominees are given a little silver pin in the shape of a spaceship as a nomination souvenir, and Mike had dozens of them, which he wore at science fiction conventions pinned to his jacket, a formidable space armada. He pinned the spaceships representing Hugos he had won pointing upward, and the ones he had lost pointing downward—a quiet little joke of his.

We were friends for thirty years or so, and whenever we could we got together for lunch at the world science fiction convention—usually at a kosher delicatessen, if we could find one, where I would have my traditional pastrami sandwich and beer, and Mike, who liked neither pastrami nor beer, would eat something else. I don't think food per se mattered very much to him. What mattered to him was science fiction. As reader, as writer, and, fairly late in his life, as an editor of the handsome magazine you are holding right now, he served science fiction ably and well, and he will be missed.

APPRECIATION

by Kristine Kathryn Rusch

Here's what I didn't get to tell him. Of all of the people who've helped me in my career, Mike Resnick was one of maybe three who helped me the most. With the exception of my husband, Dean Wesley Smith, Mike might have helped me more than anyone else.

I didn't get to tell Mike this because he didn't want me to. I would say thank you every single time he reached into my life and offered me an opportunity. I told him how much I admired what he had done, and I asked him for advice more times than I want to think about.

He turned away from the thanks, or he made a truly tasteless joke. He didn't want to hear it. He wasn't doing it for the thanks. He was doing it... because he was Mike.

So what did he do? He sent me stories, almost from the start of my editing career. Me, an untested baby editor. When I became the editor of The Magazine of Fantasy & Science Fiction, he sent me his best stories before he sent them to anyone else—which is gold for a magazine editor. His work taught me a lot about writing; his professionalism taught me how to be the kind of writer everyone wanted to work with.

Throughout my editing career, though, Mike was one of the few people who always remembered that I was a writer first. Whenever he was editing an anthology—and he edited a lot in the 1990s—he asked me to write for it, and never limited my topic or my word length, sometimes to his own detriment. Those 1990s anthologies cost him more than his advance, every single time.

The stories I wrote for him are among my best, because he brought that out, with the subject matter and with the one question he would ask to get the story started.

And then there was the Hugo.

Mike was one of the nominees for the Best Editor Hugo the year I won. Gardner Dozois was up for the Hugo that year as well, because Gardner was up every year, and Gardner won every year. So Mike and I used to joke about the fact that

we had no hope. I found out at the last minute that I couldn't attend that year's Worldcon, and the Worldcon demanded that I provide them with the name of someone to accept for me. I'd been talking to Mike, and he said something along the lines of, "Why not? You won't win anyway."

I mean, it was a forgone conclusion. By the time Gardner retired, he had won 15 Best Editor Hugos.

But something went sideways at the Worldcon that year, and Gardner didn't win. I did. So Mike, graciously, got up, carrying my little speech, and walked to the podium, scaring everyone in the room. They worried that maybe he had misheard. They worried that maybe he was going to do something untoward.

Instead, he very professionally and warmly accepted for me. And later told me the story of the scared faces around him as he headed toward the stage to accept an award for one of his "rivals."

We were never rivals. We were good friends. We spent time together at conventions. We went to France together for an SF convention. Mike arranged my attendance. The concom asked him who he thought should attend from the U.S., and he picked friends—including me and Gardner Dozois. Small world, science fiction, in those days.

That trip was a highlight of my life.

But the conversations with Mike were highlights as well. If I had a professional question— how much should I ask for this? How do you behave as the Guest of Honor at a convention? What do you do when you get orphaned?—I would ask Mike, and he would give me the most sensible answer of everyone.

I still use most of the nuggets of wisdom that he gave.

I also know that many people in the SF field didn't get along with him. I understand that. He was outspoken and he was himself and he was a particular brand of human being we don't see much these days: a no holds-barred man who had a masterful command of the English language and who could use it as a weapon if he chose to. He said politically incorrect things long before the phrase "politically incorrect" existed, often to deliberately shock.

That was just part of the package. Beneath it all was a heart so vulnerable that he once told me he stopped raising dogs because they had shorter life spans than humans. What he meant was that he couldn't handle the constant loss. He didn't have to spell it out. It was implied.

That vulnerable heart informed his fiction. His best stories always made me cry. Yes, he wrote some great stories that were funny, light, perfect entertainment. But when he actually wrote about the human condition, he illuminated what makes us flawed and beloved at the same time.

We won't have another voice like his, ever.

I knew that Mike was ill. But he didn't want anyone to know how ill. His wife Carol had been in communication with Dean about some stories for our Pulphouse Magazine, *and just the fact that Carol was handling business decisions that Mike usually made spoke volumes.*

Still, I was surprised to see his daughter Laura's touching announcement on Facebook. I hadn't realized death was that close.

I said to Dean that I didn't get a chance to say goodbye or tell Mike how important he was, and Dean said, "None of us did." Laura's tribute to her father bears that out. He thought, to the very end, that he would beat the disease and be back to work "soon."

A few days ago—about three weeks after Mike passed—I had a vivid dream. I was cleaning out my writing office, and there was Mike. It was so good to see him. We talked about SF and our mutual friends. We talked about the changes in publishing and how the world we knew was mostly gone.

Mike told me he was leaving on a long trip, and didn't know when we would talk again. I asked him if Carol was going with him. He didn't answer. I asked him when I would see him again. He said he didn't know.

And then he headed for the door. As he started to leave, he stopped, the way he sometimes would, and said that he had forgotten to tell me a few things. He came back and I took twenty-plus single spaced pages of notes, ending with an admonition to write a short story for one of the few remaining markets left.

Then we said good-bye and I went back to work....

Only I didn't. I woke up and burst into tears, because if we had had a goodbye, it would have worked like that. A discussion about the things we loved, about our mutual interests and friends, about the business we both adored. He would have given me much more advice and wisdom than I ever gave him, and he always assigned me a story. Always.

He wouldn't have let me say thank you, not really. He never did. And he never will.

But now that he's not here, dammit...Mike. Thank you.

From the bottom of my heart.

Larry Hodges, an Odyssey workshop grad, has sold more than one hundred stories. His four novels include Campaign 2100: Game of Scorpions, *published by World Weaver Press, and* When Parallel Lines Meet, *a Stellar Guild team-up with Mike Resnick and Lezli Robyn.*

BLOOD WARS

by Larry Hodges

I've heard the jingle "Have a pint and a smile!" a million times and I'm sick of it. As the CEO of Dracu-Blood, Inc., it's all I hear all night at the office, and in my daytime dreams during the day. And now they're playing a new, even more irritating version of it—"I'd like to buy the world some blood"—at the staff meeting here a thousand feet up on the hundredth floor of the Dracu-Blood Corporation in New York City. It was 1:00 a.m., shortly after lunch.

"Can you shut that racket off!" I cried.

"But it's the latest jingle!" said the advertising director. She wore a red three-piece suit along with the company's red Dracu-Blood tie that featured a smiley human face. She's even taller and paler than the average vampire, and wears her hair in a black spike that curves forward and makes her look like a scorpion about to sting.

"I like the old jingle," I lied. "Besides, remember what the owner did to your predecessor when he tried a new jingle?" I reached forward and smashed the vPad and the table with my fist. The music stopped. The only sound was the ventilator that pumped the fresh dry dust scent into the room. "Now, everyone, give me a rundown of today's problems."

"VETH is still picketing us, forty days now," said the security director in her white three-piece suit and red company tie. She's about five hundred years old, which is old even for a vampire, and has the wrinkles and scars to prove it. She's barely four feet tall—I think she has dwarf blood. "Free-Range Blood keeps them supplied with blood." I rolled my eyes at that—Free-Range didn't believe in caging animals, I mean humans, and so kept them in a huge, enclosed zoo, where they were free to walk about and do whatever humans do. They advertised their blood as "free range," and after just one year already had three percent of the market; we had fifty-one percent.

"Blast them with our advertising jingle," I said, shaking my head. Vampires for the Ethical Treatment of Humans. What a joke. "They'll be gone in hours. Next."

"Vampu-Blood released their latest sales figures," said the balding sales director, wearing an orange three-piece suit and, of course, the red company tie. He was one of those rare fat vampires, who went through bottle after bottle of Dracu-Blood all day long at his desk—said he couldn't think otherwise. "They are closing the gap—Vampu-Blood now has forty-six percent of the market, only five percent behind us. We need to do something if we want to stay the number one blood company in the world."

"Release our own sales figures, but inflate them." We had to keep up our image as the dominating number one.

"But if we do that," said the sales director, "our sales plus Vampu-Blood and Free-Range will add up to more than one hundred percent!"

"So?" I asked. "Next."

"There's a report out in the *London Cryptkeeper* that vampire deaths from strokes are rising," said the publicity director, who wore a yellow three-piece suit—what is it with us vampires and three-piece suits?—that matched his way-too-long hair, and of course the red company tie. "They are linking it to the high salt content in Dracu-Blood."

"Human blood has a high salt content!" I exclaimed. "*Duh!* What do they expect? And why are they blaming it on us—we're not the only blood seller, just the biggest."

"Are you trying to argue with the masses using facts?" asked the publicity director.

"Of course not," I said. What a foolish idea.

"The health kick is spreading to vampires all over the world," said the sales director. "If only there were a way to tap into that, our sales would explode."

There are those moments in life where everything comes to a halt, your life is suddenly in danger, and your thoughts reach peak clarity. That happened now, and it started with a loud *crash* as the door to the room was torn off its hinges and slammed to the ground. Against the opening was only a silhouette.

It was impossibly tall, impossibly thin, and gave off an aura of impossible danger and the smell of death.

Dracula, the owner of Dracu-Blood, entered the silent room in his black seven-piece suit and, of course, the red company tie, walking over the fallen door and kicking a chair in his way into the wall, which tore open, leaving a five-feet wide opening into the room. Disgusting fresh air blew into the meeting room.

"Vampu-Blood has almost caught Dracu-Blood in sales," he said in a raspy whisper from God. "Vampu-Blood stock has almost caught Dracu-Blood in value. People are drinking Vampu-Bloods in the clubhouse at the Sucking Golf Club. *My* golf club."

He slowly elevated until his feet were level with the table I'd broken. He lightly walked across its remains until he stood in front of me. He glanced about at the others sitting at the table, then down at me.

"If they pass us in sales," he whispered, "you will all die." He raised a foot and slammed it down on the table, which crumbled into ashes. He lightly levitated to the ground. Then, with a sudden motion, he grabbed the advertising director and flung her red form out the opening in the wall. In a blur he was beside it, staring down at her and willing her into immobility so she could not transform or fly. We listened to her screams as they fell away and then, seven and a half seconds later, there was a *plop* and then silence.

"I didn't like the new jingle," he whispered, giving us a sweeping look. "Hire a new advertising director immediately." Then he floated across the floor and out the door.

Clarity of thought told me what we had to do—increase sales—but not how to do it. For inspiration I visited the farms that morning after work.

"How are you doing…M44551?" I asked, reading the name off the sign on the cage. I sniffed the air; B-Negative, though I could barely tell over the human stench that even this clinically white and antiseptically clean building couldn't hide. Metal bars made up the cage, which was just large enough for its occupant and a treadmill. The cages went in each direction as far as the eye could see.

"I'm doing great!" said M44551. The naked man lay immobile in bed, his arms and legs strapped to the sides, eyes glued to the TV positioned directly over him. Twice a day, under close supervision, he was released from his bonds to walk on the treadmill for fifteen minutes. He was grossly fat, as that led to both higher volume and a more flavorful blood. A pair of tubes attached to his lower regions to remove waste products. Another tube came out of his right arm, which drained the blood that would become Dracu-Blood, still the best-selling brand on the market. And it had to stay that way.

"What are you watching?"

"*Days in Our Cages*," said M44551. "A human pulled his hands free and tried to leave his cage, but another grabbed him through the cage bars and held him while others screamed for help. The keeper gave the bad human a good lecture, and only five minutes of electroshock! And the ones who stopped him got chocolate ice cream as a reward!"

"And what does the story teach you?"

"That the keeper is good, and if we're good, they'll treat us good! I remember back before you vampires took over how much I used to like to be good, and my mommy would let me drink sugar sodas, but then I got fat, and they got mean and made me drink sugar-free sodas, and they were bad, and my mommy was mean! You let me eat and drink what I want!"

He looked up at the ceiling. "Computer, Captain Sugar King Cereal!" He opened his mouth as a scope dropped out of the ceiling. It positioned itself directly over his head and began pouring the sugary cereal into his mouth, along with periodic squirts of high-fat chocolate milk. His face flushing, the man ate an impossible amount before he finally closed his mouth, with the last flakes and milk droplets bouncing off his face. Another scope came out of the ceiling and vacuumed up the extra flakes and milk. I could see the man's reflection off its metallic sides—humans were magical in that way.

"Why did your mom make you drink sugar-free soda?" I asked.

"Mommy didn't want me to be fat, said it was unhealthy. But I don't care. People should have a choice. If someone else wants to drink some tasteless sugar-free drink, that's fine, but don't force it on me. Let the customer choose."

Let the customer choose. It struck a chord in my mind. Right now the choice was between Dracu-Blood and Vampu-blood, not including the few weirdos that chose Free-Range. Maybe these humans weren't so stupid after all.

"Can I go back to watching TV?" M44551 asked. "They're showing a rerun of *As the Blood Flows* that I really like. Computer, sugar chocolate strawberry cola please!"

The scope began squirting into his mouth as I left.

☼

Dracula called a staff meeting the next day. It was in the same room as before, with the big gap still there. The ventilator was in a losing war with the opening, pumping in dry dust scent that was quickly overpowered by the incoming fresh air. I wanted to puke.

"Do you have a solution to our problem yet?" he whispered.

The temperature dropped twenty degrees in the ensuing silence.

"Is there anything new from the advertising department?" Dracula asked the new advertising director I'd hired that morning, a tall black vampire with twenty years' experience selling coffin bedding.

"Well, we have another jing—"

She was out the gap and screaming to her death before she could get the "le" sound out.

"How about the publicity department?"

"We can double our promotions budg—"

The publicity director fell to a screaming death.

"Are you all stupider than humans?" Dracula whispered. "They at least had the brains to come up with sales ideas. Do I need to replace you with farm animals?" He slowly ran his eyes over us. "Sales? Nothing?" Dracula asked. The sales director opened his mouth but was on his way out the gap almost before I realized I was next.

"*Salt-Free Blood!*" I blurted out.

"What?" Dracula asked, nonchalantly reaching out and plucking the screaming sales director out of the air by a leg and holding him out the opening upside-down.

"You mentioned humans," I said. "They used to have sugar-free drinks as a health drink. They let everyone choose what they wanted to drink,

healthy or non-healthy. We need to do the same. Why can't we sell salt-free blood? Health-conscious vampires everywhere will go for it—it's a whole new market segment no one's ever gone after. Let the customer choose!"

"We've never sold anything except pure blood!" cried the dangling sales director. "It'll confuse the customer and destroy our brand name!" Dracula nonchalantly released him and he fell to his screaming death.

"It'll end the protests," said the security director. "In fact, we'll get free publicity everywhere."

"I like it," Dracula whispered. "You're the new advertising director. Change into red immediately after this meeting." The security director, now the advertising director, cringed. Dracula turned to me. "But won't our blood be tasteless without salt?"

"We can sell flavored blood," I said. "Chocolate, cherry, orange, citrus, and so on."

"Great idea," said Dracula. "You are now CEO slash product director."

"I don't like the name Salt-Free Blood Red," I said, wondering if there was a salary increase with my added job title. "We need something better, healthy sounding."

"We'll call it the Doctor Red line, all salt-free," the new advertising director said. "Chocolate Doctor Red, Cherry Doctor Red, and so on. For the truly adventurous, why not one spiked with just a touch of garlic for spice?"

"Garlic Doctor Red," mused Dracula. "Excellent! Have both salt and salt-free versions of each flavor. Maybe even sell by blood types. Both of you, start work on the new products and on a new advertising campaign. Oh, and one more thing."

"What's that?" asked the advertising director.

"We're going to need a new advertising jingle."

Copyright © 2020 by Larry Hodges.

MIKE RESNICK—APRECIATIVELY

by Jody Lynn Nye

[This was originally written for the WindyCon 2018 program book when Mike was Guest of Honor. I have adapted it as a memorial. (sigh)]

If you happen to have been hanging out in a con suite and hear a man with a slightly nasal but resonant baritone voice talking very loudly about breeding dogs, the Cincinnati Bengals, or horse racing, there's a good chance that you're within earshot of a longtime professional and maybe the hardest working writer in science fiction, Mike Resnick. If you looked for a broad grin bracketed by Azimovian mutton-chop sideburns, I hope you pulled up a chair, and joined what I know would have been an interesting conversation.

You might look at Mike as something of an overachiever. In the fifty-three years since he began publishing science fiction, Mike turned out around fifty novels in eleven different series plus twenty-six others, alone or in collaboration. He put out a host of nonfiction books; edited dozens of anthologies, alone or with a co-editor; published mystery novels; written screenplays (one almost produced!); and edited magazines including Jim Baen's Universe *and* Galaxy's Edge. *On top of those, he published over 280 short stories as of 2018, and could easily have added two dozen more in the interim. He submitted his work not only to English-language markets, but to countless foreign publishers as well. He was also one of the fiction judges for the Writers of the Future, the largest speculative fiction contest in the world. He and author Barry Malzberg carried on a witty, years-long conversation in the pages of* SFWA Bulletin *on the state of publishing and other topics of interest. Mike was well known for his sense of humor, and has published novels, short stories and anthologies with a humorous theme, such as* Shaggy BEM Stories, Girls for the Slime God, *or* This is My Funniest. *He made* Galaxy's Edge *a friendly venue for first-time writers, as well as hitting up his old friends for second rights on stories that he thought should be reprinted. My husband and I wrote the Book Recommendations column for him for four years.*

His delightful wife, Carol, was his constant advisor, and partner in crime on convention costume design, most notably their "The Avengers of Space" burlesque tableau, four costumes constructed for less than a hundred dollars which won Best in Show at NorthAmeriCon. Their daughter, Laura Resnick, is also a successful science-fiction and romance writer, a Campbell-award winner, and a columnist for Novelists, Inc.

Mike was nominated for more Hugo awards than anyone else, thirty-seven times, and won five of them. He won the Galaxy Award from China for Most Popular Foreign Author as well as numerous other awards, both domestic and international.

As well as writing individual works, Mike enjoyed collaborating with seasoned pros. Most recently, he published Gods of Sagittarius *with 1632 series author Eric Flint. Mike and I talked for years about working on something together and had begun writing an adventure novel. I had looked forward to the project, and it will be an emotional wrench to have to finish it on my own. Mike was a good friend. We didn't agree on everything, but he respected my opinion.*

Hanging out with Mike you have might spotted a number of other female writers. This is not just because Mike is a wonderful raconteur and a charming man, but he has also made a long practice of sharing his byline with many up-and-coming writers, often women he called his "Writer Daughters," including such co-authors as Campbell-nominated Lezli Robyn (who now succeeds him as editor of Galaxy's Edge). *He also mentored new male writers as well, such as Martin Shoemaker, his entire literary family often referred to as his "Writer Children." Working with Mike gave talented newcomers a boost in visibility as well as guidance from one of the most experienced pros in the business. In 2017, the Writers of the Future recognized Mike's generosity with the L. Ron Hubbard Lifetime Achievement Award.*

Mike and Carol traveled widely, especially in Africa, bred prize-winning collies, and were a part of SF fandom since the 1960s. He was one of the founders of Chicago's major regional convention, WindyCon, and attended nearly all of them up until last year. He had a story for every occasion and was happy to share them with anyone who would listen. I'm sorry there will be no more from him, but Mike's literary legacy will also be measured in those with whom he shared his talents and wisdom over the years.

REMEMBERING MIKE

by Stephen Leigh

Mike's record of publications and awards speaks for itself. But I'd like to celebrate the person, not the writer—though Mike was indeed had a huge presence within the field. We were, of course, aware of Mike before he moved to Cincinnati, seeing him at various conventions here and there, but we really got to know him (and Carol and Laura) when he moved here, taking up residence at the kennel he and Carol owned and ran when they first moved here, and becoming part of the local sf fannish community, the CFG (Cincinnati Fan Group). Mike and Carol would became an important part of the CFG, hosting meetings and large fannish gatherings. Mike and Carol would rarely fail to show up at CFG meetings (though Mike would generally leave around 10:00 PM because that was his "writing time."

Mike would come to have a well-deserved a reputation for taking younger writers under his mentorship, including a few in the CFG, and helping them along in their career. Although at the time I first came to know him, I'd already published several short stories and a handful of novels, Mike still did the same for me: giving me advice, helping me to see avenues within the publishing world that Mike (much better connected than me) knew but of which I was unaware, inviting me to be in some of the short story anthologies that he and Marty Greenberg were editing at the time for DAW Books, and so on.

And knowing that I'd used swords and fencing in my early novels and stories, Mike—who studied fencing and competed in tournaments in his college days—tutored me in the basics of foil and saber (and beat me soundly in the process whenever we dueled.) I still remember sweaty afternoons on the porch of their house at the kennel property, with Mike exhorting me to "Lunge. Again! Deeper! Bend those knees!"

I mention all this to point out just how incredibly generous Mike could be with his knowledge, *his expertise, and his time to those who showed an interest. There are several writers out there who owe Mike that same debt of gratitude. Mike was a fervent believer in the concept of "paying forward"—because generally when someone further up the ladder extends a hand back to you to give you a boost up, the only way to really repay them for their kindness is to extend your own hand back down to those who are below you and endeavoring to climb the same ladder, and give them the same gift of time and knowledge that you were given.*

That is, I believe, the finest tribute any of us can give to Mike and the best way to celebrate his life is this: if you knew him, pay your debt to him forward. Be willing to help others the way he helped you. I can tell you that without a doubt, that's what he'd want.

The world is a lesser place without you, Mike.

APPRECIATION

by Jack McDavitt

Mike was one of a kind, a brilliant writer, a friend who was always there, a colleague who led by inspiration. He was much more than simply a supremely gifted writer. He was a Presence. When we were collaborating on The Cassandra Project, *he was somehow seated beside me while I worked. There were times when I could sense his nodding, that "Yes, this was the way to handle it," and occasionally sighing while I struggled to install a fix.*

I miss him already. But in a sense he will always be close by. Maybe that's because it was his nature. Maybe it's because his books constitute a major component of my library. They've made it possible, in his words, to touch the sky.

It's hard to imagine what my life would have been like without him. Except to know it would have been a colder place.

Eric Leif Davin has appeared numerous times within the pages of Galaxy's Edge. *Two of his previous stories were selected for "year's best" anthologies from Baen Books. He is the author of* Pioneers of Wonder: Conversations with the Founders of Science Fiction *and* Partners in Wonder: Women and the Birth of Science Fiction, 1926-1965.

THE STARRY NIGHT

by Eric Leif Davin

They call me mad, but they did so even before I came to this asylum in Saint-Remy-de Provence. The peasants in Arles tried to commit me. They thought me strange because of what I did, what I saw, what I painted. But, strange though it seemed to them, I only painted what was there. I make no apologies for that. Nor do I complain about their opinion of me. To suffer without complaining is the only lesson one should learn in this life. I am ready to play the role of a madman, if such it must be.

I do miss Arles, though, my room, the fields, the cypress trees, the ever-changing sky. I even miss the peasants, though I doubt if they miss me. I painted them all as I saw them in my own rough-hewn way, with bold strokes and rich expressive colors. I painted a large picture of the village church, the building with a violet appearance against a flat, deep blue sky of pure color. The stained-glass windows are like ultramarine colored spots; the roof is violet and orange in parts. At the front is something green in bloom and the sun-burnt sand is pink colored. Some said the church did not look like that at all, but I painted what was there.

I went into the fields every day, setting up my easel amid the waving corn stalks, in the vineyards, in the olive groves, amid the cypress trees which pointed straight upward like spears planted in the ground. It's amazing that nobody has yet painted them as I see them, like flaming green tongues; in their lines and proportions they are as beautiful as Egyptian obelisks. One has to see the cypresses against the blue or, more correctly, *in* the blue, to properly appreciate them.

But it was in Arles that the fits began. For a long time I was perfectly fine. And then there would come a nebulous stage, followed by blankness. Then I was on the ground, looking up at the sky, with curious peasants standing over me, concern on their faces. The peasants said I raved and gibbered, as I lay prostrate on the ground. They thought I was mad, but I think it is a form of epilepsy. It consoles me that I can look upon my illness simply as an illness like any other, and thus accept it as such. It allows me to go on with my work, capturing the fields and sky, the sun, the stars as they actually are, which is all that matters.

But after the peasants of Arles tried to commit me to a hospital for the mentally ill, I could no longer remain there. Thus, I came here, to this refuge in Saint-Remy. They leave me alone here, and I am free to come and go as I please, unattended. As in Arles, I go into the fields every day. I must be out of doors; I must see nature as it really exists. It is the ripe moist excesses of nature that connects me with life, and I work endlessly to capture its reality. It is not so much the language of painting as that of nature which one must listen to.

Thus I go out and see the endlessly flat landscape, the vineyards, the harvested cornfields. All this is multiplied to infinity and spreads like the surface of the sea to the horizon. I see it all, and then, led by nature's hand, I try to capture this life spread before me in my paintings, as it really exists. This means wrestling with the colors and, in doing so, I discover that the colors take on a life of their own, and thus are ideally suited to express the principle of life. It is not so much what I see that is represented on the canvas, but life itself expressing itself on the canvas through the colors. I do not use colors to copy reality. They are, themselves, reality itself.

But it was not only during the day that nature revealed itself to me. I also went out at night, for nature at night, the sky at night, is also nature's reality, as much as the daytime sky. I cannot paint in the darkness of night, of course, but I can see what is before me, and I can remember.

So it was that I went out last night to see nature's nocturnal truths. The sky was clear as I climbed the hills overlooking Saint-Remy. I turned and looked down on the town spread out below me, the houses, the orchards, the spire of the village church.

And then I looked at the sky above me, and nature's night sky abruptly revealed itself to me. Some kind of fantastic cosmic display suddenly erupted above me. Two enormous spiral nebulae appeared from opposite sides of the sky and flowed into each other like waves and entwined themselves with each other. Amid the myriad blazing stars, eleven stars grew to impossibly enlarged sizes and their aureoles of light broke through the night. A weirdly unreal moon grew and seemed to multiply itself, so that its light competed with the light of the giant stars. A broad band of light, perhaps the Milky Way, spread across the lower horizon from one side of the valley below me to the other. The sky itself turned a deep blue and appeared to be roiling in turmoil.

Below me the sleepy earthbound village seemed oblivious to the staggering splendor of the cosmic powers curving and circling each other in the sky. It seemed to me an apocalyptic vision, an expression of the insignificance of humanity and the infinity of nature. I felt myself being drawn upward into the embrace of the universe, surrounded by spiraling stars and streams of flowing light. I looked down at the receding earth, and realized how small and insignificant we are, mere microbes on a dust mote spinning in the endless void of space.

But I also realized that, insignificant as we are, we are not separate from the universe. We are part of it, we are stardust itself, and so we are infinite, because we are part of the whole. We are here on earth, and yet we are everywhere, as far as the eye can see, for we are part of the universe. It is within us, and we are within it. I saw it all with great and comforting clarity.

Then it all faded into blankness, and I found myself lying prostrate upon the cold, damp hillside, gazing up into the night sky. The stars shone down upon me like diamonds in velvet, but the transcendent vision I had witnessed was gone.

I came directly home and painted rapidly and furiously until dawn, painting quickly with a flowing flood of brush strokes before the vision faded. When the dawn came, it appeared to me that I saw the sun with new eyes, as if a new world was revealing itself before me.

Later that morning the director of the asylum stopped by my room to visit me, as he often does, especially if I have gone out the night before. He surveyed my painting, still on its easel, the wet paint not yet dry. Hmm, he said, stroking his pointed Van Dyke beard. He removed his pince-nez glasses and polished the lenses with a handkerchief taken from his breast pocket. Then he replaced his pince-nez on his nose and peered more closely at my painting. "Very interesting, Vincent," he said. "And what do you call this new painting of yours?"

What could I say? I am a painter, not a poet. Words could not express what I had seen in the night, what was there. Nor, it seems, could my painting. It was merely a feeble representation of the infinite revelation that I had witnessed. If my painting did not speak for itself, nothing I could say could adequately explain it. My words would be dismissed as the ravings of the madman they take me for.

So, I simply smiled at him, shrugged my shoulders, and merely said, "The Starry Night."

Copyright © 2020 by Eric Leif Davin.

Eric S. Fomley's stories have appeared in Daily Science Fiction, *Flame Tree Press, The Black Library, and many other places. You can read his other fiction or contact him from his website ericfomley.com.*

THE ALTAR

by Eric S. Fomley

The Donovan family was notoriously reclusive in Tahoma county. So imagine my surprise when Melina Donovan walked into my carpentry shop and slapped a check for two million dollars onto my counter.

My heart skipped a beat. "Woah, what's this for?"

"Do you handle commissioned work?"

"Of course, we do most of our business outside the business." Mostly it was installing cabinets for older folks or building stairs, and that paid a very small fraction of what she was offering.

"Excellent. My family has a critical job that needs done by tomorrow."

"That's a very short time frame, ma'am. I have some other projects that I need to get squared away." Though for two million dollars, those other projects could wait. But I didn't tell her that.

"We are prepared to pay you another two million upon completion of the job."

My head was starting to swim now. Four million was enough money to sell the business and not have to work another day in my life. This would take the top priority. I cleared my throat. "All right then, what's the job?"

"We need a twenty-foot altar constructed behind the Donovan Manor. We have the blueprints and dimensions all squared away as well as the required lumber. My pa was going to handle the construction himself, but his arthritis hasn't been treating him well these past weeks and we are running behind schedule. My family wants the job handled by professionals so we would like you to finish it. But it *must* be done by tomorrow."

It didn't seem too unreasonable, especially if all the measurements were done and everything I'd need was out and ready. But it didn't make any sense.

Who would pay so much money for something that could be handled in a day or two by anyone decent with a hammer?

"If you don't mind my asking, what's your family need with an altar in the middle of the woods?"

"To save the world."

I started laughing but her straight face didn't break. "Wait, you're serious?"

"Something to know about me and my family, Mr. Delemonte, we take what we do *very* seriously."

Something about the way she said that sent a shiver down my spine. The whole situation was odd. But if she was willing to pay me a fortune for a rushed job to help further her religious thing, it really wouldn't matter to me how odd it was tomorrow.

"Well, I'll see to it that my co-owner and I handle it so." Clyde would be skipping around our shop when he heard this.

"Do we have an agreement then?" She extended her hand.

It was an easy request, and if I'd had anything to drink I'd have thought I imagined the whole thing. But I grasped her hand and smiled. "Consider it done."

"Good. I'll look forward to seeing you this afternoon."

I could see she wasn't about wasted time. "We'll be there."

"Remember, we need this done by tomorrow. There can be *no* exceptions to that."

"Tomorrow. I got it. You can count on us."

She gave me a curt nod and walked out of the shop. I was left scratching my head wondering how in the world I was holding a check for a fortune in my hand over something so simple.

I turned the truck down the gravel road. The trees were thick on either side and I drove slow, watching for deer.

"George, you're sure the check was good?" Clyde asked for the twelfth time since we'd left the shop.

"Yes, I'm telling you it was good. It already cleared the account. And we get another two mill when we finish."

"Damn. Who pays four million for something that doesn't even take a day to build?"

"Beats me, but I'm not complaining."

"Hell no, today might be the last day I work." He grinned over at me.

I tried not to let my own excitement show. It was a lot of money, but something didn't feel right about it. I knew some rich people could be loose with their money but I'd never heard of someone being *that* loose. Something didn't piece together for me.

"I'm not getting my hopes up yet. Let's just get this thing built and make sure we're not getting ourselves too deep into something." For all we knew, the Donovans had some multi-year and quite expensive project sitting in their backyard that they *really* wanted us working on for the money they paid.

The dirt road ended at a narrow driveway. I turned in and was surprised when I saw Melina standing at the end of the drive in front of a nineteenth-century brick mansion.

"Clearly she doesn't have anything else to do today," Clyde muttered.

"That's so weird. This altar must be a pretty big deal to her."

Clyde laughed. "It's a pretty big deal to me now!"

Melina walked up to the car as we got out. "Thank you for coming so quickly, George, and you must be Clyde?"

"Yes, ma'am," he said as she took his hand.

"If you'll follow me I'll show you to it." She led us around the back of the house where a pile of lumber lay next to a table saw and toolbox. "It's all here, everything you should need. If there's something else we can get for you just let me know." She pointed to the back porch. "I've got some lemonade up there if you get thirsty. I know it's hot and I wouldn't want to keep you boys from getting done today."

I shot Clyde a look and saw him conceal a smile. I could tell we were both thinking that these people were awfully pushy. Clyde was the type that might have said something, but I had a feeling the money involved kept his mouth shut.

Melina handed me the blueprint. "It should all be pretty self-explanatory, but please don't hesitate with questions."

I scanned over it. The altar was fairly large, but nothing too out of the ordinary. I handed it over to Clyde and smiled at Melina. "We'll get started right

away. It doesn't look like too much so we'll get it in no time."

"By tomorrow is all I ask."

"Will do."

She went to the back porch and sat in a rocking chair. That's when I noticed all the people watching from different windows of the house. I shuddered and nudged Clyde.

"Hey, we got watchers."

He looked up at the house and back at me with wide eyes. "These people are fucking weird. What's so important about this damn altar?"

"They gotta make their sacrifices." I grinned.

"I guess. Let's just get this knocked out and get outta here."

"No argument here," I said.

We got a good way through it when I broke for lemonade and let Clyde continue the work for a minute. I walked up to the back porch and the people scattered from the windows. Melina sat in the rocker, watching Clyde progress as I poured a glass.

"Where do you keep the animals?" I asked.

"The animals?" She looked up at me.

"Yeah, you know, for the sacrifices. Where do you keep them?"

She laughed. It was the first time her serious demeanor broke into something else. "We aren't sacrificing poor animals. Why on earth would we do that?"

The look of genuine amusement on her face puzzled me. "If you're not sacrificing animals, then what's this altar for?" A sick feeling formed in my stomach.

"We're going to sacrifice ourselves. For the Jixt."

I thought I was going to throw up. "I beg your pardon?"

She smiled. "Can you keep a secret, Mr. Delemote?"

I thought about that for a second and nodded.

"Do you believe in aliens?"

"No, ma'am, I think they're better left to the movies."

"I thought not. Most people don't. But most people haven't seen what our family has seen. The trials we've gone through for the sake of everyone else."

"Are you meaning to tell me you've seen aliens?"

"Not exactly, but my great great great grandfather did. They took him up in their starship. He learned things, horrible things that they were planning to do to us people on Earth. My grandfather bartered with them, made them a deal that they could have the bodies of him and his family to use or study as they saw fit so long as they left our world in peace. They agreed, sent him back to Earth, and told him they'd be back. They gave him the time and place, right here on the very same farm some hundred and fifty years into his future. So we've been getting ready. And come tomorrow when they show up, we'll lay out on that altar, take arsenic, and offer our naked flesh to the creatures of the heavens for the sake of mankind. My grandfather was a hero, and you're helping us fulfill his promise and for that, we're forever grateful." She smiled. "See, didn't I tell you we were going to save the world?"

I looked into her eyes and my stomach twisted into knots. She wasn't joking. "That's insane. That's completely fucking insane. You're gonna take the advice of some guy that's been dead at least hundred years and kill yourselves?"

Her eyes narrowed into slits. "Now, Mr. Delemonte, I didn't ask for your opinion. Nor did I ask for your judgment. My grandfather prophesied this future and my family knows what we have been called to do. This is what we've lived for. We are going to save the world. My family has offered you and your friend a lot of money to see this through and we expect you to come through, true to your word. You understand that, don't you?"

I nodded. My head was swimming. I couldn't believe what I'd just heard.

"Good. See to it that the yard is tidied up when you two are finished." She smiled and returned to watching Clyde.

I left the porch and told Clyde what I'd heard. "I'm not sure we should be doing this."

Clyde grabbed my shirt and spun me so my back was to the house. "Please don't screw this up. Now, these people are offering to pay us an enormous amount of money to build them some godforsaken altar. Whatever they choose to do with it is on them."

"So you're willing to let them kill themselves?"

"It doesn't matter what they do, it isn't any of our damn business. Aren't you religious?"

"I believe in God."

"Well there you go, how would you feel if someone came walking around telling you what to do with your beliefs?"

"My beliefs don't involve me killing myself or my family."

"It doesn't matter. Just build the altar, collect the money, and go home. That's it, that's all we have to do here. If they choose to get suicidal on it, then that's their choice. It's not ours to make for them. Plus, who's to say that if we quit now that they won't just go find someone else to finish it?"

"At least my conscience would be clear."

"Would it? Are you willing to bet four million bucks on that? And how do you know that she wasn't just pulling your leg? And if she wasn't, what do you think her and her family might do to us if we get in the way of their 'sacred' ritual?"

When he put things like that I wasn't so sure. But even if I quit now and walked away I knew it would still nag at me. "No, you're probably right."

"That's that then." Clyde spun around and went back to setting the final boards.

We finished the altar by sundown and Melina's kind demeanor returned as she gave us the second check. Clyde piled into my truck as giddy as a schoolgirl and cradled that check like it was his newborn child.

"Now, was that so hard?" he asked as I pulled out of the driveway.

"No. You were right," I said. But I couldn't shake the sinking feeling in my heart.

I dropped Clyde off at the shop and went home.

It was late, but sleep eluded me. I couldn't stop replaying in my mind what Melina had said. She was so sincere and genuine in her explanation, and her animosity to my questioning made it feel all the more real. I wish I could've just taken the money and forgotten about the Donovans. But I couldn't leave it alone.

By the time dawn broke, I was speeding down that dirt road back to Donovan Manor. I'd phoned the cops when I left about an attempted mass suicide. I wasn't sure what I'd find when I pulled into the woodland drive, but when I ran around the corner of the mansion I was both shocked and relieved to see several police officers wrestling the naked Donovan family into cuffs.

Melina saw me and her eyes narrowed. "How could you do this? You know what will happen if this doesn't go through. We trusted you."

There wasn't anything I could say. I just wanted to keep these people from hurting themselves. The way I saw them act with the police made me realize that I'd made the right choice. These people needed help. My heart sank thinking about how they could be so lost to the world around them. How they could be so twisted into doing this.

Melina was the last Donovan detained. One of the officers waved me over. He had scratches on his cheek and blood leaked from a cut under his eye.

"Were you the one that tipped us off about this shit show?"

"Yes, sir. I run Delemonte Carpentry. The Donovans contracted me to build this altar."

"I'm gonna need you to start from the beginning for me and write a statement about what all's been going on here."

There was a sound like thunder. Louder.

I looked up and a chill seized my heart. "Oh my God."

It was the shape of a skyscraper, huge even from its place in the clouds. And out of its sides poured hundreds, thousands of tiny black dots. *Ships*, I realized. Beams of green light shot out of each ship, millions of beams painting the sky green for an instant before they hit the surface.

The forest around me exploded. I clamped my hands over my ears, collapsed to my knees, and screamed.

The Jixt were here. And the deal the Donovans made with them was void.

Copyright © 2020 by Eric S. Fomley.

APPRECIATION

by Kevin J. Anderson

I'm glad Mike wrote his stories down. Somehow, I have a hard time imagining that when I go to DragonCon or Writers of the Future that Mike Resnick won't be there holding court to a crowd of new writers, telling story after story of science fiction fandom, his experiences at conventions or with old publishers, legendary editors. He spoke in a booming voice, laughing, entertaining, always holding our attention.

Mike and I collaborated on a short story, "Prevenge" (I think just about everybody collaborated with Mike on a story at one point or another). After I outlined the story and started writing a draft, Mike wrote back to me, sternly lecturing, "This isn't a short story. It's a novel! You're just writing a stripped-down novel." I tried again, and again he said, "This isn't structured like a story, it's a novel!"

We eventually hammered it into something that he called a short story, even though I had to be dragged kicking and screaming. My brain must think in novels instead of short stories. At least it turned out to be a good story, published in Analog.

Mike was also a judge and instructor for Writers of the Future, and we would see each other every year in Hollywood, spending evenings in the hotel bar, surrounded by students and talking until long after midnight (which was Mike's most active time, even though I was turning into a pumpkin). One of the projects for the WotF contest winners is that they have to research, plot, and write an entire short story in a day. At one event I remember sitting in the bar with the students who were wide-eyed and shaking, bedraggled, exhausted, and amazed at what they had done. One student remarked that he couldn't believe he had actually written a short story in a day. I let them have their moment of glory, and then said, "I always write a short story in a day." I turned to Mike. "How long does it take you to write a short story?" Mike shrugged. "A day. If it takes any longer than that, it's not cost effective."

Mike had such a large backlog of novels, and after Rebecca and I founded WordFire Press,

Mike asked if we'd be interested in reissuing them, maybe put together a couple of new short story collections. I was thrilled to have Mike Resnick on our list of authors, and he was happy to have his old books back in print again. We published First Person Peculiar, Away Games, The Dark Lady, The Outpost, The Soul Eater, Walpurgis III, *and two non-fiction volumes of* The SF Professional *essays.*

Mike was a good friend and great company, always willing to give his boundless energy to help and mentor new writers. What is the next generation of writers going to do without him?

OUR WRITERS OF THE FUTURE WRITER'S DAD: HELPING WRITERS BECOME AUTHORS

by John Goodwin, President, Galaxy Press

"It's a given that when you've had a successful career, you pay back. But in this field, it's almost impossible because, by the time you've been a remarkable success, everybody who helped you is either rich, or dead or both. So you pay forward."—Mike Resnick, 2018

And Mike Resnick demonstrated just how seriously he took this philosophy to heart in how he operated as a writer, editor, and friend to so many.

I was introduced to Mike by Kevin J. Anderson who recommended him as a contest judge. This was back in August 2009 with just enough time to invite him to attend that year's awards ceremony, which back then was held in the fall.

Mike agreed and so became a Writers of the Future writing contest judge in 2009. In subsequent years, he proved himself a willing mentor to each new group of winners, many of whom became "Mike's Writer Children."

Two years later, Mike stated in an email, "I've been 'adopting' a beginner or two almost every year since about 1990. I collaborate with them,

get them into print, vet their early stories before they submit them, and recommend markets to them (and them to editors). I imagine I'll choose one or two each year I'm a judge; it's my way of paying the field back, so you can understand how pleased I am to be working with an organization devoted to that cause."

That same year he provided an article for L. Ron Hubbard Presents Writers of the Future Volume 27 entitled, "Making It." In it, he shared what he saw a commonality amongst writers. First, a love of writing. Second, a constant study of the field. Third, talent. And fourth, perhaps the most essential quality which he defined as a fire in the belly. Over the course of our relationship, he personally took twenty-five winners under his wing to publish while co-authoring stories with fourteen winners.

In 2013, Mike sent an email announcing that he was editing a new magazine called Galaxy's Edge while proudly listing eleven finalists from the contest he would be publishing in the first five issues, as well as the three finalists in his Stellar Guild line of books. He ended his email, "So I've found a bunch of talent here, and I hope you'll keep asking me back. I pledge to continue doing my best for them."

In 2017, while accepting the L. Ron Hubbard Lifetime Achievement Award, he stated that since the 1990s he had done everything he could to help "Mike's Writer Children" and how proud he was of what he had written—but those books were in the past. He was expecting to be proud of numerous books under contract which, for all practical purposes, are the present. He closed his acceptance speech, "And this is the Writers of the Future. By definition, they should be less concerned with the past and the present than they are with other things. And because of that, I, on behalf of my writer children, and I hope twenty years from now, their writer children, proudly accept the Writers of the Future Lifetime Achievement Award."

I already miss Mike, but his legacy lives on through his writer children who now pay forward helping writers become authors.

A former diplomat, teacher and web designer, Philip's stood for parliament, sung, rowed, ridden in steeplechases and completed a forty-mile cross-country walk in under twelve hours. His short stories have been published in the USA, Canada and the UK. His novels are The Prophets of Baal *and* The Family Demon.

CADMUS P.I.

by Philip Brian Hall

This old guy staggers into the office, wheezing like a broken pair of bellows. The slaves who work the treadmill are on lunch break, so the elevator's out and he's had to climb the stairs. He's wizened, bent and leaning heavily on a stick, but he's wearing Tyrian purple embroidered with silver thread. Rich dude, huh? Potential client?

Electra's fussing around like she thinks the graybeard's fixing to have a heart attack on the premises. "This is Mr. Agenor, Cad," she says, anxiously pushing the oldster into a seat before he can keel over. "His daughter's been kidnapped."

"That so?" I smile in a welcoming way. "I'm happy to help, sir, but kidnapping sounds like a police case."

"No police," Agenor gasps. "No police."

"No? May I ask why not?" I expect the usual, you know, kidnappers threaten to harm his daughter if he calls the fuzz—put out her eyes, wall her up in a tomb or something like that. Happens all the time in the best soap operas by Sophocles.

"There's no police on Samothrace, son, only temple guards." He slumps forward, resting his head in his hands.

"Right," I say. "I knew that." I tell Electra to bring him a restorative.

I hate to look unprofessional. Fact is, Electra and me, we're new in the PI business; saw a gap in the market on a nice sunny vacation island; just opened yesterday. The frescoes on the office walls smell of wet paint and the doorman's still waiting for his spear.

"What makes you think your daughter's been kidnapped, sir?" I ask.

"Well, son," he raises rheumy eyes and squints at me, "she was carried bodily out of the house, screaming her head off."

"That does sound pretty suspicious," I agree. "Anyone get a good look at the perpetrator?"

"Sure, *I did*. I can describe him perfectly."

"Well, that's great, Mr. Agenor!"

"Yep. He was a big black bull with real long horns."

"Your daughter was abducted by a bull?"

Yeah right. Okay. It takes all kinds. Gotta start somewhere. A pity it has to be a guy who turns out to be drunk and delusional.

But then I get a brainwave. "How'd the bull carry her away?" I ask.

"Why, on his back of course." The old guy looks at me as if I'm stupid or something.

"And how did the bull get her *up* on his back, sir?"

Agenor gives me a blank look, then a light comes on behind his eyes. Maybe there's someone home after all.

"I see what you mean, son. I never thought of that."

"That's why I'm a detective, sir." Score one for client's first impressions. If my chiton had lapels I'd be polishing my nails on them. I push my luck. "Did you happen to hear *what* your daughter was screaming as she was carried away?"

"Didn't make any sense." Agenor mimes waving a hat in the air. "Sounded like *yee-ha!*"

"I see." Well, I'm congratulating myself on cracking our first case, yeah? This private eye game could be money for new rope. Yeah, about that. See, rope's only just been invented so there ain't no old rope yet.

"Were you and your daughter in Crete recently, sir?" I ask enigmatically.

"Why, yes we were! How'd you know that?" He looks at me with admiration.

"I told you, sir. I'm a detective."

"Amazing." Agenor shakes his head in wonder.

Electra brings in a big amphora of ouzo and two earthenware cups. She carefully stirs an equal quantity of water into the wine. You don't want to drink wine without water, you know—drives people crazy. Something to do with offending Dionysus.

"Electra," I say. "We're gonna get this girl back. But meanwhile we need a cover story. Get hold of the town gossip. Let's start a rumor Europa's been abducted by Zeus disguised as a bull. People will believe anything about the gods."

"Right you are, boss."

I beckon her closer and whisper in her ear. "Then book me a first-class stateroom on the next galley leaving for Knossos. Charge it to expenses."

I turn to the client. "Do you have a picture of your daughter, sir?"

The old guy pulls out a locket, flips open the lid to reveal a miniature portrait of a good-looking broad with long blonde ringlets.

"This is Europa."

"If I may borrow that, sir?" I smile.

"Sure." He nods and hands it over. Heavy gold. Guy must be good for a big fee.

"Now Electra will take you through the contract clause by clause, sir. If you find it's difficult to remember, we've composed a little poem to help you. I think we can promise you a speedy outcome to this case."

Yeah, right. So much for the best-laid plans. As it turns out, a storm forces my galley to shelter in a bay not far from Delphi. The captain says we're likely to be stuck awhile, so I figure I'll take a stroll up the mountain—maybe see if The Oracle has any news of Europa.

It's quite a climb up Mount Parnassus through the pine woods, but surprisingly cool near the summit. The air's fresh and last year's decaying cones crunch underfoot as I climb. Deer spook away from me showing their white scuts and bouncing off, oddly soundless, through the bracken. All very bucolic and pleasant but a bit too much like effort. I'll add it to the client's bill.

Eventually the Doric portico of the great temple, the one they call *The Big Apollo*, looms up ahead; it's situated on a rocky outcrop clear of the tree line. At the top of a great flight of white steps, four fat marble pillars support a triangular pediment maybe fifteen feet off the ground. It's the biggest building I've ever seen. I'm seriously impressed.

All of the sudden I hear a woman's voice. "You Cadmus?" she asks.

"Who wants to know?" I look all around, seeing no one.

"They call me Pythoness. That's cause I'm madder than a box o' snakes. I'm the priestess of Apollo."

I still can't figure where the voice is coming from. Is the dame hiding behind a tree?

"No, Cadmus. You can't see me. Though to tell the truth invisibility's a bit of a pain in the ass. People never listen properly, and I can't even point to things, right?"

"Yeah, I know," I sympathize. "Electra and I got a similar sort of problem to help folk remember our contract. You know, I'm wondering about diagrams? What d'ya think? Maybe some symbols to stand for words?"

"Say, that's not a bad scheme, Cadmus." The Pythoness sounds impressed. "That could help with my problem too. I appreciate it. In return I'll tell you something I wasn't going to. There's no point you chasing after Europa. She's been abducted by Zeus."

"Ah, no, you've misunderstood, Pythoness." A surprise, because I hadn't expected the news to get abroad this fast. I must tell Electra. That girl's got brilliant PR skills. "The Zeus thing was a cover story we put about to protect the family's reputation. Their daughter actually ran off with a bull rider from the Cretan Rodeo."

"You think?" This time Pythoness don't sound so impressed. "Look dummy, the bull carrying Europa disappeared over the horizon, right?"

"That's right. Witnesses all said the bull ran away."

"Cadmus," she speaks slowly and plainly as if addressing a kid of five. "Samothrace is an island. It's surrounded by sea. Did the bull swim?"

"Ah! Now you come to mention it... No."

This is embarrassing. It seems I didn't crack the case after all. Old Agenor will never swallow the ocean cruise on expenses and I'm going to be short of funds to pay the captain when we eventually arrive in Crete, which is now a place I don't want to go anyway.

"You know, if people learn I missed a clue like that, I'll never work as a detective again."

"Just as well *I* got a job for you, then." She chuckles, you know the way priestesses do. "Apollo says you can found a new city in his honor. All you have to do is follow the Moon Cow."

"Moo Cow?" I echo.

"*Moon Cow*, Cadmus, *Moon Cow*! What did I just say about *listening*?"

"Sorry."

"Oh, look, don't worry, you'll know it when you see it. Just follow the cow. When she lies down to rest, that'll be where Apollo wants the new city."

This sounds like another serious hike. I'm not keen.

"This PI business is not exactly all I'd hoped for," I say. "Too much like farming. I've had enough farming."

"You think you got problems?" the Pythoness replies. "Just think how much trouble future scholars are going to have following your story in oral history."

"I'll maybe work on my symbolic communications idea," I say, nodding.

"Do that. And here, take this." A toy dragon falls out of a tree and lands at my feet.

"What's this?"

"What does it look like? It's a scale model of a dragon, you idiot. Hey, d'ya notice what I did there? *Scale* model, d'ya geddit? Oh, never mind. When you find a real one, pull its teeth out. Then plant the teeth just like seeds where you establish your city."

"You want me to sow dragon's teeth?"

"Hey, you catch on quick, Cadmus. Plant the seeds and you'll reap something you're gonna need. Courtesy of The God."

I don't know. Follow the bull; follow the cow; pull a dragon's teeth? I'm a PI not a veterinarian. I shake my head and give a deep sigh. It never happens like this in the cartoons they paint round all the most expensive Grecian urns. Still, whatever Apollo wants, Apollo gets. You don't argue with The God.

I wander back down the mountain and, lo and behold, I come across a cow, also wandering, in this case down the main street of a cute village. The settlement sits on top of an exposed foothill of Parnassus, so I guess it gets a lot of sun at noonday. The locals seem to deal with this by having their houses inside out: all blank whitewashed walls on the outside, but with inner windows opening on to shady central courtyards. Real neat. Great idea.

The cow's all brown but with a white mark on its side just like a waxing crescent moon.

"Hey, you Moon Cow?" I ask hopefully.

The cow looks at me out of sorrowful deep brown eyes. "Moo," says the cow.

"See? I knew I was right before," I say. Then I fall in behind.

You ever try walking behind a cow? Like, cows are sl-o-ow, folks. They go nowhere in a hurry. By the time I've been following the cow three days I figure we're well over the border into Boeotia, my sandals are scuffed, my feet are dusty and sore and I'm dropping for lack of sleep. I've also collected quite a crowd of hangers-on who're all fountains of wit; they're pointing and laughing and they've run through all the cow-jokes in the known world half a dozen times.

We've also passed half a dozen great sites for a settlement. I try to catch the cow's attention. "Hey, Moon Cow—how about here?"

"Moo," says the cow. That'll be a no, I guess.

Then all of the sudden the cow slumps down, exhausted. I figure this must be the place. It's a nice sheltered position on an open hillside. There's plenty of vegetation so I figure there's fertile ground and good grassland for pasture. I see a tree-clad ravine over to the east; I figure there should be a stream running down inside the cleft, so I tell a couple of my irritating followers to go and fetch us fresh water.

"Why?" they say. "We're tired too."

"Hey, you want to be citizens of my new city or not? We have to make a sacrifice to Apollo so he'll bless our foundation."

"We could sacrifice the cow," one of them says helpfully.

"You wanna rethink that idea, sonny," says the cow, getting up again. "I'm not tired. I could walk for weeks." Okay, when the cow finally speaks, she's making more problems. Typical!

"Relax, he's joking!" I say. I turn back to my guys. "Go get the water. We'll make camp."

They're back in two minutes. They don't have any water.

"Get your own water, cowboy," they say. "That there stream's guarded by a dragon."

"A dragon?" I groan. Then a thought strikes me. I rake about in my rucksack until I find the model. "Did it look like this?" I ask.

"Well, leaving aside that it breathes fire and is twenty feet high, I guess there might be a passing resemblance," says one.

"Yes!" I exclaim. And I rush over there as fast as my weary legs can carry me.

Sure enough I find a huge scaly dragon with huge yellow teeth and a great big red-spotted, white handkerchief tied around its badly-swollen jaw. It's sitting beside the fast-running stream in the bottom of the deep rocky ravine and bathing the swelling with a sponge it keeps soaking in the cold water.

"Go away!" hisses the dragon, smoke and flame gushing from its mouth. "Can't you see I'm in pain here? My mouth feels like it's on fire."

"Dragon," I say, "this is your lucky day. It so happens I'm a dentist specializing in dragon's teeth."

"Dummy, I'm a dinosaur. Dragons are a myth."

"What's a myth?" I ask.

"You got a *lithp* or *thomething, thonny?* I got a toothache, that's what's *amyth*."

Cows, dragons, suddenly everyone's a comedian. "Never mind," I say. "Look, I just administer a general anesthetic, extract the offending molar and *Hey, presto*! Bob's your uncle!"

"You're thinking of some other dinosaur," says the dinosaur, shaking its head. "I don't have any uncle named Bob. All my relatives are called Rex. It's a family tradition. I'm T Rex. My uncles are called A Rex, B Rex, C Rex..."

"So!" I enthuse. "We might be related. My name's Cadmus Rex." A pardonable exaggeration, right? It'll soon be true. "I give family discounts."

"You do? And can you really fix my toothache?"

"Absolutely!" I assure him.

"I'm not sure about this." The dinosaur shakes his huge head again and burns off a swathe of vegetation. "I've never had a general anesthetic. How does it work?"

"Like this!" I say, smashing him over the head with a rock.

The dinosaur drops down insensible and I'm soon busy extracting his teeth. When I'm finished I wrap them in his spotted handkerchief and set off back for the campsite. I'm annoyed to find no tents pitched and all the guys asleep. The cow's nowhere to be seen.

"Dammit!" I fling the teeth on the ground in fury. "Do I have to do everything myself? Wake up you jackasses. Where's the cow?" I roust out the two guys who'd failed to fetch the water.

"Er, boss..." The talkative one rubs his eyes and points behind me.

"What?" I turn round to see where he's pointing. Where I'd thrown the seeds on the ground a whole troop of soldiers have sprung up from the earth, fully armed and armored. They look warlike. They look bloodthirsty. They don't look amused. I gotta think fast.

"Quick," I say to my guys, "collect all the trash you can find in camp and put it in this dragon's handkerchief. I'll stall them. Do *not* take long!"

I stride toward the scowling troopers with a smile on my lips. "Hi, guys! I'm Cadmus Rex. I guess you're all here to apply for jobs in my new city guards? That's amazingly prompt of you; we ain't even built the city yet. But I'll tell you what, if you'd like to line up just over here, I'll be happy to begin the selection process early."

I carry on my spiel for a minute or two until one of my guys sneaks up timorously behind me and hands me the handkerchief, knotted together to form a bag, full of trash from the camp.

"Now this is how it's going to work, fellers," I call out to the soldiers. "You see this scrap of dragon skin here?" I peel off a piece of dinosaur that unaccountably seems to have become stuck to my chiton and wave it at them.

"Now I'm going to mark some magic symbols on this piece of skin, guys, and these symbols say *THE BEST*, right? I'm hiding the piece of skin inside this bag, right? And whoever brings it to me is going to be declared officially *THE BEST* of you, which makes him commander of the city guard with all the privileges and perks pertaining thereto. You all got that?"

Just as well the Pythoness already got me thinking about the symbolic code stuff. So I scrawl some symbols on the skin and stuff it in the bag. Though I say it myself they're neat designs. I might be able to work this up into a proper system. But not right now. I heave the bag high as I can in the air and it falls down to earth in the middle of the troop.

Well, right away they all start in fighting each other. Oh! That is some kind of a brawl. There's one *Dis* of a noise; shouting and bawling; arms lopped off, legs lopped off, heads lopped off. In the end the ground's covered in blood and assorted body parts and there's only five guys left standing. Just about the number I reckon I'll need for city guards.

Hey, I'm some inventor, yeah? I just thought up a great system for whittling down job applicants. I think I'll call it *aristo-cracy*—that's Greek, yeah? It means when I'm in charge there'll be plenty of jobs for the boys.

Luckily, these boys are all too bushed to fight any more right now. One of them grabs the wreckage of the bag and finds the piece of skin. He brings it to me and collapses to his knees with exhaustion.

The piece of skin is a bit torn. Out of the seven symbols I'd scrawled, only six are left. *THE BES...* Well, adaptation to circumstances is my middle name. That's after Cadmus and before Rex, right?

"Miraculous!" I say. "A clear sign from The God that our city is to be called *THEBES*. You, sir—what's your name?—are officially selected commander of Thebes' first ever civil guard. You can be police commissioner. That means every criminal you catch can be sold into slavery and you charge a commission on the sales. How does that sound?"

"Sounds okay," the new police commissioner grunts.

"But first off I have to go to Samothrace and fetch my secretary, Electra. The rest of you, just get busy building. Nice whitewashed-stone houses built round central courtyards. Windows only on the inside. You got that? When I get back I want to see a proper garden city. Police Commissioner, you're deputized in charge."

"Are you going to give me some more magic symbols, sir? Sort of certificate of my authority?" he asks.

"Sure thing," I say. "But with all this stuff I have to write down, I'm going to need some more hide to scrawl them on."

I scratch my chin and consider. "Tell me, Commissioner, do you have any experience skinning dragons?"

✿

HISTORICAL NOTE: *(If you must.) The legendary hero Cadmus, founder of Thebes, discoverer of parchment etc., was also credited by the Ancient Greeks with inventing writing. It's too early to tell whether this will turn out to have been a good thing.*

Copyright © 2020 by Philip Brian Hall.

---

*Joe Haldeman is a multiple Hugo and Nebula Award winner, the author of an acknowledged classic (*The Forever War*), and a former Worldcon Guest of Honor.*

COMPLETE SENTENCE

by Joe Haldeman

The cell was spotless white and too bright and smelled of chlorine bleach. "So I've had it, is what you're saying." Charlie Draper sat absolutely still on the cell bunk. "I didn't kill Maggie. You know that better than anybody."

His lawyer nodded slowly and looked at him with no expression. She was beautiful, and that sometimes helped with a jury, though evidently not this time. "We've appealed, of course." Her voice was a fraction of a second out of synch with her mouth. "It's automatic."

"And meaningless. I'll be out before they open the envelope."

"Well." She stepped over to the small window and looked down at the sea. "We went over the pluses and minuses before you opted for virtual punishment."

"So I serve a hundred years in one day—"

"Less than a day. Overnight."

"—and then sometime down the pike some other jury decides I'm innocent, or at least not guilty, and then what? They give me back the hundred years I sat here?"

He was just talking, of course; he knew the answer. There might be compensation for wrongful imprisonment. A day's worth, though, or a century? Nobody had yet been granted it; virtual sentencing was too new.

"You have to leave now, counselor," a disembodied voice said. She nodded, opened her mouth to say something, and disappeared.

That startled him. "It's already started?"

The door rattled open, and an unshaven trusty in an orange jumpsuit shambled in with a tray. Behind him was a beefy guard with a shotgun.

"What's with the gun?" he said to the trusty. "This isn't real; I can't escape."

"Don't answer him," the guard said. "You'll wind up in solitary too."

58

"Oh, bullshit. Neither of you are real people."

The guard stepped forward, reversed the weapon, and thumped him hard on the sternum. "Not real?" He hit the wall behind him and slid to the floor, trying to breathe, pain radiating from the center of his chest.

As the cell walls and Draper faded, a nurse gently wiggled the helmet until it came off her head. It was like a light bicycle helmet, white. With a warm gloved hand, she helped her sit up on the gurney.

She looked over at Draper, lying on the gurney next to hers. His black helmet was more complicated, a thick cable and lots of small wires. The same blue hospital gown as she was wearing. But he had a catheter, and there was a light black cable around his chest, hardly a restraint, held in place by a small lock with a tag she had signed.

The nurse set her white helmet down carefully on a table. "You don't want to drive or anything for a couple of hours." She had a sour expression, lips pursed.

"No problem. I have Autocar."

She nodded microscopically. *Rich bitch.* "Take you where your things are."

"Okay. Thank you." As she scrunched off the gurney, the gown slid open, and she reached back to hold it closed, feeling silly. Followed the woman as she stalked through the door. "I take it you don't approve."

"No, ma'am. He serves less than one day for murdering his wife."

"A, he didn't murder her, and B, it will feel like a hundred years."

"That's what they say." She turned with eyes narrowing. "They all say they didn't do it. And they say it feels like a long time. What would you expect them to say? 'I beat the system and was in and out in a day'? Here."

As soon as the door clicked shut, she opened the locker and lifted out her neatly folded suit, the charcoal gray one she had appeared to be wearing in the cell a few minutes before.

The blow had knocked the wind out of him. By the time he got his voice back, they were gone.

The tray had a paper plate with something like cold oatmeal on it. He picked up the plastic spoon and tasted the stuff. Grits. They must have known he hated grits.

"They didn't say anything about solitary. What, I'm going to sit here like this for a hundred years?" No answer.

He carried the plate over to the barred window. It was open to the outside. A fall of perhaps a hundred feet to an ocean surface. He could hear faint surf but, leaning forward, couldn't see the shore, even with the cold metal bars pressing against his forehead. The air smelled of seaweed, totally convincing.

He folded the paper plate and threw it out between the bars. The grits sprayed out and the plate dipped and twirled realistically, and fell out of sight.

He studied the waves. Were they too regular? That would expose their virtuality. He had heard that if you could convince yourself that it wasn't real—completely convince your body that this wasn't happening—the time might slip quickly away in meditation. Time might disappear.

But it was hard to ignore the throbbing in his chest. And there were realistic irregularities in the waves. In the trough between two waves, a line of pelicans skimmed along with careless grace.

Maybe the illusion was only maintained at that level when he was concentrating. He closed his eyes and tried to think of nothing.

Zen trick: four plain tiles. Make each one disappear. The no-thing that is left is just as real. Exactly as real. After a while, he opened his eyes again.

The pelicans came back. Did that mean anything?

Maybe he shouldn't have thrown away the grits. You probably get hungry in virtual reality. But you couldn't starve to death, not overnight. No matter how long it seemed.

He gave the iron bar a jerk. It squeaked.

He tugged on it twice, and it seemed to move a fraction of a millimeter each time. Was that possible? He looked closely, and indeed the hole the bar was seated in had slightly enlarged. He could wiggle it.

"Trusty?" he shouted. Nothing. He walked to the steel door and shouted through the little hole. "Hey! Your goddamn jail's already falling apart!" He peered through the small peephole. Nothing but darkness.

He sniffed at the hole, and it smelled of drilled metal. "Hey! I know you're out there!"

But what did he really know?

✿

She popped her umbrella against the afternoon shower and was almost to the parking place when a young man came running out. "Ms. Hartley!" He was waving a piece of paper. "Ms. Hartley!" She stepped toward him and let him get under the umbrella.

"Your objection was approved. You can bring him out any time!"

She glanced at her watch. He'd only been in VR for about twenty minutes, counting the time she'd spent dressing. "Let's go!" Two months passing each minute.

Security at the courthouse door took an agonizing five minutes. But the young man raced on ahead to make sure the room was ready.

She crashed through a door and rushed up the single flight of stairs rather than wait for the elevator. The sour-faced woman was blocking the entrance to the VR room.

"Get out of the way. Every second, he spends a day in that awful cell."

"You know this won't work if he doesn't believe in his own innocence. If he blames himself in any way."

"He wasn't even *there* when his wife was murdered!" The woman's eyes searched the lawyer's face. "Look! I've been a defense attorney for eighteen years. I know when someone's lying to me. *He didn't kill her!*"

She pushed on in and the young man was standing by a chair, next to the gurney that Charlie Draper lay on, holding the white helmet. "Here. You don't have to lie down. Just put this on."

✿

Crappy system can't even make an illusion that works.

He went back to the iron bar and rotated it squeaking in its concrete socket, and gave it a good rattle. Concrete dust sifted down. He seized it in both hands and gave it all he had. "Bitch!" He squeezed it as hard as he had Maggie's neck, and jerked, with the strength that had snapped it and killed her.

The bar came free in his hands. A piece of concrete fell to the floor with a solid thunk. "You call this a…"

A large crack crawled up and down from floor to ceiling. With a loud growl, half the wall tilted and fell piecemeal into the sea. "Wait." A fine powder was drifting down. He looked up to see the ceiling disappear. "No." All four walls crumbled into gravel and showered to the sea.

✿

When they took the helmet off her, there was an older man, dressed like a doctor, standing there.

"It's a temporary thing," he said. "He's resisting coming out of it. For some reason."

"I didn't go to the cell. I didn't go anywhere," she said, peering inside the helmet. "It was all just white, and white noise, static."

"You're out of the circuit. The electronics do test out. But he's not letting you make contact."

She looked into her client's vacant eyes. She touched his cheek gently and he didn't respond. "Has this happened before?"

"Not with people who know and trust each other. But we'll get through to him."

"Meanwhile…every ten hours is a hundred years?"

"That's a safe assumption." The doctor opened the manila folder in his hand and looked at the single piece of paper within. "He signed a waiver—"

"I know. I was there." She lifted her client's hand and let it drop back onto the sheet. "He's a…social kind of guy. I hope he's not too lonely."

✿

There was only the floor and the iron door. He touched the door and it fell away. It turned end over end once, and slid flawlessly into the water, like an Olympic diver.

Above him, a perfect cloudless sky that somehow had no sun. Below, the waves marched from one horizon to the opposite. A line of pelicans appeared.

He tried to throw himself into the water, but he hit something soft and invisible, and fell gently back.

He screamed until he was hoarse. Then he tried to sleep. But the noise of the waves kept him awake.

Copyright © 2011 by Joe Haldeman.

THE ENGINE OF THE NIGHT

by Barry N. Malzberg

It becomes a simple deal, at least in the abstract, as you edge toward or beyond the Biblical span in the mortality racket; it becomes quite clear, whether you like it or not, and the deal is this: either you are deserted by those you love or they are deserted by you; either you do the chapters from Lamentation *or they are stuck with the rotten task. It's a rough deal, a Hobson's Choice in reverse, but I do not know any third path, not unless there are metaphysical aspects still unknown to me. Or maybe supra-religious aspects which strike me as unacceptable.*

I have already done the Locus *thing, which should have been available well before this will meet the internet or print edition. This is Mike Resnick, arguably one of the ten most important science fiction writers to emerge with the category since 1926 and I felt I had to take note. He was indomitable. He has been part of the landscape. Indeed, he has* been *the landscape for over forty years. He was the property manager, the property, the open-ended bonds and the maintenance crew in synchrony. There is no way to write this, good or bad.*

Mike was my second most important collaborator (between Bill Pronzini & Kathleen Koja), and similarly my second most prolific: a novelette, a handful of short stories and fifteen years of 4500 word columns—62 of them for the Science Fiction Writers of America Bulletin, *through which we investigated, argued over and reached only partial solution to the many problems of the category and its writers. I grumbled in and out of those dialogues. He was forceful and unforgiving and not unwilling to mock my positions; I responded by sulking, nattering and making occasional announcements of readiness to quit—all of which I was dissuaded from and that was a goddamned good thing because we did good work in those columns through a fifteen year period of the greatest change, not only in publishing but in the Republic.*

We did not get the job done but nobody gets this kind of thing done (anybody remember Murray Kempton? Pete Hamill? Jimmy Breslin? Max Lerner? even James Thurber?) and all you can do is be true to your moment. We were true to many moments and the measure of the work we did in those columns is that it was so much of their time that it must necessarily perish. *It was not for the ages, it was* of *the ages, Shakespeare's Ages of Man and at the end sans teeth, sans heart, sans perhaps even soul.*

Enough. He was the best friend I ever had, the most loyal, the most trustworthy: uncompromising enough to tell me bluntly when I was full of shit, but always there for me. He was there for me for forty years, longer than I knew either of my parents. He was—self-plagiarizing for the only instance from my Locus *tribute—the best person I ever knew. I did not deserve him. Our wretched, magnificent, flawed, brutal, brilliant, and utterly pointed field did not deserve him either. But we got him, we will have him as long as we persist, and some day the Expedition from Ganymede will sort out the whole damned thing. Meanwhile, there is a lot of work there, much of it magnificent. Try "Mwambi in the Squared Circle."*

George Nikolopoulos is a master of the short-short, these days known as flash fiction. His Galaxy's Edge *story, "You Can Always Change the Past", has been selected to appear in Baen's* The Year's Best Military and Adventure SF.

I AM SALVADOR

by George Nikolopoulos

I woke up from the strangest dream to see a small boy standing next to my bed, looking at me. He seemed no more than two years old.

When he saw that I was awake he said nothing; he just motioned me to follow and walked out of the room.

I got out of bed and followed him. No more melting clocks, and yet it felt like I was still dreaming.

The boy wore a white nightshirt that resembled a miniature version of mine. His footsteps made no sound on the wooden floor.

We went out to the porch and walked to the barn. It had rained in the evening, one of the first autumn rains; the earth was damp and moist under my bare feet. A crescent moon had risen in the east, casting enough light to let me see where I was going.

We reached the barn and still he hadn't turned once to look at me or made any sound, and yet I followed like a dog on a leash.

After all the silence, the sound of the creaking door when I entered the barn almost made me jump; he'd squeezed in through the opening but I was larger and had to push the door open on its rusty hinges.

The barn smelled of hay and fresh manure. As my eyes slowly adjusted to the darkness, I could see the boy clearly. He'd stopped walking and stood right there looking at me. He seemed oddly familiar.

"Who are you?" I said. My voice sounded thin to my own ears.

"Yo soy Salvador Dalí i Domenech," he replied.

I wanted to laugh, and yet I didn't feel like laughing. The whole scene was so eerie that nothing seemed beyond the bounds of possibility.

"I am Salvador Dalí *i* Domenech," I said.

He smiled, and I realized why his face was so familiar.

"You were named after *me*," he said. "You were born nine months after my death."

He didn't sound like a boy of two; but he was a ghost, if his claim was true. I was eighteen, and he was older than me. My older brother, who died at the age of two, nine months before I was born.

I remembered my mother taking me to his grave when I was five. She'd told me I was his reincarnation. At the time, I'd believed it; yet now he stood in front of me, so it seems that after all I wasn't.

"Why are you here?" I asked. "Aren't the dead supposed to be...*somewhere*?" Heaven, hell, purgatory; anywhere but here. I was jittery. I should have never left my bed. Was I still dreaming?

"I was born to be the greatest painter of all time," he said. "I wasn't supposed to die that young. My death was a mistake of the Fates. It was wrong. *Terribly* wrong. It has to be made right."

I looked at him, eye to eye. He was so small. I'd heard of ghosts, but nobody comes back from the dead. "*I* am Salvador Dalí," I said. "You can rest in peace; your destiny will be fulfilled. *I'm* the one who's going to fulfil it. *I will be* the greatest painter of all time."

He snorted. "So I was promised, but I'm afraid it's not going to happen. I've seen your paintings. You're not nearly good enough. That's why I'm here."

I was incensed. How could this puny boy speak of me like that? Ever since I could remember, I'd always been painting. My paintings were so lifelike, you could hear them breathe. *"I am Salvador Dalí!"* I thought. *"The one and only!"* Even so, he was my older brother—or had been, anyway. I had to treat him with respect, even though he was just a ghost now.

Showing respect to the little rascal was too hard for me, however. I looked at him haughtily. "So you think you're better than me?" I said. "Prove it. Show me how great you are."

Instead of replying, he showed me his hands. I looked at them, uncomprehending. He extended his right hand as if to shake, so I shook it; or at least I tried. My hand passed right through his. It was the strangest sensation; it left my hand tingling and numb.

"I am a *ghost*," he said. "Do you think I can hold a brush? But I'll show you what I mean." He pointed at a horse, sleeping in the barn. "Draw this horse for me," he said.

I always kept my drawing material in the barn, the one place where I had privacy to paint. I took out my brushes and some canvas, I lit a candle and I drew the horse. I showed it to him, proudly. It was an exact replica of the sleeping animal. Though I said so myself, my sketch was magnificent. It looked as if you could wake the horse and it would start whinnying.

"*That's* how good I am," I said with a smile. "Have you ever seen a painting so true to life like this one?"

He smiled back. "As I said, you aren't *nearly* good enough," he replied. "Is this how a horse looks to you?"

I stared at him, incredulous. Of course it was. "What do you mean?" I asked.

"You must learn to see the true essence of the horse," he said. "You must see *through* the horse. But don't worry, I'm here to teach you. Salvador Dalí is destined to become the greatest painter this world will ever know—and you'll never be able to make it happen without my help."

✿

So he taught me. Every single night he came to my room, and I got out of bed and followed him to the barn. Not once did my parents—*our* parents—wake during all those night forays, for weeks on end.

He taught me how to see through *his* eyes. His was a strange world, but I was drawn to it like an insect to the light. I saw the horse transformed right before my eyes. Its legs became spindly, spidery. It reared; it towered above me. Its mane writhed like fire. Its face became mad, beastly.

The whole world was transformed. It became a landscape of melting clocks, flying tigers, men who looked like insects, ships with sails of butterflies. A world of illusions and visions. And it was *his* visions I now painted.

He'd been right, after all. I had been painting perfectly; I could paint any single thing in the world and my painting would look exactly like the real-life model. But this gift wasn't enough. Others had been able to do that, and still others would be in the future. It was his bizarre visions that would make me the greatest painter in the whole world; and so I, like an overgrown sponge, absorbed everything he taught

me and I was thankful for it. I never once questioned his motives for teaching me; he was my brother.

✿

"You're ready now," he finally said, after a month of weird visions and sleepless nights. "You're better than any painter ever was. You've become a true master."

I smiled, in my pride and glory.

"You won't need me anymore," he went on to say. "I've taught you everything I know. I should be getting ready to move on..."

"I'll miss you," I said—and I honestly meant it. "Thanks for everything, brother. I'll never forget you."

"But I want something from you, in exchange for teaching you. It's only fair, after all, isn't it?"

The way he said this made it sound ominous, but I wasn't alarmed. "What do you want?" I said. "I owe you so much, you may ask for anything."

"Only a trifle." He chuckled; somehow this creepy sound coming from such a little boy made my hair stand on end. "I'll just be needing your *body*," he said—and he floated upward. Before I could react, his hands were at my throat; but still they couldn't hurt me. They weren't solid, they felt like mist. And then they passed through the skin of my neck and they were there *inside* my throat, clutching at my windpipe. "Stop it," I said. I was having a hard time breathing. My throat was on fire. "Stop it right now!" I wanted to say, but no words left my mouth. I struggled to shake him off, but I couldn't. I tried to get hold of him but my hands passed right through him. I started seeing black spots. I began to lose consciousness.

My last thought was, "*I am Salvador Dalí! I am...*"

✿

I got up and looked at my hands. They seemed so *elegant*. I stooped and picked up a brush. I held it fast. To be able to *hold*, after so many years of frustration—*after so many years of death*. I laughed. "I'm back!" I shouted into the night. "Salvador Dalí is back!"

Scott lives with husband, Mark, in Sacramento. He started reading sci-fi at nine, and as he grew up, he wondered where all the queer characters were. Eventually he decided to write them himself. A Rainbow Award–winning author with thirty-five publications, he runs QueerSciFi.com and is an associate member of SFWA.

EVENTIDE

by J. Scott Coatsworth

I felt a little sick. Okay, a lot sick—like something had wrenched my stomach out of my gut and pulled it halfway to Mars.

Not far from the truth, as it turned out.

I reached for my stomach. My furry belly was a little thicker than I would have liked—too much processed sugar, Peter said. That and the whole no exercise thing.

What did I eat this time? My memories were a bit fuzzy.

I remembered bright lights and a sharp antiseptic smell. And a keening whine.

I opened my eyes. The light above dimmed of its own accord.

That's weird. And the smell…kind of antiseptic?

I sat up, and my fingers sank into the soft blue mat beneath me, leaving an impression when I lifted them up which just as quickly disappeared.

I was naked. *What the hell?*

Alarmed, I looked around as my eyesight cleared.

I was alone in a plain white room. White walls curved into a white floor and ceiling, and only the "bed" had any color—a bright blue pad on a raised pedestal. There were no doors or windows.

I pushed myself up and my head spun. My stomach clenched, and I felt sick.

The room swam around me, darkening, changing.

I've been sick. I was certain of that, but the details were vague. I fell back, cushioning my fall with my left hand. "Hello? Peter?"

"Hello, Tanner Black." The reply was warm, cordial. Feminine, maybe? Hard to tell.

"Hello." My head ached. "Where am I? Who is this?" The walls continued to flow.

"I am Sera. You are in an awakening room. Welcome to the Seeker."

"Welcome to *where*?" None of this made any sense. *Where's Peter? He must be looking for me.* I tried to get up again and a searing pain clenched my gut.

"Please lie down, Mr. Black. You have not fully recovered yet, and your room is not ready."

Recovered from what? I wanted to argue, but suddenly resting seemed like an eminently sensible idea. I *was* tired, and my head hurt.

Maybe just a short nap.

I pulled my feet up and lay down, wishing for my comfy feather pillow.

The foam conformed to my body, hugging me. *So comfortable.*

That thought faded as sleep took me, and the light went out.

✧

I woke slowly.

I lay still for a while, hoping not to alert whoever or whatever had brought me here to the fact that I was awake.

The last thing I remembered was being in bed, in our little bungalow near the river. With Peter. A strange keening sound rang through my mind, mixed with the smell of hospital disinfectant.

Is this heaven?

I opened one eye, looking at the ceiling.

It was no longer white. Instead, it was coffered, the stained oak paneling that Peter and I had chosen when we'd renovated my den.

I was dressed in khakis and a polo tee.

"Good morning."

I sat bolt-upright, looking around for the source of the voice.

The voice from before. Sera?

She was on the far side of the room, a woman so perfect that I found myself aching at the sight of her in all the wrong places. It was strange. I was pretty much a Kinsey six, a gold-star gay.

Peter and I had joked about the whole "gay men liking hot female celebrities" thing more than once. *"I'd switch teams for Ariana Grande. Voice like an angel."*

That was Peter, ten years younger than me. Always up on the latest thing. Me, I was more of a classic type. *Angelina Jolie, any day.* But this woman? I would have let her have her way with me. *Is that weird?*

Then it struck me. This *was* my den. *How did she get here? How did I? Why can't I remember?*

Sera stood by the window, running her tapered fingers over the books on my bookshelf. She was tall, her skin tawny, her face smooth and unlined, and her eyes were golden and almost too big.

"Good morning….Sera? What are you doing in my house?" Maybe the white room had just been a weird dream.

"Yes. And this is not your house. Not exactly." She set the leather-bound book she'd been leafing through back on the shelf and sat down in the russet-red Tom Ford leather chair in the corner.

I laughed nervously. "Not my house?" What the hell was she talking about?

"It will all make sense soon."

Sure it would.

It was fall outside—the maple leaves outside were red and gold. *Is it November already?* The antiseptic smell was gone, replaced with something like lavender.

"So if this isn't my house…what is this place? Heaven?" Maybe she meant they'd foreclosed on our place, though I didn't remember that. Was she a Realtor? I frowned.

She looked at me strangely for a second, and then smiled. "No. This is neither heaven nor hell. You have some strange concepts."

I didn't know if that *you* meant me, or maybe humankind? Or…? "Where are we, then?" If this wasn't my study, the resemblance was uncanny, right down to the scuff in the bamboo floor where I'd dropped one of my granite bookends.

"We'll get to that. First, let's talk about where you are *from*."

"Dammit, this *is* hell." Heaven wouldn't keep me waiting like this. *Maybe hell is a waiting room.* Weird how she talked so formally, no contractions.

Sera laughed again. "Really, it is not. Suffice it to say that it's a long *time* away from your own."

In a galaxy far, far away… That sounded a lot like sci fi. "Is this Milliways? If so, I wanna meet the meat."

Her eyes unfocused again, and then she laughed even harder than before, but her laugh sounded a bit odd. "A surprisingly apt guess."

I hadn't expected *that*. Douglass Adams would be proud. "So am I dead?"

She smiled. It looked like maybe she was trying to reassure me, but it was more like a grimace. "Tell me about where you came from." She seemed eager to press ahead—if she'd had a watch, she would have been glancing at it furiously. "I promise all will be explained."

I sighed. Now this was sounding like therapy. I rubbed my chin, thinking. "My husband and I live in a little yellow house in Sacramento." *Peter, where are you?*

"What's Sacramento like?"

"It was kind of a cow town. Not as bad now as it was twenty years ago."

Her eyes unfocused, a gesture I was coming to realize meant she was accessing information. "Ah, I understand. Do you like it?" She was taking notes. I could feel it.

I nodded. "More than I thought I would. I came from San Francisco—that's a big city by the ocean. Sacramento is…was?…calmer. Less crazy."

Sera rubbed her chin, looking lost in thought. "And your husband?"

"Peter?" I laughed. "He's a pain in the ass." I couldn't bring myself to talk about him in the past tense.

She started to unfocus.

"It means he's difficult, in an endearing way." Peter was my everything, even if I wanted to kill him at least twice a week.

"I understand."

I looked around again at the den, feeling closed in. Just before this—there'd been a white room like the one I woke up in the first time. Clean, slick, soulless. "I think I was sick."

It was a statement, not a question. There'd been chemo. Weeks of nausea, followed by weeks of recovery.

Sitting in The Chair. The Cancer Club.

Memory washed over me.

"What you in for?" The skinny woman had a purple bandana wrapped around her head, her freckles vivid on pale cheeks.

I stared at the tube pumping poison into my veins, wishing I were anywhere else. "Prostate. You?"

"Breast." She touched her flat chest, flashing me a mischievous smile. *"What do you think of my rack?"*

My face flushed. "I don't know…"

"It's all right. Just messing with you. I'm Anna Kirkpatrick."

I nodded, relieved. "I'm Tanner. You have a nice Irish name."

She grinned. "Yes, from my father's side. You?"

"Good British stock. Long time back."

"Welcome to the Cancer Club." She was sweet. We talked about books we'd read, our families, our cancers.

Three weeks later she was gone.

I opened my eyes and looked down at my hands. *Cancer.*

Sera nodded, like a therapist. "Cancer sounds like a terrible thing."

"You don't have it…here?" How did she know? *Where am I? When am I? Is any of this real?*

"No. We did once. Something similar—a cellular malfunction. It was a long time ago."

I looked up, hopeful. "Figured out the secret?" *Maybe they cured me after all.*

Sera looked down at her hands, not meeting my gaze.

"I…I died, didn't I?"

"Yes."

I bit my lip. "So. This *is* heaven." Sera was an angel. Not that I was particularly religious. And yet, here I was.

"Let me show you something." She stood and touched the window. It shimmered and changed, the trees and golden afternoon sunlight vanishing.

It was an almost indescribably beautiful vision, hard to render in words.

It was a play of colors, every one of them in the Pantone chart. Or an explosion, sparklers of light playing across the screen. Or maybe a bursting of bubbles.

Or a grand symphony the likes of which Beethoven might have conceived, if he'd worked for Pixar.

It was all of those things, and none of them at all.

I stumbled toward it, reaching my hand out to touch the cool, clear surface. "It's breathtaking." I tried to take it all in.

She nodded. "The screen filters out the escaping radiation. Otherwise you'd be dead."

I already am. I didn't say it. *I should be grateful for whatever this is.*

Mom would have shaken me by the scruff of my neck—*Do you realize how lucky you are?*

Then again, maybe this was all just a dream. "What is it?"

"It's the end of all things." Her lips were set in a grim line.

I stared at her. She looked serious, and also a little broken.

I wasn't good at reading women. I wanted to comfort her, but I held back.

This is *Milliways.* Without the fine dining and self-introductory cows. But the end of the Universe, nevertheless. Or maybe some chemo fever-dream. "Why am I here?"

My stomach rumbled.

Traitor. It didn't matter. *I don't need food. I'm already dead.* Though for some reason, I suddenly had a massive craving for a burger and fries.

Sera touched the window, and autumn returned, though somehow its beauty seemed washed out now. "I'll make you a deal. Let's share a meal. And for every question of mine you answer, I'll answer one from you."

Answers from an angel? Who wouldn't want that? I wished Peter were here to see this. "Deal."

She waved her hand. The alien bed sank into the floor, and in its place, another Tom Ford chair and a small wooden table arose, matched to the stained maple paneling on the walls.

"Fancy." I knelt to examine the table. It was beautiful, hand-crafted. Shaker construction, if I guessed right.

She shrugged. "I suppose. Replication is quite mundane to me. What should we eat?" *Move this along,* her posture said.

There was an aura of sadness around her. I had caught a glimpse of it at the window, but now it was as clear as the autumn leaves.

Outside it was moving from late afternoon into evening.

"What are my choices?"

"Anything you want."

I narrowed my eyes. "You must have quite the kitchen."

She laughed, a little of the sadness lifting. "No, just a good replication system."

"Okay." If this was heaven, it was the strangest version I'd ever heard of. "A McDonalds cheeseburger, fries, and chocolate shake." Everyone knew Mickey Dees had the best fries, even if I didn't eat them anymore. *I am already dead, after all.*

Her gaze went faraway again, and then she touched the bookshelf. After about ten seconds, it split apart, and there was a nook with an orange tray, complete with paper liner and the items I'd asked for. Two of each. "You're joining me?"

She nodded. "When at Rome…"

I laughed, but didn't correct her. Prepositions were a bitch in any language.

I took a bite. *Oh my God.* The cheeseburger was amazing, fake cheese and pickle juice dripping down the side of my mouth. I'd forgotten how good processed food could be.

Sera took a bite and frowned.

"Don't like it?"

"It's…interesting." She pulled off the bun and stared inside. "What's that?"

I squinted. "*That* is a pickle. One of humankind's finest inventions." It took me a second to realize she'd used a contraction.

Sera picked up the pickle and sniffed it. "I'll take your words for it."

I smiled. She was still a little rough on idioms.

I popped one of the fries into my mouth. They were perfect—hot, crispy, salty. And underneath the carton… I stared. "Is that…the Hamburglar?"

Another data check. "Yes, it is."

I laughed. It was patently absurd.

Here I was, vaunted sci fi writer and climate change scientist from the early decades of the twenty-first century, sitting in my den at the end of the Universe, talking pickles with some future human/alien goddess, while a cartoon drawing in a jailhouse jumpsuit grinned at me from a plastic orange tray.

Sera laughed too, and soon we were doubled over squeezing our sides.

"The…the…Hamburglar. And holy shit, Grimace?"

Tears were coming from her eyes. "Why are we laughing?"

"This whole thing…it's just so *weird.*"

The laughter trailed off, and we stared at each other in companionable silence.

However different we were, we had just shared a moment. A *human* moment.

I took a sip of the chocolate shake. It was already starting to melt. "So…assuming I believe what you've told me, what do we do now?"

"Ask me a question." She sat back, her arms resting on the arms of the chair. "Then I'll ask you one."

This was like having a genie. *Do I get more than three questions?* I had to make each one count, just in case. "Can you read my mind?"

Sera shook her head. "Not exactly. I can access a copy of your memories—the one we used to replicate you. It helps me answer some of your questions, and to know what to ask next."

Let's test that. I want to kill you with my bare hands.

I waited to see if she reacted. But she seemed as serene and calm as before. She was either telling the truth, or she was a better actor than me. "Your turn."

"What do your people think about life after death?"

I sat back, staring at her. It wasn't what I'd expected. "That depends. Some of us think there *is* one. Many of us, actually. There have been many wars fought over different interpretations of that very question."

"And you?"

"That's technically two questions."

She smiled enigmatically and said nothing.

"Well, before today, I would have said no. You get the time you get, and then your atoms are dropped into the cosmic washing machine to be cycled out into something new." *What if I was wrong about that?* Was this place the afterlife, or some kind of elaborate scam?

Sera nodded, giving me nothing.

My turn. "Why am I here?"

"That's a fair question. My kind—you can call us Seekers—we've always sought knowledge across our galaxy. Wherever that search took us. Now that the end is near, think of this as…" That glazed look again. "Ah yes. Our last hurrah."

So I'm a science project. "Okay, but why…"

"*My* turn." Her grin was almost mischievous. "What's Earth like?"

If this whole thing *was* a chemo dream, it had me fooled.

I closed my eyes. "It *was* beautiful. Lots of wild space, so many animals and plants. When I was a kid, I used to run outside in the monsoon rains barefoot in the street, the pavement rough under my feet, heavy drops falling from the sky. And the creosote smell in the air as the water rushed past." I could still smell that musty odor. I missed those simple pleasures. "Dad took me to the White Mountains once. I snuck out of the tent at dawn to smell the pine needles, and my breath made clouds in the air." I could still see the sunlight filtering like the strings of a harp through the trees. "Can you *see* it?"

Sera closed her own eyes, and a wistful smile crossed her face. "Yes. It's beautiful."

"It was. We ruined it. Too many people, too much greed."

She stared at me like I was an insect on a pin, her fingers tapping her knee.

Time was growing short. I could feel it. I squirmed. "My turn."

"Go ahead."

"Why *me*? There are so many smarter people, better representatives of the human race." *Einstein. Mother Teresa. Hell, even Oprah.* My eyes narrowed. "Are you really human?"

Sera laughed. "That's two questions." She rubbed her chin, as if considering how to respond. Just like I had. "You were chosen because you live in a pivotal time for your kind."

"So I'm important?" I scratched my head.

"My turn again." She picked up one of the now-cold fries and nibbled at it. "What's the biggest challenge facing your people?" She sipped her milkshake, waiting for my response.

She looked so *normal*. It made me laugh.

"That's funny?"

"Technically two questions. But I'll allow it." I grinned. "I laughed because you reminded me of a girl I used to date. Before I came out."

Her eyebrow arched, but she didn't ask the question.

"And unquestionably the climate. We've done everything we can to destroy it, and no one seemed to care. I studied these things, and believe me, you'd be scared shitless if you knew half of what I knew." In some ways, it was a relief to be dead—it was no longer my responsibility.

"That's very common. Civilizations often destroy themselves with the very things that lifted them out of the primordial mud." She scratched her head absently.

Just like I did.

"You're really *not* human, are you?"

She set down her shake and her eyes sparkled. Legit sparkled. "No. What gave me away?" Technically it was a question. But it was an answer too.

I was a scientist. I knew the odds. "The end of the universe would be millions, probably billions of years away from my time. The likelihood that humans would still be around to see it…plus you're copying my gestures. Like you're just learning them."

She laughed. "I think I like you humans."

You humans. It was a friendly laugh, but knowing it originated from someone, or something, alien sent a shiver down my spine.

"To answer your question, no, the Seekers aren't human. We never were. We're not really one race at all. Our progenitors evolved on a small world circling a red sun, a billion years ago. After all this time, even the names of our origin race and planet are lost."

I whistled. I had a hard time imaging a million years, let alone a billion.

I suddenly felt very young.

"And to answer your next question…I don't know how old I am. I stopped counting a long time ago. A couple million years? I'm an aggregate—a creature born of a thousand worlds and a thousand cultures that survived their childhoods. Bits of me collected over time, and now I am the sum total of all that came before. All we were able to save. So *age* is a rather meaningless measure, don't you think?"

I stared at her. It was more than I could take in, having a cheeseburger and fries with one of the caretakers of the universe.

She reached out to touch my forehead. "Show me your favorite memory?"

It was like an electric shock.

✿

It was summer, in New York, hot and humid in the way that only the East Coast in July can be, well over ninety degrees and muggy as hell.

I was sitting on a bench in Central Park, in the middle of one of my periodic unsuccessful attempts at getting in shape. It had been a week now and I was still gasping for breath.

Today's attempt had ended badly, with me sitting there panting on the bench, head between my knees, feeling lightheaded and weird.

I was thirty-five and single.

"Want some water?"

I looked up, half-expecting a gym rat, some muscly guy who would drive me back into full-blown body shame.

Instead, he was aggressively *normal*. Light brown hair, brown eyes, nice features, someone you wouldn't think twice about if you saw him crossing Fifth Avenue. He was dressed in athletic shorts, his shirt was tucked into the back of his pants. He had a nice chest, but nothing like you see in the magazines.

Lots of freckles.

"Thanks." I took the water and uncapped the bottle, gulping it down gratefully.

"Hey, don't drink too much. Your body has to play catch-up."

"Not mustard?" I groaned at my own terrible pun. These things just slipped out sometimes.

He must think I was an idiot.

He laughed and held out his hand. "Peter."

I shook it. "Tanner. Tanner Black."

"Oooh. Porn star name."

"Yeah, well." I gestured at my own lackluster form and shrugged.

He sat down on the wooden bench next to me. "Late New Year's resolution?"

I nodded. "Friend's wedding next month."

"Oh God, I hate those." I handed him back the bottle, and he took a sip. "Gorgeous day." He glanced up at the cloudless sky, a stunning deep blue.

"Damned sweatshop, if you ask me."

Peter laughed again. "Yeah, it *is* pretty bad." He looked at me, and then looked away again.

"What?"

"Nothing."

"Hey, you wanted to ask me something, or say something. Spit it out."

"Okay." He ducked his head. When he looked back at me, he was biting his lip. "I know it's quick. But…you wanna go out sometime?"

I snorted. *Nobody* wanted to go out with me. "Yeah, right."

"I've been watching you. Not like in the creepy stalkery way. But these last couple days. I was trying to work up the courage to ask you. I know you're way outta my league."

You gotta be kidding me. I'd never had *anyone* tell me I was out of their league.

I looked him over again. He was actually kind of cute, in that quiet, intelligent way I liked. He was funny. And hell, he liked *me*. "Why not?"

He grinned again, and pulled out a sweaty piece of paper from his pocket. "Here's my number. Call me." Then he leaned over and kissed my cheek, got up, and ran off.

I watched him run. He was beautiful.

Maybe the universe had a plan for me after all.

I opened my eyes.

Sera had a lopsided smile on her face.

"What?"

She seemed ever more human. "When was that?"

"Twenty years ago. We've been together ever since."

She nodded.

I felt like I'd just passed a test. "So did we make it?"

"Humanity?"

"Yeah."

She stared at me for a moment, her golden eyes fixed on mine. "Honestly? We don't know yet."

I laughed harshly. "How can you not *know*? This is the end of the universe, right? All the stories have been told."

She bit her lip, a human gesture she seemed to really have taken to. "This isn't *your* universe."

I stared at her. "What?" My head ached.

"You're not really here. Not the original *you*. You and your kind are a thing still to come…" Sera waved her hand, and the window changed again to show the End of All Things. "That's your future, not ours."

I stared at the screen. "I don't understand."

"Our universe is in the final stages of collapse. The Seekers' time is coming to an end. We found a way to reach forward into your universe to continue our mission. Into *your* time, to find places where we might intervene to set young races like yours on a different path before they self-destruct. *If* they are worthy."

"To pay it forward." I was shaking.

Sera's eyes glazed, and when they refocused, she nodded, flashing me a grateful smile.

I had been chosen to represent my entire race. How could I even begin to accept that?

And yet…*humanity must still have a chance.*

I got up and paced around the room, full of nervous energy. "How many?" I demanded. How big was this…ship? This place?

"Races? A hundred thousand or so. Only a small fraction will reach the stars."

"Show me?"

She nodded and took my hand.

My consciousness expanded outside the room.

In the next one over, a creature that looked like a golden beetle—albeit seven feet tall—chittered with another of its own kind in a room that was best described as *organic.* Beyond that, in a grassy glade, something rustled its purple leaves or feathers in what I had to assume was a query.

As my consciousness expanded, the scene repeated itself over and over, and soon I was swooping up above it all to see the ship.

It was vast, a white amorphous thing, more like a cloud than a hard, physical structure.

It billowed and shifted, all the while being drawn inexorably forward toward its ending.

"Enough." Instantly I was back inside my own body, though I suspected it was no more than alien binary code. I sank back into my seat, overwhelmed by the scale of this effort.

We seemed to have given up on the every-other-question thing, so I plowed ahead. Something else was bothering me. "Couldn't you have just read my mind—or my memory copy—to find all of this out?"

She sat back. "Yes. We could have. We did, in fact. But it was important to see what kind of creature you really are. We find that's easiest when we speak to the being itself. You come to life—you are so much more than just your memories."

That made sense. I noticed she'd switched to plural pronouns. "What about you?"

"What about us?"

"If you could pluck my consciousness from a future universe, surely you could survive the end of this one yourselves."

She looked down at her hands. It was hard to believe that she wasn't human.

"Our time is over. We have accepted that. We've explored all there is to explore." She looked up, and her eyes swirled white, like the ship. "You're at the beginning of your potential. You have so much more to learn and explore. We're jealous."

I laughed. "Some of the physicists say we've discovered almost everything."

"So bold. So confident. You've only just scraped the surface." She frowned. "It's time."

"The End?"

She nodded. "In a few moments, the Seeker will be sucked into the burning heart of possibility, and a few moments later, your universe will be born."

I shuddered. "What will happen to me?" I kicked myself mentally. Her entire race—races?—was dying, and I was worried about myself.

Hell, I was already dead. What did it matter?

"You'll be sent home."

Where I was already dead.

We stood together and watched as the carnival lights engulfed us.

Sera reached out and took my hand as we approached the End. The brightness swelled to unbearability, searing my vision.

She squeezed my hand tightly, fingers warm in mine. Her eyes were wet.

I'd never asked her real name. I opened my mouth—

—and found myself laying on a bed in a hospital room. Something beeped in a steady rhythm next to me. Sunlight filtered in through pale green blinds.

Peter sat in a chair, bent over, head in his hands.

Was this some kind of after-death, out-of-body experience? *I am dead, right?*

I opened my mouth, but only a croak came out.

Peter looked up, stared at the heart-rate monitor and then at me. His eyes went wide. "Tanner?" He reached me in a second.

I looked at him. "Water."

"Tanner. Holy shit. Doctor Bamra!" Peter ran to the door. "Get the doctor!"

"There's nothing more he can do. Your husband's gone." One of the nurses poked her head into the room to look at me. "You need to—-" She squeaked, and almost fell over as I sat up and stared at her. "I'll go get the doctor."

Peter brought me a plastic cup of water.

I felt good. *Really* good. Better than I had in a year. My mind was clear. No more chemo brain. No more weakness or nausea.

Is this a dream?

I closed my eyes, and something blossomed inside me.

The history and thoughts and ideas from a thousand other races who had survived their adolescence flowed through my mind like a floodtide. The knowledge of a universe.

And Sera's true name. Sera meant *evening* in Italian. Her true name was unpronounceable, but *Eventide* was a more poetic translation.

She'd been the last of her kind.

"How are you alive?" Peter sat on the side of my bed, touching my hand, my chest, my face. "You were *dead*. I saw you die."

The cancer was gone. I knew that, as surely as I knew the charge I'd been given.

There were ways to save us all, to guide the world onto a better path. Even now. "You're never going to believe me."

"Try me."

I kissed him. His face was wet, and he shook as I pulled him into my arms.

"I don't understand."

"I know." I squeezed him tight. "It's going to be okay."

It was our turn to claim the stars.

Copyright © 2020 by J. Scott Coatsworth.

APPRECIATION

by Gregory Benford

Mike was above all funny. He had endless tales, jokes, stories of our field and its foibles. He always told them in the spirit of how-crazy-is-all-this and laughed along with our appreciation. He worked a crowd, made them part of it all. Look at his speeches on the Writers of the Future site to see him in full, tuxedo'd glory.

Farewell to our Toastmaster supreme....

APPRECIATION

by Nancy Kress

I met Mike in the 1980's when he was Guest of Honor at a small con in upstate New York, where I then lived. We played pool in the bar. Young fan that I was, and knowing almost nobody in science fiction, I always read the fiction of anyone coming to town. Mike had not yet written the stories that would win him five Hugos (out of thirty-seven nominations) and a Nebula, but I liked what I read, and told him so.

"I'm a writer," he said, "but I'm mostly a fan. And you're a terrible pool player." Then he sank the four-ball with a bank shot.

I was, and he was. Always, over the thirty years I knew him, he defined himself as a fan. At Worldcons, he put in a perfunctory appearance at the SFWA suite and then took off to make the rounds of fan parties. This was made easier by the night-owl hours he kept. When I praised an especially gorgeous sunrise, Mike replied thoughtfully, "I saw a sunrise once. I was putting on my pajamas at the time." When we taught together on Sail To Success, the writing cruises sponsored by Galaxy's Edge, I asked to teach in the morning and Mike asked for the evening panels. When he had to get up "early"—as, for instance, to not miss the ship sailing from Miami—he grumbled. A lot.

We sometimes had differing opinions on writing, publishing, teaching, which we argued about both on panels and at shared meals (although never breakfast). Unlike a lot of people, Mike was willing to admit when he was wrong. He maintained for years that writing could not be taught. Then he was invited to teach Clarion. Afterward, he sent me an email: You were right. I was astonished at how much the Clarion students improved from their week one stories.

And he was generous. He encouraged young writers, he collaborated with them, he published them. A student of mine in upstate New York wrote a story he could not sell. On my suggestion, Mike read it and immediately wanted it for an anthology he was editing. The table of contents was already set, but Mike made room for it. The story,

"The Winterberry" by Nick DiChario, went on to be nominated for a Hugo.

Mike and I wrote introductions to each other's story collections. His fiction covered an enormous range: funny ("Travels With My Cat"), sentimental ("A Princess of Mars," his tribute to his wife Carol), bleak ("Seven Views of Olduvai Gorge"), exuberantly inventive (Santiago). His story "For I Have Touched the Sky" is one of only two SF stories that have ever made me cry. He wrote often about bigger-than-life characters, people worthy of legend and fable.

I will miss him as a writer, but even more as a friend.

Eleanor R. Wood's stories have appeared in Pseudopod, Flash Fiction Online, Deep Magic, Daily Science Fiction, *and* Diabolical Plots, *among other places. She writes and eats liquorice from southwest England, where she lives with her husband, two marvelous dogs, and enough tropical fish tanks to charge an entry fee.*

LUX NOCTURNA

by Eleanor R. Wood

The shrieking began on the first of October.

Alethea jolted awake, clutching the bed-sheets around her, heart racing with the disorientation of being dragged from sleep. The sound died away as her awareness returned. *A nightmare*, she told herself, catching her breath as she lay back down. Sleep embraced her.

She was dreaming of a locked door when the next shriek woke her. She threw the blankets over her head in feeble protection from the long, high screeching. It was a knife against porcelain, nails on a chalkboard. Heart thumping in terror, Alethea reached a hand out to the lamp beside her bed. Light bathed the room. The shrieking stopped. The clock on her wall read 1:01 a.m.

She convinced herself it had been a fox outside her window, but sleep would not return this time. She turned off the light and snugged low into her bed, but could not shake the unease that went beyond sudden waking.

The grandfather clock in the hall chimed two. The shrieking followed once more, longer and louder than ever. The walls of the house trembled with it. It was anger and distress, frustration and wrath. It consumed Alethea's mind and left no room for rational thought. She pressed herself into her mattress, holding her breath and plugging her ears until, blissfully, it ceased again, leaving only her fear.

She did not sleep again.

She spent the rest of the night willing the dawn to arrive, watching the clock and dreading each hour, when the ungodly sound would strike again.

The sun brought no respite. Despite the brightness of the day, the terrifying screams continued, every hour on the hour, while Alethea paced the house looking for their source. She wielded her longest kitchen knife in one hand and a broom in the other, but every room was as untouched as the rest.

It was a big house: far too big for just her. But it had been in her family for generations, and her grandmother had left it to her care. She had always felt comfortable here despite the unused rooms. She could practice her music without disturbing anyone. Her nearest neighbors were at the end of the long driveway, and the peace and seclusion suited her. Besides, there was no rent and no mortgage, and she knew her piano teacher's salary would never afford her a place as spacious.

She had three students that afternoon, at the local community center. As she stepped out the door at midday, the hourly wail followed her all the way down the leaf-strewn path.

✿

Alethea was distracted through the lessons, though she did her best to pay attention to each student's progress. The big plastic clock on the wall wasn't helping. It faced her as she sat beside the piano, and as each hour approached, she felt herself tensing in readiness for the bone-chilling sound that never came. Yet even as she sat in the bright, airy communal hall, she knew that half a mile up the road, her house was trembling as it screeched.

Or as *something* screeched.

Marion, her final student of the afternoon, was learning Respighi's *Notturno*. She'd grasped the technical aspects and was now improving the dynamics that were essential to a good performance of the delicate nocturne.

"What if we try this bar pianissimo?" Alethea reached over to mark the sheet music with her pencil. "Then you've got room to crescendo up to the next mezzo forte."

"I'll give that a go." Marion played the next few bars with beautiful expression.

They ironed out a few more bars before the lesson drew to an end.

"Keep working on those dynamics. We'll aim for a proper performance next week," Alethea said as they parted company.

It wasn't until she was halfway up the hill that she realized her anxiety had fled during that last hour. Working on the Respighi with Marion had taken her mind off the disturbing events of the last day. The music was still playing in her mind, and she embraced it as she walked the remaining distance home. Whatever was wrong with her house, she would find it and fix it. That was all.

The clock chimed four as she stepped inside. The hellish scream that accompanied it made her jump, but she gathered her resolve.

"Hello to you too."

She took a cup of tea to her piano room. The room was spacious, like much of the house, and she occasionally wondered why her grandmother had insisted it be reserved solely for the piano. She felt sure she'd asked her at some point, but couldn't recall the reason. Her grandmother had been an accomplished pianist, and Alethea supposed certain quirks went with the territory.

Alethea had dragged a sofa into the room after Gran died. It felt cozier, and gave her somewhere to sit and peruse sheet music. The piano itself was a small vintage grand, still rich in tone despite its age.

She worked on her own pieces, sipping tea in between them, scrawling marks on the page as she adjusted a finger placement here, a dynamic shift there. As always, she lost time at the piano, only aware of the hour by the chiming of the hall clock. She was so caught up in her practice that she forgot the freakish phenomenon plaguing her.

At the strike of five, the spine-chilling shriek rent her music like a scythe through silk. Alethea's hands flew to her ears of their own accord as the sound pierced her skull and reverberated through her chest. It was the loudest scream yet. The strings of the open-topped piano vibrated with it, adding their own eerie hum to the cacophony. It seemed endless, a screech that rose and fell in terror and anguish.

"What are you what are you what ARE YOU?" Alethea screamed back as panic overwhelmed her.

It didn't answer. The scream died away as always, echoing through the barely-furnished room until all was still again.

Shaken, Alethea stood from the piano and turned on her heel to survey the room. Her instinct was to flee, to run and hide under her bed like a frightened child, or better yet, to leave the house and never come back. But she clenched her hands into fists and rooted herself to the floor. She would not run. This was her home.

It had been so much louder this time. She forced her trembling mind to calm and focus on cold rationale.

Was whatever *it* was getting closer? Would it simply increase its intensity until she lost her mind? Or was it just that she had been nearer to it this time?

She hadn't practiced piano since the screeching started. Although she'd explored the house that morning looking for an intruder, she hadn't been in this room during any of the hourly terrors. Dreading the thought, she decided to be here for the next hour. She would be prepared, ready to turn her ear to the sound and try to determine whether it was originating from the room.

She fetched a book and a soft blanket and made some hot chocolate. She took them to the sofa in the piano room and made herself a consoling nest to wait it out. The nights were drawing in, so she turned on the room's tall lamp and pulled the floor-length curtains. A sense of deja vu settled over her for a fleeting moment.

And then I lock the door, she thought, for no apparent reason. The front door was already locked. There was no lock on the piano room door, which stood ajar.

She dismissed the stray thought and the fading sense of familiarity and picked up her book. She read the same two paragraphs three times before putting the novel down, too distracted to take it in.

When six o'clock came, Alethea was ready. She sat up tall, holding the blanket around her and willing her heart to slow. The clock chimed. The wailing started.

As before, it filled the room and set the floor-boards shaking. Alethea leapt up and spun in place, scanning the bare bookcases, the stone fireplace, the paneled walls, the small cupboard in the far corner.

The small cupboard in the far corner was rattling.

Rattling like something was trying to get out.

She fell back onto the sofa, yanked her feet up, and wrapped her arms about her legs, clutching herself to fend off panic. She stayed that way until long after the shriek had died away. When she uncoiled, her limbs were stiff and achy. She hadn't taken her eyes off the cupboard, which had reverted to its still and nondescript self.

She didn't even know what was in that cupboard. There was ample storage elsewhere in the house, and although she was sure she had opened the piano room cupboard, she couldn't for the life of her recall what, if anything, was inside it.

Certainly it was nothing that could rattle the door from inside.

She gathered her courage and approached the waist-high door set into the wall. She had never noticed the key in its lock.

Lock the door. The thought came again, a whisper in her mind. Hurriedly, without thinking, she grabbed the key and turned it, chilled to find it had indeed been unlocked.

"There's no handle on the inside of the cupboard," she whispered to herself in reassurance, pocketing the key and stepping back from the door.

She played the Respighi *Notturno* that evening, over and over. She told herself it was in preparation for her next lesson with Marion, but in truth, the piece continued to calm her in a way none of her current repertoire did. The more she played it, the more relaxed she became, until the hourly shrieks became more of a nuisance than a terrifying ordeal.

Eventually, fingers aching, she left the piano, found herself something to eat, and went to bed. The shrieks continued, interrupting her sleep and spiking her tension once again until she sat, bleary-eyed, waiting for the sunrise.

"Top of to-do list: buy earplugs," she muttered to herself as the second of October dawned, crisp and bright.

✿

As the days continued, the hourly shrieking became a background part of Alethea's life. She taught, she played, she barricaded the piano room cupboard. She convinced herself managing the problem was as good as solving it, but it was a lie she couldn't maintain for long.

Yet the only way to take it further was to open the cupboard. The prospect alone froze her into immobility. She would play the Respighi, feel better, and ignore the problem until the next hour chimed.

She made a list.

What Might Happen

- Whatever is inside comes out, is grateful for its freedom, and leaves.
- Whatever is inside comes out, wraps its claws around my throat, and drags me into the abyss.
- Nothing is inside. This is all in my imagination.
- I keep playing piano at the problem until it disappears.

That last one was Alethea's half-hearted attempt to make light of the situation, but somehow it resonated with her. *Keep playing.*

Keep playing.

By the tenth of October, the hourly shrieks were getting under Alethea's skin. She was sleeping well enough due to her ample supply of earplugs, but during the day she longed for the wailing to cease. She couldn't immerse herself in a task, she couldn't find peace within her own home, she couldn't invite anyone over. She longed to leave, but to what end? The quiet would only be temporary.

She packed a bag on the morning of the thirteenth, after the ten o'clock screech caught her unawares. She was brewing tea as the sharp, haunted cry pierced her silence. She startled, splashing boiling water over her hand. She barely heard her own cry of pain over the din. A sob of fear and frustration caught her throat as she rushed to the cold tap and drenched her scalded skin.

"I can't do this anymore," she said as the wail echoed away. "I want my life back."

You always say that.

Deja vu? A whisper from her subconscious? She shook it off and went to pack some overnight things.

She stood in the hall, her bag by the front door, keys in hand. The clock read half past ten. She didn't know where she was going, only that she had to be gone. But as she stood in the large en-tryway, cozy with the familiarity of years, a spark of anger ignited.

"I live here," she said aloud. "*I* live here, not you!"

She would not be frightened out of her own home. She would not. She threw her keys down on the hall table and stormed into the piano room.

"Damn you. Damn you," she said as she pulled the stack of dining chairs away from the offending cupboard. Its key was in her pocket. Always in her pocket. She pulled it out and turned it in the lock, refusing to contemplate what she was doing. She paused on the handle for a fractional moment, and then summoned her anger and swung the door open with a roar of defiance.

She sat back onto the floor in deflated astonishment. Before her was a bare cupboard, dusty and unused. Two empty shelves spanned its width. A piece of old carpet lay on the bottom. Nothing else was there. No forgotten paraphernalia, no useful items. No hellish creature from the depths.

Just an empty cupboard.

Alethea's anger turned on herself. Had she really been so stupid? So afraid of a forgotten, empty cupboard without so much as a wispy cellar spider lurking inside? The tension of every hour of the past fortnight snapped within her and she tore at the rectangle of carpet, ripping it out, bashing at the cupboard's floor and walls, daring something else to be hiding within.

The carpet fibers made her cough. The walls and floor were firm and unresonant. There were no hidden hollows. There was nothing in the cupboard. She sat, staring at it for an endless moment, October's panic and weariness suddenly a futile, foolish nonsense.

Tears stung her eyes. She levered herself up from the floor, about to slam the cupboard door shut. The grandfather clock began to chime eleven.

The back wall of the cupboard *shifted*. It blurred. The painted plaster swirled away, like the reverse of milk stirred into coffee, leaving empty, fathomless black. The shriek began, deafening Alethea and breaking her mesmerized stillness. It echoed up from that incomprehensible darkness, threatening to pull her in even as it strove to come out. She threw her full weight against the door, slamming it shut, thudding the lock home, yanking out the key and flinging it across the room.

The shriek's anger was palpable this time, as if it knew its freedom had been thwarted. It went on, and on, and on, long after the clock's chimes had died away. Alethea became aware of her own petrified keening, a high whine at the back of her throat as her mind struggled to process the horror seared into it. All the while, the cupboard door rattled and shook in its hinges.

There's something in there.

It needs to get out.

I have to stop it. I have to stop it.

As if on autopilot, she stumbled to the piano. Her burned hand protested as she flexed it, but she had to play. She couldn't even have said why.

The trembling opening notes of Respighi's *Notturno* filled the room. The high melody came in, sweet, elegant, almost ethereal in its beauty. Alethea's panic faded away. The music swept through the shriek, dampening it, subduing it, overpowering it with haunting beauty. As she spread the piece's final chord, the only sound left was its resonance through the piano's strings.

Silence.

Peace.

Calm.

Alethea took a deep breath and went to find some lavender oil for her burn.

☼

By the next morning, her skin had blistered and any movement added additional pain to the dull throb of her injury. She managed to get an appointment to see the nurse at her local surgery, who diagnosed a second-degree burn and prescribed rest and painkillers.

"I'm a pianist. I need to play," she said.

"Not for a couple of weeks at least," the nurse said. "It will heal, but you need to give it time."

Alethea fought dread as she walked home. She loved the autumn, but even the sweet scent of falling leaves couldn't soothe her. She felt sure the Respighi had helped keep the Thing at bay, but if she couldn't play, she couldn't test it again. Nor could she restore her own calm with the music.

She taught the afternoon's students as usual; her injured hand didn't prevent her giving direction and guidance. When she got home, she plugged her ears and sat on her bed with a book, ignoring the shrieks as best she could.

The next day, she ran through practice with her right hand only. At the hourly wail, she tried the right-hand part of the Respighi, but it made no difference to her anxiety and had no effect on the eldritch thing in the cupboard. She gave up on her practice and closed the piano room door as she left.

☼

It was getting louder. It sounded closer. Its volume was now as tremendous upstairs as it had been in the piano room. In the piano room itself, Alethea needed ear plugs to protect her hearing. She continued her one-handed practice, but she didn't touch the Respighi. She needed her left hand to heal first.

She protected the blisters, she applied lavender and aloe when she could stand to, and she moved her fingers gently to prevent them stiffening.

You're running out of time, her paranoid mind insisted.

"Out of time for what?" she asked herself, wishing Gran was still here. She'd be sure to know the answer.

☼

By the final week of October, Alethea's nerves were strung to breaking point. She lived with hourly bone-rattling screams and the terror of whatever was making them. She had piled furniture in front of the locked cupboard, but it still rattled every hour as something tried to get out. She didn't know what she was supposed to do, but she knew she had a responsibility. She simply couldn't work out what it was.

She snapped at a student one day. She never did that. She wasn't eating properly, though her appetite had always been good. Her dreams were full of piano music that she couldn't recall when she awoke. When her unwanted house guest shrieked its frustration, she just as often screamed her own in return.

"I can't do this. I can't," she sobbed into her pillow one night.

Yes, you can, my love. Yes, you can. Only a few more days.

Her grandmother's soft voice was a balm to Alethea's disturbed mind. She didn't even wonder at it. She embraced the calm words as she drifted into sleep.

✿

At midnight on the thirty-first of October, Alethea sat bolt upright in bed. She was sound asleep one moment, wide awake the next. She could hear the shriek through her earplugs, which was nothing new these days. But something was different.

"It's Samhain," she said, knowing it meant something.

Suddenly the knowledge flooded her mind, the heady recollection of a forgotten dream, the astonishment that she'd ever forgotten.

"It's Samhain, it's Samhain!" she yelled, leaping from her bed and flipping a light switch. "And I know the piece. I know what I have to play!"

But her hand...

She looked down at the healing skin, blisters long gone though pink flesh remained. She flexed her fingers. There was tightness, but the pain had eased. It would do.

"When my arthritis gets too bad, you'll have to take over," Gran had told her. "I won't be able to do this forever, just as my own grandmother couldn't. I stepped in then, and soon it will be your turn."

Every year, the same. Every year, they had to keep the demon at bay. Every year, this was their charge.

The memories filled Alethea as she pulled on her dressing gown and went downstairs. The memory of remembering, at midnight every single Samhain—never before the date, never after. The memory of her grandmother showing her what had to be done.

"Why do we forget, Gran?" she had asked. "What's the use of that? A whole month, terrified and anxious, when we've faced the same thing every year. If we knew what was going on, surely we'd be so much better prepared?"

"You'd think so, wouldn't you?" Gran had answered. "I asked my Nannie that question. She told me what I tell you now: 'Every year, you will find the piece that subdues them. Every year, it is different. And if you search for it, aware of the desperate need that rests on your choice, you will never find it.'

"So we forget everything, every year. While we play, while we practice, while we immerse ourselves in our music as we always have, the piece that will work comes to us. We discover it organically, and we know it when we do."

Respighi's *Notturno*. She would play it twenty-four times today, once each hour, diminishing the otherworldly being with every performance. It was at its strongest now. But so was she.

"Hello, my friend," she greeted her piano. "It's us against the forces of darkness again. You ready for this?"

It sat, squarely, in the center of the room that was its purpose. Alethea caressed its keys and played a few simple pieces, warming up her stiff left hand, easing it back to familiarity. She yawned, made herself a hot drink, splashed water on her face. There would be no more sleep tonight.

At a quarter to one, she took the cupboard's key from her pocket. She knew what she had to do. She'd done it many times, recalling each occasion with the strange knowledge that she would forget them all again for the rest of the year. She placed the key in the lock and opened the door. The blank sides and bare shelves looked as benign as they had the last time. Only this time, she knew what was to come, she knew what it meant, and she knew what would happen if she did nothing.

Leaving the door wide, she went to the piano and sat down. The minutes between now and the hour seemed poised with tension. Alethea tried to relax her mind. The first hour was always the worst. But she knew and loved the piece. She would get through it. She focused on the cupboard, just past the top of the piano. She heard the hall clock's gears turning as it prepared its single chime. The back wall of the cupboard began to swirl away. And from the void, the beginning of a hellbeast's cry as it fought its way into her world.

Alethea's fingers knew their part. Her left hand played the soothing opening bars, so at odds with the horrific shriek filling the room, filling the house, filling her mind. She caught her first glimpse of movement from the blackness, and tore her eyes from the monstrous sight she recalled too well from another Samhain.

She looked down at the keys, at her fingers gliding across them, creating a sound of such purity that no monster could breach it. She no longer needed the sheet music. Respighi's *Notturno* was safe in her mind and the muscles of her hands. At the first crescendo, the shriek wavered. At the second, it began to retreat. By the end of the piece, it had ceased completely. Alethea looked up, heady with the wave of music, to see that the cupboard was a cupboard again and the world was safe, for this hour at least.

Twenty-three to go. But she knew that with each one, the thing beyond would lose strength, fading away until it was gone for another eleven months. Her burned hand ached a little. The new skin was tight against her ligaments. By two o'clock, it had eased, but a seed of anxiety at its resilience settled in Alethea's mind.

Had she performed this ritual with an injury before? She didn't think so. Under normal circumstances she would ease back into her playing gradually, as her hand continued to heal. But she didn't have that luxury. She had to play now, every single hour.

As the dawn light filled the room and turned to a golden autumn morning, she played. As the afternoon drew on and evening's shadow began to fall, she played. At the first sounds of costumed children on their yearly sugar-hunt, she played. She could afford to ignore her doorbell. A thrown egg meant nothing against the horror that would be unleashed if she missed the next hour.

She applied ice to her throbbing hand in between. She pushed past the pain, heedless of the danger of long-term damage. And all the while, the shrieks waned as her music entered the cupboard and penetrated the depths beyond.

By seven p.m., Alethea was battling exhaustion as well as pain. Her left hand ached constantly now, and she was starting to lose mobility. Halfway through the piece, she messed up one of the bass chords and faltered for the first time. An edge of panic crept past her defenses as the shriek rebounded, leaping at its first opportunity. Her eyes betrayed her, flickering to the open cupboard as her hands fumbled for the next bar. The darkness itself seemed to be moving, forming a shape. A hideous face loomed from it, and she dragged her gaze back to the keys and found her melody despite her thundering heart. Her instincts screamed at her to flee, but she couldn't.

She wouldn't. She merged herself with the music and smothered her primal terror.

The shriek faded again. Alethea caught her breath and retrieved her ice pack. Only five hours to go.

This time she massaged her hand with clove oil after icing it. She swallowed painkillers. She drank coffee. She would see this through, just as she had every year. As her grandmother had, and hers before her, stretching back generations. None of them had failed. She was damned if she would relinquish their legacy. At eight o'clock, she imagined her maternal ancestors surrounding her piano, lending her strength, granting her the collective stamina of their Samhains.

She didn't falter again.

At eleven o'clock that evening, she played the *Notturno* with a sense of loss. Its purpose was almost complete. Despite her aching hand and tingling fingers, she would only play it one more time with such import. The shrieking darkness fought to overcome her music, and failed yet again. Shattered but relieved, her annual vigil nearly at an end, Alethea poured herself a glass of wine and waited for the final hour.

At midnight on the first of November, she played Respighi's *Notturno* against the demon's final stance. Halfway into the piece, the terrorizing thing was gone.

Until next year, she thought.

She finished the piece.

How lovely. She would make it a part of her permanent repertoire.

She yawned and flexed her stiff hand. So tired... so late! She stood from the piano, headed for bed.

The cupboard was open. *That's odd*, she thought, and closed it.

She never used that cupboard.

Copyright © 2020 by Eleanor R. Wood.

APPRECIATION

by Tina Smith

When I first interacted with Mike it scared me a little. I'd sent several judges for a contest an email to let them know I was excited to meet them at the conference I'd be attending, and Mike didn't just respond with a "Thanks! See you there!" like everyone else—nope—he wrote me back a letter asking me more about myself. I knew then he was different. But also, being a female on the internet talking to a virtual stranger, I was cautious. Turned out Mike was genuine. He really wanted to know more about me—like he had so much work to do and needed to get started! He wanted me to know about the writing community. Nobody can doubt he was a fan as much as a writer. We met in person and he promptly introduced me to everyone I was too intimidated to go right up to; I was new to the writing world, I wanted to be sure I wasn't too forward. He right away observed I wasn't shy. I held conversations and he explained to me that every writer he thinks has what it takes to become successful has a "weakness"—something that would hold them back.

He did eventually figure out my weakness, and man did he work on me over the years. It's been really difficult to go through my past emails and messages with him these last few weeks. I know he came to realize my weakness was also one of the things he liked about me from the start, but I don't really want to talk about me. I want to tell you about Mike. I don't think it's a secret that Mike's weakness, if we can call it that, was new writers. It devastated him to see anyone fall through the cracks. He saw a hole in the field, and nobody was filling it the way he thought it needed to be and he stepped right in. And yeah, he couldn't help every single new writer. He was only one person (maybe that was the weakness that held him back—did he need a couple of MikeClones to help?). But he took an obvious pride in being the first to publish someone he thought would "make it." When we'd talk, he'd brag about writers he knew. He'd brag on his "Writer Children." Scrolling through my old messages he bragged about his wife—that she was the smartest person he knew. He'd brag about his daughter—that she had a spirit and mindset that he admired. He didn't outwardly say these things, it was the stories he'd tell about them that really made it apparent.

And I just remember being in awe of him, that he thought so highly of people around him or how he'd talk about his favorite writers like C.L. Moore as if they were still alive—because to him they were. Mike is like that for me—so vibrant in personality I can still feel him when I read his stories.

I think, if we do anything to honor Mike's memory, it would be to continue paying that goodness and positivity in our writing community forward. He's started a thing that, like his stories, will live on through its message and intent. And that's a truly amazing legacy.

Janis Ian is a singer-songwriter with ten Grammy nominations and several Grammy and Audie awards. She also writes science fiction because Mike Resnick forced her into it. Their co-edited book of short stories, based on Ian's songs, by her favorite authors, was a Publisher's Weekly *pick. She is grateful for Mike's generosity of spirit, and his faith in her talent.*

HIS SWEAT LIKE STARS ON THE RIO GRANDE

by Janis Ian

My heart was broken long before we met, so when love came sneaking up, it was completely unexpected.

I'd grown up in the shadow of The Wall, but never given it much thought. It had always been there. It would always be there. I was grateful to be living on this side, where the Rio Grande provided water for the agricultural station my father ran, and kayaking provided some small relief from the late April humidity. I loved seeing the *huisache* bloom, their feathery yellow flowers mirrored in the river's edge. My favorite time of day was early morning, before the worst of the heat. I would sit in my secret place and watch the sunlight glisten on the river, pretending the sparkles were stars that had fallen to earth the night before.

When I was young, I'd sometimes "borrow" my mother's binoculars and focus on the migrant families working the fields to the north. They fascinated me, the way their children seemed to run everywhere without any sign of supervision. The way the women carried naked infants in slings across their breasts. The way they'd stop occasionally to nurse, or hold the infant aloft as it did its business in the grass. I'd never seen an adult woman's breasts before, and as mine began to bud, the thought of what they'd become fascinated me.

And I must admit, I loved to look at the men as they worked bare-chested in the sun. Loved the way a drop of sweat would make its way from the nape of a neck to the top of the shoulder blades, then along the alley between, down and down and down, until it finally disappeared into parts unknown. Loved

their wiry muscles, bunching and flexing as they grabbed at the plants, making my own still-forming parts throb and pulse. I had no name for it, this feeling of desire, but I gloried in it nonetheless.

I fell in love with Roger when he asked me to the tenth-grade dance. I'd been hopeful, but still, it came as a surprise. I was nothing to look at, although my lineage was good. Father a supervisor, mother a tracker—both respectable jobs, requiring intelligence, stamina, and leadership qualities. And, as Roger pointed out one starry night, a certain ruthlessness. Laughing, he said I'd managed to inherit them all, and some lucky fellow's children would benefit from it one day.

That actually made me blush.

We dated all through high school, progressing from dry, fumbling kisses to "cupping," as we called it. Roger would cup my breasts in his hands and tenderly kiss them through the fabric of my brassiere. In turn, I'd cup his balls through the fabric of his Bermuda shorts, lifting and assessing them until I could see his penis straining at the front, begging to be freed.

To this day, even seeing Bermuda shorts on a department store mannequin gets me all hot and bothered.

But we never went "all the way." We were saving that. I wasn't sure for what, but it seemed like the right thing to do. My parents liked his parents, his parents liked my parents, and the backgrounds all checked out. Still, something in us hesitated. I used to think it was because we knew it would never work out in the end, but perhaps it was just cowardice.

I cheered for him at the football games, when his tight end went on the offense to break the line. I helped with his Spanish, since his tin ear made it nearly impossible to understand his labored sentences. He wanted to be a tracker, like my mother, and I encouraged him to get the best education possible. I knew a tracker needed grounding in geology, and topography, and half a dozen other subjects unavailable at our local community college. When he dreamed about attending Texas A&M, I even wrote the application for him.

He broke my heart on graduation day, taking me out to a beautiful dinner at the best our little town had to offer. Making sure it was public, so I couldn't make a scene. Telling me without a shred of shame that we'd been great for high school, but now it was time to move on. Saying that as much as he'd enjoyed the fooling around, withholding himself had seemed the best way "to not get tied down."

He thanked me for being a good sport.

He paid the bill.

He pulled out my chair.

He walked me home, and left me alone at the door.

I didn't cry that night. I was too ashamed. When my parents asked how the evening had gone, I simply said I was tired, and made my way upstairs. I fell asleep almost immediately, and my dreams were filled with bronze-skinned men. We walked through the fields naked, letting the tall plants brush against our skin, weaving and waving and caressing without end. Strong arms lifted me into the wind, higher and higher, reaching toward the sky until I finally let go in one huge, orgasmic rush, and shuddered back to earth.

The next morning, I left early and went to my favorite place. There, hidden by the blackbrush and clapweed, I wept until my eyes were too puffy to see. I rinsed them in the river and made my way home.

That evening, I announced to my family that I'd broken up with him. "He's just too slow," I said. "I've kept it from you because I didn't want to cause tension, but I had to write his college application for him. I had to walk him through Spanish class too. I don't know how he'll manage in college, but I don't want to find out the hard way." He'd been fine for high school, I added, but it was time to move on.

And move on I did. Through my mother's contacts, I managed to get an internship at LICE, our Local Immigration and Customs Enforcement. I began learning about the migrant workers who populated our fields, everything from their immigration status (H2-A visas, allowing them to stay as temporary workers) to breeding habits (birthrate dropping steadily, no one knew why). I learned that the word "temporary" didn't have much meaning anymore because we needed them there to plant and harvest year-round. The migrant workers had become the breadbasket of America, and we couldn't let them go.

Because of Mother's status in the field, I was trusted with information most interns never saw. There were problems with The Wall, problems nobody had

foreseen. No one knew if there were similar issues on the other side; they'd cut off all communication in my great-grandparent's time, when it was first built. But there were plenty of problems on our side.

I'd always been taught that the snipers were there to keep people from coming over the wall to our side. Now, I learned they were there mainly to keep people *in*. Trackers like my mother were occasionally permitted to "go over" but the migrant families who'd been here when The Wall went up stayed, generation after generation, whether they liked it or not.

The distant gunfire we'd occasionally hear wasn't from LICE agents defending our borders. It was from LICE agents shooting desperate workers as they tried to climb The Wall and get out.

I was troubled by what I learned, troubled enough to discuss it with my parents. Of course, they already knew all about it. My mother explained what a mess the country had been in before, terrorists running rampant and drug culture invading even the whitest homes. The Wall went up, immigration cracked down, and the country returned to its previous peaceful state.

Wasn't I grateful I never had to worry about being raped when I walked home at night? Didn't I understand that keeping those people here was, in a sense, saving them from the gang warfare that infested their own homeland? Besides, none of them were really Mexican anymore. That was just a myth, like Palestinians claiming parts of Israel as "home." True, the migrants weren't really American either, but at least they had food, shelter, and a place to live.

Put that way, it all made sense. And I had a steady job waiting for me, if I keep my head down and didn't make waves.

I rose through the ranks, from intern to watcher to head of Enforcement and Education. I had my own desk, name plate and all, with an official title. I wouldn't say I was happy, but I was certainly settled.

And then came Gabe. Gabriel Alfonso Alvarez, to be exact. Fourth generation green card holder, the right handed down from his great-greats in a direct line after the moratorium on new citizenship applications went into effect. Those original green cards, usually held by university professors or tech geniuses, were a closely guarded privilege. Even the head of our field office had never seen one before.

It had only been a few years since Roger's betrayal, but during that time I'd convinced myself it was for the best. I'd slammed the lid on my desire so hard I barely felt anything, even when I touched myself. The occasional bout with a vibrator was enough to release any built-up tension. As for the men around me, when I compared them with what I saw through my field glasses, they were pasty-faced and bloated. It would feel like being stroked by a dead fish. I'd set sex, and all thoughts of sex, completely aside.

So the hot flush that ran from my toes right up my hairline when Gabe first spoke my name was a shocking reminder that I still harbored a craving for contact. I managed to stammer something intelligent, like "How on earth do you know my name?" before lapsing into red-faced confusion.

Laughing, he pointed to the plate on the front of my desk, saying, "You would be 'Señorita', then? Not 'Señora'?"

"Yes," I responded in my best I'm-the-teacher-here-don't-get-out-of-line voice.

He sighed dramatically, slumping for effect. "A pity. Your offspring would be beautiful."

Beautiful.

He thought I was beautiful.

Not "genetically clean," or "well groomed," but "beautiful."

I don't know that I'd ever spoken to a Hispanic person before, other than the women who cleaned our house over the years. They patiently let me practice my language skills on them. "Buenos dias, señoras," I would say, and they'd respond with "Buenos tardes, señorita." I would ask, in halting Spanish, how their day was going. "Bueno, señorita, bueno. Estamos muy contente," they'd say, and we would be finished with the lesson.

I still dreamed of them, though, as I had all my life. Dreamed of Hispanic men, their golden bodies glistening in the sun. Wondered whether drops of their sweat had watered the tomato I brought to my mouth. Slowly savored a peach, licking the skin and imagining the sweet salt of their perspiration on it. And here he was, calling me "beautiful."

I was lost.

Not that I was blind, nothing of the sort. I looked at him long and hard before agreeing to anything permanent. There were concerns. Gabe had tried his hand at half a dozen jobs, but never settled on anything. He had a small inheritance from his parents, and it was enough to provide the necessities but not much more. Despite his obvious intelligence, he had no real drive. He'd come here, to our little town, hoping to find his passion.

And then, he found me.

I'd like to say it was love at first sight, but it was more like instant lust. He asked whether I was seeing anyone, then took me to lunch. We stayed through dinner. He walked me home, striding confidently through the town, oblivious to the stares and whispers. He moved sinuously, muscles obeying without thought. I could feel them through the sleeve of his shirt when I took his arm. It was like walking with a tiger.

I want to be clear. I loved him then, as he was, and I love him now, as he is.

We dated for several months while my parents ran the usual checks. I understand it was much the same during the age of AIDS, when two people interested in sex would go to the doctor together and get tested. Protective measures. After all, no woman in her right mind wants to get pregnant and then find out her child's genes also came from an anarchist or, God forbid, a terrorist.

Gabe came up clean in every respect, for three generations back. No questionable antecedents. No criminal elements. Nothing but your basic hard-working American dreamers.

After that, events moved along by themselves. We married with little hoopla, took our honeymoon in San Antonio, then settled down. Thanks to my parents, he was able to get a job supervising workers in the broccoli fields. He seemed to enjoy himself.

As for me, I was deliriously happy. Every pent-up emotion came roaring out the first time he touched me. I think I even fainted for a moment.

He was an incredible lover, knowing just how far to push and just how long to make me wait. And he was inexhaustible. We'd make love first thing in the morning, have breakfast, go to work, come home, make love again, have dinner, and sometimes make love for a third time. There wasn't a spot in the house we hadn't tried, from the guest shower to the kitchen table.

We didn't plan on children, at least, not yet. I wanted him all to myself. I loved to watch him, shirtless in the Texas heat, as he mowed the yard. I needed to feast my eyes on his skin and imagine what the night was going to bring. Just the sight of his fingers buttoning a shirt made me wet. Absurd as it sounds, watching him take out the trash made me weak at the knees. I was in perpetual rut, and it showed no sign of ending.

Back at work, things were different. There was tension around the border; whispers of trouble passed desk to desk when no one else was listening. More and more of the migrant workers were dying, of old age, of illness, of simple neglect. We saw the reports and were told to ignore them. "Don't worry. They breed like rabbits," one supervisor said.

But that wasn't true. The migrant laborer's birth rate had begun falling a year after they were told they were permanent guests here, and the decline had continued. According to the Homeland Security statistics, we had less than half the workers we'd had three generations back—and almost twice the regular population. Asking Americans to work under those conditions was unthinkable. Paying a decent wage, which might allow migrants to send their children to school and work their way out of the fields, was unaffordable. Americans wanted cheap food, be it soda pop or Brussels sprouts, and they didn't much care how they got it.

The anxiety I felt at work began to surface in our home. As Gabe moved around, from broccoli to tomatoes to sweet corn and snap beans, he began to know individual families. He'd come home each day and tell me their stories as we lay sweating in the heat, exhausted by foreplay and its aftermath. He worried over them. He felt helpless.

There was one little boy he kept returning to, a seven year old named Hector. The child was obviously very bright, Gabe said, but he'll never have the chance to be anything but a "potato puller."

When Gabe started talking about changing the system from without, if it couldn't be changed from within, I realized his kind heart might be his undoing.

I worried over it incessantly. The more involved he became with the migrants, the more I begged him to distance himself. He began to resent what he termed my lack of empathy. I began to resent his willingness to throw away everything his family, and mine, had worked for over the years.

"Aren't you grateful to your ancestors for making sure you never have to live like that?" I'd ask. "Don't you owe them something for their bravery, their willingness to rise above their beginnings and make this their permanent home?"

And he'd respond that the workers' families had been brave as well, coming to a new country where they didn't even speak the language, working in the fields, hoping *their* children would have a better life too.

We'd argue, pushing and pulling, going around in circles. I'd bring up our future children; he'd answer that he didn't want them growing up in a world where only those who already had could have more. I'd tell him that for every bright little child in the fields, there were a hundred slow-moving dullards who were fit only to till the soil. He'd tell me that if my parents hadn't gotten enough protein, I'd be a dullard as well. And so on and so on.

Frustration grew on both sides until I reached for him one morning, and he pushed me away. I rubbed against him, whispering in his ear, but he rolled over and ignored me.

A few nights later, he came in late, immediately hopped in the shower, then fell asleep on the couch. When I woke him up to bring him to bed, he said he'd forgotten his hat that morning. He thought he had a bit of sunstroke, but just in case he was getting sick, he'd stay on the couch.

And so, slowly but surely, the love making stopped. I felt like I was losing my mind. My body was used to constant satiation, an erupting geyser that was suddenly capped off. The pressure began to build. I could relieve myself just so many times before I began feeling like a narcissist. Frankly, I only found my own body interesting when Gabe was playing with it. Otherwise, relief was a mechanical necessity, and I hated it. I was desperate for something that would take my mind off my body, and not finding it at home, I looked for it at work.

So when a rumor went around about a special meeting coming up, I was all ears. The affected employees had to sign a full non-disclosure agreement, on top of the multiple secrecy papers we already signed off on every year. There were dire warnings about what would happen to anyone found taping, or filming, or even taking notes. We talked about it in the restrooms and around the water cooler, speculating on what could make the administration so nervous.

They held the meeting in our regular conference room, but the windows were blacked out and once we were all in, the door was locked. A U.S. marine stood at either side of the door, weapons at the ready. All four senior department heads were there, north, south, east and west. There were a few local employees like myself, along with several representatives from the agriculture and chemical industries. And there was a slew of government officials, with buzz-cut scalps and chests full of metal.

Last to enter was the Surgeon General, who told us all to sit down while he made his opening remarks.

He explained that the birth rate problem among migrant workers had finally come to the attention of the FDA (Food and Drug Administration), who'd contacted the CDC (Centers for Disease Control), who in turn had called in the NSA (National Security Administration). The security people then reached out to all the scientists under their command, demanding an answer that would ensure America's continuing food supply.

The scientists had finally come up with an answer.

Once they had it down on paper, it went to the Secretary of Defense, and from there to the Joint Chiefs of Staff. Finally, the National Security Council, who advised the President directly, were brought in. They informed the President of their conclusions. He, in turn, heaved a sigh of relief at such an elegant solution and green-lighted it immediately.

After that, the army Chief of Staff took the floor. He reminded us of our patriotic duty. He said that just as The Wall protected our nation's borders, we were the human wall that guarded the rest. While we might not like it, we had to face the fact that stringent measures were called for. We needed to safeguard our country's future, not just for ourselves, but for our children. While the solution might appear drastic at first, he was sure we'd come to understand that it was all for the best in the end.

In closing, the Chief of Staff said, "Let there be no confusion here. We will not take away anything that will be missed."

Then he introduced a team of army neuroscientists, telling them with a grin to "keep it simple, keep it basic, keep it quick."

The lights went out, and projections of human brains appeared on the walls. There were specific sections, colored pink and blue and green, labeled ventromedial prefrontal cortex, left anterior cingulate cortex, amygdala. The youngest in the group pulled out an old-fashioned pointer, and proceeded to tell us what each area did. It was incredibly boring.

When the lights went back on, the older neuroscientist took over, explaining that thanks to government-sponsored research, they'd recently made a few tremendous advances in technology. For instance, they could now isolate precise regions of the brain. Not just overall areas dealing with specifics like math, or speech, but the more fluid areas. The parts that governed free will. Happiness.

Sexual desire.

Operation MASS, or Migrant Attitude Selection Service, would ensure that only the most necessary areas of the brain were targeted. Husbands would still love their wives, and children would continue to love their parents. The only changes would be in their overall happiness quotient, and their increased desire to "go forth and multiply."

There were snickers all around when he said that, because any Sunday School student knew the phrase from Genesis 1:28, Biblically polite short-hand for "Get you some nookie, and fast!"

Under the guise of free dental check-ups, workers' heads would be held still so x-rays could be taken. At the same time, a guided laser operating outside the detection range of the human eye would swoop in, destroying some bits of tissue, and exciting others. The patient would feel nothing but the dental plate clenched between his teeth.

As he droned on, the army people paying close attention, the rest of us were busy trying to figure out how this would apply to our own jobs. Sure, we'd be a necessary part of convincing the workers to go in for check-ups in the first place, but how exactly would that be done?

The obvious answer was to have some of the field supervisors volunteer to go first. That way, the migrants could see it was safe and painless. They'd even be given the day off with pay, courtesy of a grateful

U.S. government. The chemical companies would foot the bill for that, while the agri-business corporations would cover the cost of dentists, laser technicians, and mobile units.

Of course, the lasers wouldn't be used on the supervisors. That was out of the question.

We all agreed that this was an incredibly elegant solution, and the meeting was adjourned. Except for me. I needed just a little bit more information, and the junior neuroscientist was kind enough to provide it. He even let me take a few notes, after I mentioned my parents' positions and the length of their tenure.

The first thing I did when I got home was apologize to Gabe for nagging him about the migrant workers. I admitted I'd been wrong. They deserved his attention, and our support. I was going to speak with my parents and the head of LICE about it, personally. There had to be some way to give boys like the one he'd told me about a chance to escape the vicious circle their great-greats had left them in.

Next, I apologized for taking my sexual frustrations out on him. After all, he was my husband, not my boy-toy. He deserved to come home to welcoming arms and a supportive spouse. I'd do better in future, but for now, just to even things up a bit, any first moves would have to come from him. The look of relief on his face almost made me ashamed of what I planned to do, but fortunately, it passed.

We made love a couple of times that week, and I reveled in it, while reminding myself that it could end at any moment. I would never let that happen again.

The free dental exams were first announced over loudspeakers on the water trucks. Then came billboards in English and Spanish, as well as bilingual flyers. They even left bags of candy out for the children, with dates and times of the upcoming examinations written on the wrappers. It did my heart good to know this was happening all over the country, even in cities like New York, where the trucks were rolling through Chinatown making announcements in Mandarin and Cantonese.

The day before the check-ups were to begin, I suggested to Gabe that he attend them incognito. "Dress like one of the workers," I said. "Let another

supervisor go first, and you spend the day among your friends, reassuring them. They won't believe the other bosses, but they already trust you. After they see you come out looking the same as when you went in, they'll feel a lot better about things."

He praised me for being so compassionate, and got up the next morning to put on the clothes of a *campesino*. I even accompanied him to the mobile station, though of course I couldn't stand with the migrant workers—as much as he'd told them about his *gringa* wife, I might still engender mistrust. So I watched from the sidelines as he went in, and waited until he came out.

He was smiling, pointing to his mouth, opening it wide and saying, "Ah-h-h-!" to the children. He gave out sugarless chewing gum, reassuring everyone in Spanish. There was much back-slapping and many looks of relief all around.

For the rest of the day, Gabe and I stood and watched as they filed into the mobile units with their families.

When it came time to go home, I looked at him and said, "What would you like to do now, dear?" and he said, "I don't know, *mi esposa*…but for some reason, I've never felt happier in my life. What would *you* like to do?"

It's been two years now, two years that feel like a constant honeymoon. The workers are content, and as they say, "breeding like rabbits." There are babies underfoot wherever I look; the fields will soon be full of children earning their keep.

Meanwhile, Gabe is content to go to work, eat his meals, and make love whenever and wherever I ask. We even managed a quickie in a two-person kayak one cloudy morning. True, he isn't terribly pro-active about it, but so long as I remember to tell him what I want, he comes through like a champ.

Sometimes I knock off early and sit on our veranda, watching him in the fields. The children love Gabe, and the adults all tip their hats. Once in a while, he gets down in the dirt with them, yanking and pulling and lifting the baskets high over his head as he leads everyone toward the waiting trucks. Beads of sweat collect at the nape of his neck, then run down his back in rivulets, sparkling like stars on the Rio Grande.

APPRECIATION

by Toni Weisskopf, Publisher, Baen Books

Mike Resnick was a fan. Oh, of course he was a professional writer and editor, and rightly lauded for his work. But to me, like me, he was a fan. He loved science fiction fandom, and he loved the literature, and he loved being part of it all.

If I recall correctly, I met him and Carol, both together, at my first Windycon, which would have been 1987 or thereabouts, and got autographs from both of them. I was emerging out of the cocoon of Southern fandom and about to become part of Midwestern fandom as I more-or-less attended college in Ohio. This was very much Resnick territory. He was a fixture at Midwestcon and the con circuit surrounding Chicago and Cincinnati. And, as "Another Satisfied Eleanor Wood Client" (as the ubiquitous badges declared), he had a lot of books out over the next decade, and he went to even more conventions. So if you attended cons at all east of the Rockies, you inevitably ran into Mike.

He was one of those I considered my "late night stalwarts," still awake, still smoking cigars, still telling tall tales, in some invariably freezing corner of the con hotel—him and Jack Chalker, and Dave Locke, and a few others. And there we, the hardcore partiers, would find ourselves after 2a.m., enthralled. And I use the fannish sense of "party," which is to say sitting around talking about cool stuff.

Mike was one of the great fannish raconteurs, and he knew a lot about a lot of stuff—to include Broadway musicals. When I told him my then-husband, who also loved show tunes, had never seen Sweeney Todd, he immediately sent me a bootleg video to remedy that unfortunate gap.... His articles with Barry Malzberg accurately captured his conversational style, and were wonderful windows onto science fiction's professional past, remembering contributors who all too often were left out of the official histories. Like lady editor Bea Mahaffey. Someday I hope to be so remembered.

I got to work professionally with Mike on a couple of projects, the one closest to our hearts being an Edgar Rice Burroughs tribute anthology. And I got to work with Mike twice on one of Shahid Mahmud's floating workshop cruise jaunts, where the relaxed pace let him and Carol and me talk in the light of Caribbean day. And I got to see Mike experience his first DragonCon, which was a hoot. He saw, as I do, that it contains multitudes, including multitudes of readers—all potential Mike Resnick fans.

I never did take up his invitation to come to Cinci and explore his extensive photo archives for pictures of Bob Tucker, and I regret that. I will miss his affectionate banter, and his big, generous personality, and I really wish this were a convention program book appreciation and not a memorial tribute. He left big shoes to fill.

Alex Shvartsman is the author of an epic fantasy novel Eridani's Crown *(2019). His short stories have appeared in* Analog, Nature, Strange Horizons, *and here on the pages of* Galaxy's Edge. *He's the editor of over a dozen anthologies and of* Future Science Fiction Digest. *His website is www.alexshvartsman.com*

GODS PLAYING POKER

by Alex Shvartsman

I wait for the trickster gods to arrive in an expensive hotel suite. I sit at the head of the mammoth poker table that has been brought in by section and assembled on site, all ornate wood and green felt. Trays of exotic fruit and bottles of aged spirits line the walls. My skirt is ironed and my blouse starched. Everything in the room is prepared for their once-in-a-decade reunion.

They pop in all at once, wearing human forms by accord and tradition. Six men—and it's always men, cocky rule breakers and rapscallions and black sheep among their own pantheons—greet each other warily, partaking of food and booze. They ignore me completely.

They're the winners, the ones who are at least temporarily at the top of the heap, possessing of enough clout and power among their fellow trickster celestials to claim the honor of being invited to this gathering. I recognize most of them from the last few sessions—a decade isn't enough time to significantly alter their fortunes. Even so, a pair of the gods from the last time have been replaced by their more successful peers.

One of the newcomers, a Pacific Islander dressed in a gray hoodie, nearly seven feet tall and wide as two men, walks over and introduces himself. His name is Daucina and he flirts with me half-heartedly until Coyote comes over and whispers a few stern words in his ear. Daucina nods politely and skulks off in search of conversation elsewhere. The dealer is not to be the target of their games, also by accord. They need me free and clear of their influences.

After a brief period of mingling they take their seats at the table, ready for the main event. Their game of choice these days is Texas Hold 'Em. Over millennia they've played games of all kinds, from throwing bone dice to flipping gold coins to stacking ivory tiles. What matters is the combination of luck or skill. And, of course, the stakes.

They place their buy-ins onto the felt, neatly stacked chips that glow with warm amber light. Ambrosia packed by magic into the physical form. Immortality itself.

I can't help but eye those stacks hungrily. My fee is a small percentage of the bets. Not so much for a god, but enough to stay young and healthy, and to show up decade after decade to host their game. A rake of far greater value than any ever collected by a human casino.

The game begins slowly; the gods are cautious as they try, yet again, to feel out each other's tells, to take advantage of each other's fleeting moods and flights of fancy. Loki drags his long-nailed fingers across the felt. Regal Anansi leans back from the table as he observes the others. A newcomer whom I don't recognize stares at the cards through thick lenses of his unnecessary glasses. He looks like a nerdy, lanky teenager, complete with a constellation of zits on his left cheek. Stone-faced Sun Wukong dexterously stacks and unstacks his chips with his left hand. But it's not in any of their natures to be reserved—or display an overabundance of caution—for too long. The bets become larger, the mood thaws, and soon the inevitable boasting begins.

"I'm the greatest trickster in history," declares Loki.

As usual, his pronouncement is met with sneering and disdain.

"When Prometheus gave humans fire, I taught them to make gunpowder," Loki reminds them. "When they invented the car, I encouraged the road system that created the traffic jam."

This is true. Trickster gods harness their ambrosia from the suffering of humankind. They gather bits of it like droplets of sweat that form on humanity's psyche. From the perspective of humans, what they do is deplorable, but I can no more fault them for this than I can blame a lion for sinking its teeth into a wildebeest. A predator has to eat.

"The internal combustion engine is a gift that keeps on giving," says Loki. He goes on to describe in great detail his efforts to undermine wind and solar, to make people afraid of nuclear energy, and to keep the coal plants running.

As he regales them with details of his machinations, the game continues, and Daucina tries to cheat.

He subtly manipulates the probability field to increase the chance of spades being revealed on the flop. It requires effort, but I counter his spellwork with practiced confidence. I don't call him out, though. Not a session goes by without one or more of the players trying to pull something like this. Cheating is in their nature; they're as likely to attempt it as the scorpion is likely to sting the frog ferrying him across the lake. Part of my job as hostess is to prevent such shenanigans, and I'm very good at what I do.

By the time Loki finishes his story, many chips have exchanged hands and Daucina, who bet heavily on the chance at the flush he never made, is knocked out. He casts surly glances at Coyote, having incorrectly guessed at who had foiled his magic. Sun Wukong hangs on by a thread, his stack having dwindled to a handful of chips.

"You can always bet on humans innovating their way into trouble," says Loki. "Remember Set and how hard he tried to prevent the Industrial Revolution? The old curmudgeon hasn't sat at this table for centuries!"

"You're a one-trick reindeer, Loki," says Coyote. "Sniffing out ways to subvert human technology is amusing, but it's not nearly as effective as meddling in their politics. One can start a war by encouraging a disgruntled peasant with a gun, or initiate a coup by whispering the right words into a king's ear." As he speaks the words, he calls Anansi's bet and reveals a pair of kings. "I'm the best at that, and that makes me the greatest trickster in history."

The others jeer again, but less loudly. Coyote's track record is self-evident.

"I've recently convinced an entire nation to exit an alliance that was clearly beneficial to them, throwing their government and economy into utter chaos," says Coyote. "Here's how I did it."

Cards are dealt and chips exchange hands as Coyote regales us with the tale of his latest accomplishment. It is a master class in manipulation and subtle power moves that would make Machiavelli weep bitter tears of inadequacy. Even the other gods are

ensnared. They all pay attention to his words and his methods, no doubt already thinking of ways they can apply what they learned to their own ongoing schemes. All except for the lanky teenager who looks intensely bored by the proceedings, like a young child forced by his parents to attend Sunday church services. When Coyote wraps up his tale he snorts derisively.

"You seem to disapprove of my methods, Veles?" asks Coyote. His manner is amicable but I recognize a subtle edge to his voice.

Veles was a minor Slavic deity who got himself killed when followers of the Abrahamic god took over his lands and he stubbornly refused to adapt to the new reality like the rest of them. He was a bearded old warrior covered in scars, but now that I look closer at the new Veles I recognize those same intense blue eyes behind his glasses. More often than not, the gods are reborn, even if the process might take a few centuries.

"I have no quarrel with your methods." Veles's voice is nasal and squeaky, but it carries the underlying rage of someone who hasn't forgiven the universe for rendering him irrelevant and killing him a thousand years ago. "But you think too small. You all think too small even as you rest on your laurels, even as you meet for no reason but to congratulate yourselves on your so-called accomplishments."

"I've only been back a short while," says Veles, "but in that time I've accomplished more than the lot of you have in centuries. I've undermined the meaning of universal truth and replaced it with disposable almost-truths an inferior mind can choose among to best suit their worldview. I've suppressed civil discourse and encouraged a level of vitriol seldom seen before. I've convinced a few to carry out terrible acts that in turn stoked the hatred of millions."

And then, in that nasal voice, Veles explains just how he did it.

By the time he is done, even the other gods appear subdued. The merriment has gone out of the room, and instead of toasting joyfully they are brooding into their drinks. Anansi stares at Veles unblinking, even as all the others avoid looking him in the eye.

"Why are you looking at me like that, spider?" asks Veles.

Anansi takes a long time before he finally answers. "For a moment I thought you might be him. But no, your methods are too blunt, your thirst for vengeance too consuming."

"Who?" asks Veles.

Anansi leans forward and lowers his voice.

"Lucifer. Satan. Beelzebub. The prince of lies with a thousand names and a face recognized by none. We may try our best but he's the greatest trickster of us all. Always has been."

The others look uncomfortable; those names are not brought up at these meetings by tradition rather than law. Their shoulders slump and they bury their faces deeper in their drinks. All except Veles, who laughs.

"Look around, you doddering fool. The greatest of us are here, but Lucifer is not. You know why? Because there's no such thing. Satan is a myth our kind invented to feel better about our own inadequacies. A caricature of a trickster to counterbalance the Abrahamic god and to scare human children at bedtime. But you were right about one thing: if there's a superior trickster, a prince of lies to sit on the throne of thorns and lord over gods and humans alike, you're staring at the right celestial."

The others jeer half-heartedly at this display of bravado. Despite Veles's accomplishments, it's not in their nature to concede superiority willingly to any one among them, and especially not one so young. His braggadocio breaks the spell woven by his tale.

The evening draws to a close. One by one, the gods wink out of the room until I sit alone, once again, a stack of precious ambrosia chips left in front of me. Enough to last me a decade without the risk and trouble of having to procure more on my own.

I've seen gods like Veles rise and fall, fortunes shift over time like dunes in the desert. Every decade there's a slightly different group, another set of terrifying tales told around the gaming table. The gods come wearing the latest human fashions and speaking the latest human jargons. They leech from humanity not only its suffering, but its very zeitgeist to give themselves form and meaning.

That is one thing that remains a constant. Another constant is me, always their dealer, their enabler, their trusted and unobtrusive servant who ensures they keep competing to earn their seat at the next gathering. That they share their experiences and latest machinations, thereby making each other even more effective at spreading misery and suffering across the human realm. That they think themselves clever and powerful, and are never inclined to peek at who's pulling the strings from behind the curtain.

After all, the greatest trick I ever pulled was convincing the world I don't exist.

Copyright © 2020 by Alex Shvartsman.

IN MEMORY OF MIKE RESNICK

by Eleanor Wood

To say Mike Resnick was extraordinary, is like declaring that on a clear day the sky is blue. He was a brilliant writer who added immensely to the science fiction and fantasy world; he helped introduce so many new authors to the field via Galaxy's Edge *and the Stellar Guild series, and at conventions was generous with his time, speaking with fans and writers. I had the great fortune to become Mike's agent in 1983. What a long and wonderful ride this has been!*

Mike Resnick, along with editing the first seven years of Galaxy's Edge *magazine, was the winner of five Hugos from a record thirty-seven nominations and was, according to* Locus, *the all-time leading award winner, living or dead, for short fiction. He was the author of over eighty novels, around 300 stories, three screenplays, and the editor of over forty anthologies. He was Guest of Honor at the 2012 Worldcon.*

DISTANT REPLAY

by Mike Resnick

The first time I saw her she was jogging in the park. I was sitting on a bench, reading the paper like I always do every morning. I didn't pay much attention to her, except to note the resemblance.

The next time was in the supermarket. I'd stopped by to replenish my supply of instants—coffee, creamer, sweetener—and this time I got a better look at her. At first I thought my eyes were playing tricks on me. At seventy-six, it wouldn't be the first time it had happened.

Two nights later I was in Vincenzo's Ristorante, which has been my favorite Italian joint for maybe forty years—and there she was again. Not only that, but this time she was wearing my favorite blue dress. Oh, the skirt was a little shorter, and there was something different about the sleeves, but it was the dress, all right.

It didn't make any sense. She hadn't looked like this in more than four decades. She'd been dead for seven years, and if she was going to come back from the grave, why the hell hadn't she come directly to me? After all, we'd spent close to half a century together.

I walked by her, ostensibly on my way to the men's room, and the smell hit me while I was still five feet away from her. It was the same perfume she'd worn every day of our lives together.

But she was sixty-eight when she'd died, and now she looked exactly the way she looked the very first time I saw her. I tried to smile at her as I passed her table. She looked right through me.

I got to the men's room, rinsed my face off, and took a look in the mirror, just to make sure I was still seventy-six years old and hadn't dreamed the last half century. It was me, all right: not much hair on the top, in need of a trim on the sides, one eye half-shut from the mini-stroke I denied having except in increasingly rare moments of honesty, a tiny scab on my chin where I'd cut myself shaving. (I can't stand those new-fangled electric razors, though since they've been around as long as I have, I guess they're not really so new-fangled after all.)

It wasn't much of a face on good days, and now it had just seen a woman who was the spitting image of Deirdre.

When I came out she was still there, sitting alone, picking at her dessert.

"Excuse me," I said, walking up to her table. "Do you mind if I join you for a moment?"

She looked at me as if I was half-crazy. Then she looked around, making sure that the place was crowded in case she had to call for help, decided I looked harmless enough, and finally she nodded tersely.

"Thank you," I said. "I just want to say that you look exactly like someone I used to know, even down to the dress and the perfume."

She kept staring at me, but didn't answer.

"I should introduce myself," I said, extending my hand. "My name is Walter Silverman."

"What do you want?" she asked, ignoring my hand.

"The truth?" I said. "I just wanted a closer look at you. You remind me so much of this other person." She looked dubious. "It's not a pick-up line," I continued. "Hell, I'm old enough to be your grandfather, and the staff will tell you I've been coming here for forty years and haven't molested any customers yet. I'm just taken by the resemblance to someone I cared for very much."

Her face softened. "I'm sorry if I was rude," she said, and I was struck by how much the voice sounded like *her* voice. "My name is Deirdre."

It was my turn to stare.

"Are you all right?" she asked.

"I'm fine," I said. "But the woman you look like was also named Deirdre."

Another stare.

"Let me show you," I said, pulling out my wallet. I took my Deirdre's photo out and handed it to her.

"It's uncanny," she said, studying the picture. "We even sort of wear our hair the same way. When was this taken?"

"Forty-seven years ago."

"Is she dead?"

I nodded.

"Your wife?"

"Yes."

"I'm sorry," she said. "I'd say she was a beautiful woman." Then, "I hope that doesn't sound conceited, since we look so much alike."

"Not at all. She *was* beautiful. And like I say, she even used the same perfume."

"That's very weird," she said. "Now I understand why you wanted to talk to me."

"It was like…like I'd suddenly stumbled back half a century in time," I said. "You're even wearing Deedee's favorite color."

"What did you say?"

"That you're wearing her—"

"No. I meant what you just called her."

"Deedee?" I asked. "That was my pet name for her."

"My friends call *me* Deedee," she said. "Isn't that odd?"

"May I call you that?" I said. "If we ever meet again, I mean?"

"Sure," she said with a shrug. "Tell me about yourself, Walter. Are you retired?"

"For the past dozen years," I said.

"Got any kids or grandkids?"

"No."

"If you don't work and you don't have family, what do you do with your time?" she asked.

"I read, I watch DVDs, I take walks, I google a zillion things of interest on the computer." I paused awkwardly. "I hope it doesn't sound crazy, but mostly I just pass the time until I can be with Deedee again."

"How long were you married?"

"Forty-five years," I answered. "That photo was taken a couple of years before we were married. We had long engagements back then."

"Did she work?" asked Deirdre. "I know a lot of women didn't when you were young."

"She illustrated children's books," I said. "She even won a couple of awards."

Suddenly Deirdre frowned. "All right, Walter—how long have you been studying me?"

"Studying you?" I repeated, puzzled. "I saw you jogging a couple of days ago, and I watched you while I was eating…"

"Do you really expect me to believe that?"

"Why wouldn't you?" I asked.

"Because I'm an illustrator for children's magazines."

That was *too* many coincidences. "Say that again?"

"I illustrate children's magazines."

"What's your last name?" I asked.

"Why?" she replied suspiciously.

"Just tell me," I said, almost harshly.

"Aronson."

"Thank God!"

"What are you talking about?"

"My Deedee's maiden name was Kaplan," I said. "For a minute there I thought I was going crazy. If your name was Kaplan I'd have been sure of it."

"I'm sorry I lost my temper," said Deirdre. "This has been just a little…well…weird."

"I didn't mean to upset you," I said. "It was just, I don't know, like seeing my Deedee all over again, young and beautiful the way I remember her."

"Is that the way you always think of her?" she asked curiously. "The way she looked forty-five years ago?"

I pulled out another photo, taken the year before Deedee died. She was about forty pounds heavier, and her hair was white, and there were wrinkles around her eyes. I stared at it for a minute, then handed it to Deirdre.

"This is her too," I said. "I'd look at her, and I'd see past the pounds and the years. I think every woman is beautiful, each in her own way, and my Deedee was the most beautiful of all."

"It's a shame you're not fifty years younger," she said. "I could go for someone who feels that way."

I didn't know what to say to that, so I said nothing.

"What did your wife die of?" she asked at last.

"She was walking across the street, and some kid who was high on drugs came racing around the corner doing seventy miles an hour. She never knew what hit her." I paused, remembering that awful day. "The kid got six months' probation and lost his license. I lost Deedee."

"Did you see it happen?"

"No, I was still inside the store, paying for the groceries. I heard it, though. Sounded like a clap of thunder."

"That's terrible."

"At least she didn't feel any pain," I said. "I suppose there are worse ways to go. Slower ways, anyway. Most of my friends are busy discovering them."

Now it was her turn to be at a loss for an answer. Finally she looked at her watch. "I have to go, Walter," she said. "It's been…interesting."

"Perhaps we could meet again?" I suggested hopefully.

She gave me a look that said all her worst fears were true after all.

"I'm not asking for a date," I continued hastily. "I'm an old man. I'd just like to talk to you again. It'd be like being with Deedee again for a few minutes." I paused, half-expecting her to tell me that it was sick, but she didn't say anything. "Look, I eat here all the time. What if you came back a week from today, and we just talked during dinner? My treat. I promise not to follow you home, and I'm too arthritic to play footsie under the table."

She couldn't repress a smile at my last remark. "All right, Walter," she said. "I'll be your ghost from six to seven."

✿

I was as nervous as a schoolboy a week later when six o'clock rolled around. I'd even worn a jacket and tie for the first time in months. (I'd also cut myself in three places while shaving, but I hoped she wouldn't notice.)

Six o'clock came and went, and so did six ten. She finally entered the place at a quarter after, in a blouse and slacks I could have sworn belonged to Deedee.

"I'm sorry I'm late," she said, sitting down opposite me. "I was reading and lost track of the time."

"Let me guess," I said. "Jane Austen?"

"How did you know?" she asked, surprised.

"She was Deedee's favorite."

"I didn't say she was my favorite," said Deirdre.

"But she is, isn't she?" I persisted.

There was an uncomfortable pause.

"Yes," she said at last.

We ordered our dinner—of course she had the eggplant parmesan; it was what Deedee always had—and then she pulled a couple of magazines out of her bag, one full-sized, one a digest, and showed me some illustrations she had done.

"Very good," I said. "Especially this one of the little blonde girl and the horse. It reminds me—"

"Of something your wife did?"

I nodded. "A long time ago. I haven't thought of it for years. I always liked it, but she felt she'd done many better ones."

"I've done better too," said Deirdre. "But these were handy."

We spoke a little more before the meal came. I tried to keep it general, because I could see all these parallels with Deedee were making her uncomfortable. Vincenzo had his walls covered by photos of famous Italians; she knew Frank Sinatra and Dean Martin and Joe DiMaggio, but I spent a few minutes explaining what Carmine Basilio and Eddie Arcaro and some of the others had done to deserve such enshrinement.

"You know," I said as the salads arrived, "Deedee had a beautiful leather-bound set of Jane Austen's works. I never read them, and they're just sitting there gathering dust. I'd be happy to give them to you next week."

"Oh, I couldn't," she said. "They must be worth a small fortune."

"A very small one," I said. "Besides, when I die, they'll just wind up in the garbage, or maybe at Goodwill."

"Don't talk about dying like that," she said.

"Like what?"

"So matter-of-factly."

"The closer you get to it, the more a matter of fact it becomes," I said. "Don't worry," I added lightly. "I promise not to die before dinner's over. Now, about those Austen books…"

I could see her struggling with herself. "You're sure?" she said at last.

"I'm sure. You can have a matched set of the Brontës too, if you like."

"Thank you, but I don't really like them."

It figured. I don't think Deedee had ever cracked any of them open.

"All right," I said. "Just the Austen. I'll bring them next week."

Suddenly she frowned. "I don't think I can make it next week, Walter," she said. "My fiancé's been away on business, and I'm pretty sure that's the day he comes home."

"Your fiancé?" I repeated. "You haven't mentioned him before."

"We've only spoken twice," she replied. "I wasn't hiding the fact."

"Well, good for you," I said. "You must know by now that I'm a believer in marriage."

"I guess I am too," she said.

"You guess?"

"Oh, I believe in marriage. I just don't know if I believe in marriage with Ron."

"Then why are you engaged to him?"

She shrugged. "I'm thirty-one. It was time. And he's nice enough."

"But?" I asked. "There's a 'but' in there somewhere."

"But I don't know if I want to spend the rest of my life with him." She paused, puzzled. "Now why did I tell you that?"

"I don't know," I replied. "Why do you think you did?"

"I don't know either," she said. "I just have this feeling that I can confide in you."

"I appreciate that," I said. "As for spending the rest of your life with your young man—hell, the way everyone gets married and divorced these days, maybe you won't have to."

"You sure know how to cheer a girl up, Walter," she said wryly.

"I apologize. Your private life is none of my business. I meant no offense."

"Fine." Then: "What shall we talk about?"

I thought about Deedee. Sooner or later we talked about everything under the sun, but her greatest passion was the theater. "Whose work do you like better—Tom Stoppard's or Edward Albee's?"

Her face lit up, and I could tell she was going to spend the next ten minutes telling me exactly who she preferred, and why.

Somehow I wasn't surprised.

☼

We skipped the following week, but met every week thereafter for the next three months. Ron even came along once, probably to make sure I was as old and unattractive as she'd described me. He must have satisfied himself on those counts, because he

never came back. He seemed a nice enough young man, and he was clearly in love with her.

I ran into her twice at my local Borders and once at Barnes & Noble, and both times I bought her coffee. I knew I was falling in love with her—hell, I'd been in love with her from the first instant I saw her. But that's where it got confusing, because I knew I wasn't really in love with *her*; I was in love with the younger version of Deedee that she represented.

Ron had to leave town on another business trip, and while he was gone she took me to the theater to see a revival of Stoppard's *Jumpers* and I took her to the racetrack to watch a minor stakes race for fillies. The play was nice enough, a little obscure but well-acted; I don't think she liked the color and excitement of the track any more than Deedee had.

I kept wondering if she could somehow *be* Deedee reincarnated, but I knew deep in my gut that it wasn't possible: if she was Deedee—*my* Deedee—she'd have been put here for me, and this one was marrying a young man named Ron. Besides, she had a past, she had photos of herself as a little girl, friends who had known her for years, and Deedee had only been dead for seven years. And while I didn't understand what was happening, I knew there couldn't have been two of her co-existing at the same time. (No, I never asked myself *why*; I just knew it couldn't be.)

Sometimes, as a bit of an experiment, I'd order a wine, or mention a play or book or movie that I knew Deedee hadn't liked, and invariably Deirdre would wrinkle her nose and express her lack of enthusiasm for the very same thing.

It was uncanny. And in a way it was frightening, because I couldn't understand why it was happening. This wasn't *my* Deedee. Mine had lived her life with me, and that life was over. I was a seventy-six-year-old man with half a dozen ailments who was just beating time on his way to the grave. I was never going to impose myself on Deirdre, and she was never going to look upon me as anything but an eccentric acquaintance…so why had I met her?

From time to time I'd had this romantic fancy that when two people loved each other and suited each other the way Deedee and I did, they'd keep coming back over and over again. Once they'd be Adam and Eve, once they'd be Lancelot and Guinevere, once they'd be Bogart and Bacall. But they'd be *together*. They wouldn't be an old man and a young woman who could never connect. I had half a century's worth of experiences we could never share, I was sure the thought of my touching her would make her skin crawl, and I was long past the point where I could do anything *but* touch her. So whether she was my Deedee reborn, or just *a* Deedee, why were the two of us here at this time and in this place?

I didn't know.

But a few days later I learned that I'd better find out pretty damned quick. Something finally showed up in all the tests I'd been taking at the hospital. They put me on half a dozen new medications, gave me some powerful pain pills for when I needed them, and told me not to make any long-term plans.

Hell, I wasn't even that unhappy about it. At least I'd be with my Deedee again—the *real* Deedee, not the charming substitute.

The next night was our regular dinner date. I'd decided not to tell her the news; there was no sense distressing her.

It turned out that she was distressed enough as it was. Ron had given her an ultimatum: set a date or break it off. (Things had changed a lot since my day. Most of my contemporaries would have killed to have a gorgeous girlfriend who had no problem sleeping with them but got nervous at the thought of marriage.)

"So what are you going to do?" I asked sympathetically.

"I don't know," she replied. "I'm fond of him, I really am. But I just…I don't know."

"Let him go," I said.

She stared at me questioningly.

"If you're not certain after all this time," I said, "kiss him off."

She sighed deeply. "He's everything I should want in a husband, Walter. He's thoughtful and considerate, we share a lot of interests, and he's got a fine future as an architect." She smiled ruefully. "I even like his mother."

"But?" I prompted her.

"But I don't think I love him." She stared into my eyes. "I always thought I'd know right away. At least that's the myth I was brought up on as a little girl, and it was reinforced by all the romance novels I read and movies I saw. How was it for you and your Deedee? Did you ever have any doubts?"

"Never a one," I said. "Not from the first moment to the last."

"I'm thirty-one, Walter," she said unhappily. "If I haven't met the right guy yet, what are the odds he's going to show up before I'm forty, or sixty? What if I want to have a baby? Do I have it with a man I don't love, or with a guy I love who's living six states away before it's even born?" She sighed unhappily. "I have two good friends who married the men of their dreams. They're both divorced. My closest friend married a nice guy she wasn't sure she loved. She's been happily married for ten years, and keeps telling me I'm crazy if I let Ron get away." She stared across the table at me, a tortured expression on her face. "I'd give everything I have to be as sure of a man—*any* man—as you were of your Deedee."

And *that* was when I knew why I'd met her, and why the medics had given me a few more months atop Planet Earth before I spent the rest of eternity beneath it.

We finished the meal, and for the first time ever, I walked her home. She lived in one of those high-rise apartment buildings, kind of a miniature city in itself. It wasn't fancy enough to have a doorman, but she assured me the security system was state of the art. She kissed me on the cheek while a couple of neighbors who were coming out looked at her as if she were crazy. I waited until she was safely in the elevator, then left and returned home.

When I woke up the next morning I decided it was time to get busy. At least I was going to be in familiar locations where I felt comfortable. I got dressed and went out to the track, spent a few hours in the grandstand near the furlong pole where I always got the best view of the races, and didn't lay a single bet, just hung around. Then, after dinner, I started making the rounds of all my favorite bookstores. I spent the next two afternoons at the zoo and the natural history museum, where I'd spent so many happy afternoons with Deedee, and the one after that at the ballpark in the left-field bleachers. I had to take a couple of pain pills along the way, but I didn't let it slow me down. I continued my circuit of bookstores and coffee shops in the evenings.

On the sixth night I decided I was getting tired of Italian food—hell, I was getting tired, period—and I went to the Olympus, another restaurant I've been frequenting for years. It doesn't look like much, no Greek statues, not even any belly dancers or bouzouki players, but it serves the best pastitso and dolmades in town.

And that's where I saw him.

His face didn't jump right out at me the way Deirdre's did, but then I hadn't really looked at it in a long time. He was alone. I waited until he got up to go to the men's room, and then followed him in.

"Nice night," I said, when we were washing our hands.

"If you say so," he answered unenthusiastically.

"The air is clear, the moon is out, there's a lovely breeze, and the possibilities are endless," I said. "What could be better?"

"Look, fella," he said irritably, "I just broke up with my girl and I'm in no mood for talk, okay?"

"I need to ask you a couple of questions, Wally."

"How'd you know my name?" he demanded.

I shrugged. "You look like a Wally."

He cast a quick look at the door. "What the hell's going on? You try anything funny, and I'll—"

"Not to worry," I said. "I'm a just used-up old man trying to do one last good deed on the way to the grave." I pulled an ancient photo out of my wallet and held it up. "Look at all familiar?"

He frowned. "I don't remember posing for that. Did you take it?"

"A friend did. Who's your favorite actor?"

"Humphrey Bogart. Why?" Of course. Bogie had been my favorite since I was a kid.

"Just curious. Last question: what do you think of Agatha Christie?"

"Why?"

"I'm curious."

He stared at me for a moment, then shrugged. "I can't stand her. Murders take place in back alleys, not vicarages." It figured. I'd always hated mystery novels where the murder was committed primarily to provide the detective with a corpse.

"Good answer, Wally."

"What are you smiling about?" he asked suspiciously.

"I'm happy."

"I'm glad one of us is."

"Tell you what," I said. "Maybe I can cheer you up too. You know a restaurant called Vincenzo's—a little Italian place about three blocks east of here?"

"Yeah, I stop in there every now and then. Why?"

"I want you to be my guest for dinner tomorrow night."

"Still why?"

"I'm an old man with nothing to spend my money on," I said. "Why don't you humor me?"

He considered it, then shrugged. "What the hell. I don't have anyone to eat with anyway."

"Temporarily," I replied.

"What are you talking about?"

"Just show up," I said. Then, as I walked to the door, I turned back to him and smiled. "Have I got a girl for you!"

Copyright © 2007 by Mike Resnick.

A FEW MEMORIES OF MIKE RESNICK

by Barb Galler-Smith

Sometimes you meet someone who makes a profound change in your life. Sometimes, if you are very, very lucky, you meet someone who makes more than one profound change in you. And sometimes, by whatever grace you may deserve, you meet someone like Mike Resnick.

He gave me so much—not just books, DVDs of some of his favorite old TV shows, or stories to read just because, but his time and patience, his consideration and encouragement. He bought three of my short stories. He blurbed the first book. He nagged me to send him stories. He supported me unconditionally as a writer. He helped me hone my skill as an editor.

I was part of his first generation of Writer Children from CompuServe's Science Fiction writing forums in the early 1990's. Our first face-time together was at Worldcon 1994 in Winnipeg. At first I was little intimidated, but he soon whipped me into shape by telling me, with a forceful voice and a stern look, that he thought I could write and so I better just pay attention, because he had things to teach me.

He took me, as he did so many others, literally by the hand and marched me around to parties at Worldcons (where he would sample any good chocolates that we passed by) and introduced me to people he thought I should get to know. Many of my writer friends today were also in the crowd of Writer Children—and every year new, talented faces. He gave freely of his time, his energy, and his wisdom.

He gave us hundreds of tips on the act and art of writing, on markets, on editors, how to be a professional, and his joy of fandom. At those sit-around times, I learned about writing—the art and the craft, how stories unfold, how to keep your butt in the chair, why to write even if you don't feel like it, and how, if you choose to persist, it can be your real job. He talked about loving to write. He told stories of previous cons and stories about some of the stars of writing, not because he'd met them once or twice, but because they really were his friends.

A multitude of Mike's friends would show up for those sit-around parties. Sometimes there were belly dancers (I will always remember the Julies!), and always a gaggle of Writer Children gathered. Sometimes he'd tell writer stories, sometimes he'd pontificate a bit, but always with humor and kindness.

Some of those stories were even true—how the Masquerade's rules changed to say "No peanut butter" and what he and his Carol wore when they won Best in Show one year. He spoke with pride about his collies, their successes, how they all got their names, and the love he felt for his dog, The Grey Lensman. He talked horse racing, too.

Mike was a funny guy and he liked funny things. He wrote some pretty funny stories with great characters, including his sometimes less-than-politically correct Lucifer Jones—one of my favorites! He remains the only person I ever allowed to call me "Blondie."

He was also serious, and could pull emotional heart stings with the best of us. In 1994, Asimov's magazine published a story by Mike called "Barnaby in Exile." I decided to read the story over lunch in an open café in the West Edmonton Mall. I remember coming to the end of the story and uncontrollably sobbing loudly. I glanced up to everyone around was staring at me in concern. I held up the magazine and could only say "good story." That moment was pivotal. And it was the quintessential example of what a good short story should do. It should move you.

Mike was pretty casual about it. He said he'd intended to grab my emotions with the matter-of-fact manner he had about everything relating to the business of writing.

Okay, he could be stubborn, and opinionated, and downright curmudgeonly, but he never pulled punches and was always honest. I admired his gumption even when I disagreed.

His best works won awards left and right and still holds the record for the most writer Hugo nominations of anyone—thirty-seven. He wore the little rocket pins on his lanyard with pride. I especially remember how delighted and proud he was when chosen as Guest of Honour for the Worldcon in Chicago in 2012.

He loved Carol before everything, and she was never far from his thoughts. He often told us how much she meant to him—his great love, friend, reader, critic, and supporter. He was intensely proud of his talented daughter, writer Laura Resnick.

Our last time together was at Worldcon 2015 in Spokane. I have regrets now, of course. They're the usual ones everyone has when you live far apart, drift into other places, and don't keep in frequent touch—when all those little things added up and stretched the times between talks to too long.

Mike was first my friend, then my writer dad, and later my editor dad. I am a better writer and a better editor because of him. The ripples of his friendships, his fandom, his professional expertise, and dedication to paying it forward will last a long time.

Thank you, Mike, for making me a part of your life for over thirty years.

NIGHTFALL ON KIRINYAGA

by Michael Swanwick

What a sweet guy Mike Resnick was! He loved to encourage new writers and to sit in the bar telling old stories. Those stories were worth hearing. Mike knew the history of science fiction as few others did and was there when much of it happened. He was a part of that history as well. His books will not fade away with his passing.

We two had a tradition whenever we were both nominated for the same Hugo Award. (Which happened a lot; Mike was nominated for 37 Hugos and won five.) Meeting at the nominee mingler before the ceremonies, one of us would say, "Since it will have no influence whatsoever on the outcome, I hope you win," and the other would reply, "On exactly the same terms, I hope

you win." Then, usually, we both lost. That exchange was my consolation prize. I'm doubly bereft to have lost it.

Resnick the author wrote at least one metric ton of fiction that his readers relished. Whom the gods favor most, they make prolific. But Mike had not only volume but range. His work could be frivolous or deathly serious, adventure-driven or literary. Even at its most ambitious it was always entertaining. I read his Kirinyaga tales, about the clash of traditionalism and Western liberalism in post-colonial outer space, as they came out and marveled at how knowledgably, how evenhandedly, he dramatized the failings of both worldviews, deftly leading to the inevitable realization that they could never be reconciled. I was convinced at the time that no resolution of the series worthy of its component stories was possible. Mike proved me wrong and I am still in awe of the accomplishment. (No spoilers here! If you're curious how it was done, the stories, by design, neatly fit together to make up the novel Kirinyaga.)

Others will write about Mike's fannish activities and his editing; about how he introduced Janis Ian to the science fiction world, convinced her to edit an anthology, and coached her through the process; of his love of Africa; of his canny business sense; of his many acts of kindness. I only want to point out, for those desirous of emulating him, how Mike garnered so many awards and nominations. First, of course, he taught himself how to write well enough to deserve them. But then, after he had mastered the art of writing novels, he kept writing short fiction. Financially, short fiction is a mug's game. The only reason to write it when you don't have to is out of love of the form—and of science fiction. Mike Resnick loved science fiction more than anything but his family.

In my every memory of him, Mike is smiling or just about to. He enjoyed life as well as anyone I know. And a man who manages to spend his life doing what he loves is a man who has lived wisely.

Now that wisdom is gone. All we survivors can do is hope to live by his example.

Joy Ward is the author of one novel. She has several stories i n print, magazines and anthologies, and has also done interviews, both written and video, for other publications.

Mike Resnick, along with editing the first seven years of Galaxy's Edge *magazine, was the winner of five Hugos from a record thirty-seven nominations and was, according to* Locus, *the all-time leading award winner, living or dead, for short fiction. He was the author of over eighty novels, around 300 stories, three screenplays, and the editor of over forty anthologies. He was Guest of Honor at the 2012 Worldcon.*

THE *GALAXY'S EDGE* INTERVIEW

Joy Ward interviews Mike Resnick

Mike Resnick is more than simply a science fiction icon. Mike has won more awards than any other science fiction writer. In fact, Mike is so good at what he does he makes the very hard work of writing top-notch science fiction look almost easy. Besides numerous books and stories in print all across the world, Resnick is also the editor of *Galaxy's Edge.*

Joy Ward: How did you get started writing?

Mike Resnick: My mother was a writer. I always wanted to be a writer. By the time I was in high school I sold my first article at fifteen, I sold my first poem at sixteen. I'm not a poet but I ran it in Facebook a while back.

Silky Sullivan came to the Derby with more pre-publicity than Secretariat and ran twelfth. I wrote "Silky at the Post" (which was my answer to "Casey at the Bat") and I actually sold it. I sold some stories by eighteen. I married Carol in college. I was nineteen, she was eighteen, and after a year of fiddling around working for the railroad I figured it was time to get a job in publishing somewhere—and it happens that the only publishing job open in the whole city of Chicago at that point was at 2717 North Pulaski Road. National Features Syndicate is what they called it, but what they did is they put out three tabloids, very much like the *National Enquirer* only worse, and three men's magazines. Within half a year this twenty-two-year-old kid is editing *The National Insider* with a print run of 400,000 a week. Our best-selling headline during the years I had it was "Raped by 7 Dwarves." I will not testify to the veracity of our stories. Because we did not publish erotic books, adult books, that meant I was free to sell them elsewhere, whereas I couldn't sell tabloid or men's magazine stuff elsewhere because we had our own publications. But I knew guys from other publishers in our field and I started doing that. By the time the dust had cleared ten years later I had sold over two hundred of them, all of them under pseudonyms. As I explained, the only place we writers wanted our name was on the check, never on the book.

You'd be surprised how many people who have gone on and made it pretty big started, learned their trade in that field because you could get very well paid while you were learning how to write. We only got a thousand a book, sometimes seven hundred a book, and no royalties ever, but if you turn out a book every two weeks or every week or so, this was at a time when the average American was making eight thousand bucks a year. We could do that every two months if we had to. We were twenty-two, twenty-three-year-old kids. You learned how to make deadlines and you learned how to differentiate characters since they were all going to do the very same thing. I sneaked through some Edgar Rice Burroughs and Robert E. Howard pastiches to legitimate New York publishers, but I didn't want to write Burroughs or Howard books, I wanted to write Resnick books.

One day in 1975 I turned to Carol and I said, "If I write one more four-day book or one more six-hour screenplay for Herschel Gordon Lewis (he was voted the second worst director in history after Ed Wood), if I do one more my brain is going to turn to putty and run out my ears. What else do we know how to do?"

At the time we were breeding and exhibiting collies. We had twenty-three champions overall, and we had twelve or fifteen dogs on the place any given day—and we figured if the two of us could care for fifteen dogs and I had time to write all that crap, think of what a staff could do. So we spent about eight months looking around the country and wound up buying the second-biggest luxury boarding and grooming kennel in America, which happened to be in Cincinnati. We moved there and within about four years it was going full force. We had a staff of twenty-one. Any given day we were boarding like two hundred dogs, sixty cats, grooming about thirty or forty dogs.

I was finally able to go back to writing, only this time writing the kind of stuff I wanted to write. I was sure there was no audience for it. That was why we had the kennel. Much to my surprise, it started selling and in 1993, when the writing out-earned the kennel for the fifth year in a row, we sold the kennel. We figured we could now live anywhere we wanted, so we looked all over the country, decided we liked it here, so we stayed in Cincinnati.

The first thing I sold after we bought the kennel was *The Soul Eater* in 1981. *Analog* called it a work of art, which surprised the hell out of me that anybody besides me thought it was any good. The next one I wrote was one called *Birthright: The Book of Man*, which I have resold a dozen times. It created a future in which I've put about thirty-five of the novels I've written since then. I wrote thirteen books for Signet and they were getting phenomenally good reviews. They were selling okay because Signet kept buying them from me, but they weren't selling any more than okay.

My advances weren't getting any bigger. It was like I was standing still doing nothing. My friend Jack Chalker finally convinced me that the problem was my agent. I had made one foreign sale in four years. So, after he convinced me, I did the smartest thing I've ever done in my career: I hired Eleanor Wood as my agent. I hired her in 1983, and she remains my agent today. The first book she sold was *Santiago*, which got me three times the biggest advance I had gotten up to that point. It made *The New York Times* bestseller list and in the first two years I had her she made twenty-six foreign sales for me, which was twenty-five more than anybody else had made for me. We have been together ever since.

I thought at the time, a rather stupid thought, that if you had something important to say you had to say it in sixty, seventy thousand words or more. You couldn't do it in a short story. I only wrote seven stories the first ten years I was writing science fiction. Then in 1986 Orson Scott Card asked me to write a story for an anthology he was doing called *Eutopia*, and by keeping to all the strictures he gave, which were interesting ones, I wrote a story called "Kirinyaga." It made my reputation. It won the Hugo. It made me decide that yeah, you can occasionally do something with short stories. It has re-sold thirty-four times to domestic and foreign venues. From that day to this I've written and sold about three hundred short stories. I found out I love doing them.

You have to understand that unlike most beginners, I wasn't one. I probably had ten million words behind me so the fact that it sold wasn't the thrill that it would be for most people. Everything I wrote sold. Most of it I didn't want to sign my name to. It was very gratifying that I was able to get away with it. I didn't have to do Burroughs books and Howard books. I could do Resnick books and sell them. That was very satisfying, and so was the fact that I had a legitimate New York publisher say, in essence, "Okay, I'll buy three a year from you, any subject you want." It was gratifying to know that I could finally write what I had been training myself to write for fifteen years, I could write stuff I could sign my name to, that when people came over and said, "What do you write for a living?" I wouldn't give them any titles because I didn't want anybody to know those titles. It was very satisfying to be able to write at a more elevated level. Howard and Burroughs were fine for their day and they wrote at the peak of their ability, but those are not the peak of most of our abilities. Totally different kinds of things.

What happened was Lin Carter was a friend of mine and he was probably the greatest literary chameleon of them all. One day I am in New York, probably around 1970 or so, having lunch with him. He was telling me what he was working on. He said, "Two weeks ago I did a Burroughs book and right now I'm doing a Leigh Brackett book. Next month I'll be doing a Robert E. Howard book." I said, "That's fine, Lin, but when are you going to do a Lin Carter book?" He looked at me and I could tell he didn't understand the question. That made up my mind then and there. I didn't want to spend the rest of my life writing Robert E. Howard and C. L. Moore, the way Lin did. So I stayed out of the science fiction field for ten years. I wrote more adult books. I wrote other things. It really made up my mind that I didn't want to write that stuff. I'd rather not write science fiction at all than imitate other people.

So it was really gratifying to be putting my own views down. This is the kind of science fiction I want to write, nobody else was writing exactly like this, and to be able to sell it and get good reviews, to have a publisher and finally a number of publishers who continually encourage me and say do more of it—well, it finally made writing both fun and satisfying.

It also meant that I knew what I was going to do for the rest of my life, and I do a *lot* of it. I'm pretty fast. One thing you learn writing in that Other Field for a thousand a book, no royalties, and publishers who may go to jail in three weeks, is that you learn how to be fast. Well, to give you an example, I'm seventy-four years old. I should be slowing down and in ways I am. But when I was seventy, four years ago, I had ten books out. Last year, at seventy-four, I sold fourteen new stories and delivered eight books as well as editing *Galaxy's Edge*. I'm not impoverished. I do it in these quantities because this is what I love to do more than just about anything else in the world.

The most satisfying part of being a writer, probably for the last twenty-five, thirty years, has not been seeing my name in print. I do that all the time. I love winning awards, and I've certainly won my share—but the real highlight is at the end of the day when I look at what I've written and it comes out pretty much the way I hoped it would when I sat down in the afternoon to write. To me, that's more gratifying than any good review or anything else. I know the difference between good and bad. I also know when I write, even though its saleable, isn't as good as it should have been and I have to go back and do it again. But again, it's really very gratifying when it comes out the way I hoped it would.

My most memorable award was probably the first Hugo I won because you never expect to win one. Nobody expects to win one.

We were sitting in the audience right behind George Effinger in 1989 and I was up for best short story. It was the first time I had ever been nominated. I looked at the field and David Brin was up. David Brin was as hard to beat in the late eighties as Harlan was in the early seventies. I knew I was going to lose to him so I was talking to George Effinger. Then Carol pokes me in the ribs and says, "Go up there. You won!"

I said no, you must have heard wrong. David Brin had a lock on it.

She says to George, who had been turning to me, "George, will you tell him he won?"

What she didn't know was that George was deaf in one ear and he had turned the good ear to me and the deaf ear was facing the stage, so he didn't know. Finally a bunch of other writers who were sitting near us told me to go get the goddamned award so we can find out who won the next one. That was probably the most surprised and the biggest kick I got. Thereafter, not that I ever felt I had a lock on a particular Hugo, but at least I knew it was possible. I didn't know that the first time.

JW: You have a love affair with Africa.

MR: Yes I do.

Off the top, it's a beautiful and fascinating continent. More to the point, it's as close to an alien society as a science fiction writer is going to find on this world. I think every science fiction fan will agree with two statements. One, if we can reach the stars we are going to colonize them. Two, if we colonize enough of them sooner or later we are going to come into contact with more than one sentient race. Africa offers fifty-one separate and distinct examples—because it was colonized by so many countries—of the effects, usually deleterious, of colonization, not only on the colonized but on the colonizers. Those of us who don't learn from these warnings—and humans aren't all that good at learning anything—are doomed to repeat them. You add that to the fact that these really *are* alien societies. How alien? In Kenya in 1900, there were forty-three languages and not one of them had a word for wheel. That's pretty alien. There are many other examples. At the same time, as a tourist, it is beautiful. The animals are beautiful.

One of the interesting things is that I made friends with our private guide. Whenever we're going to Kenya or Tanzania I will write him ahead and say I'm going to be working on this, this and this. Find me some old-timers who can tell me about whatever it is I'm researching. So we spend some time in the game parks, but we also hunt up a bunch of salty old guys with really weird stories to tell who are going to die with them untold if I don't visit them. I ultimately transform them into science fiction, and they end up in my books and stories.

My most powerful stories are about Africa, or based on things African. My five Hugo winners are about Africa, and except for *Santiago*, my better sellers are about Africa—and that's because I feel very passionately about it and it comes through.

JW: You have your writer children?

MR: That's what Maureen McHugh dubbed them. What happened was with *Alternate Kennedys*, a closed anthology. Invitation only. I had invited Nancy Kress to it. She was teaching a workshop and a kid called Nick DiChario gave her a story she thought would fit, and told him to send it to me. The story came in and I must have been in a bad mood, because instead of putting in a little note saying politely please don't do this until you are asked, I thought let me read it and see just how bad it is. By page four I knew nothing could keep it off the Hugo ballot. And nothing did. It was a Hugo nominee, and a World Fantasy nominee and Nick himself was a Campbell nominee for that story. I finally met him a few months later at the Orlando WorldCon and I said to him, "Nick, why did you send it to me?" The magazines at the time had three times the circulation of an anthology. "A story that ballot worthy should get to as many people as possible." His answer was that he had sent it to every magazine in the field and got nothing but form rejects. I thought they are crazy! They should have fired the slush readers, because it never got to an editor. No ed-

itor could read that story and not buy it. We became correspondents and friends, and about a year later he sends me a novella and a note that he was having the same trouble with this. Could I tell him what's wrong with it? I read it and the only thing wrong with it was it was by Nick instead of by Isaac, Arthur or Robert. I knew Piers Anthony was doing an anthology on that theme. I wrote Piers and told him read this, that he was going to buy it—and indeed he did.

I thought if we keep treating this poor kid like that, he's not going to stop writing—but he's going to stop writing science fiction and go write espionage or something else. We're going to lose a helluva talent. So I figured I'd better do something to encourage him. I get about eight or ten invites every year for anthologies. When they invite me it's a guaranteed sale. So I invited Nick to collaborate with me on four or five of these just to get him into print, to keep him enthused. He's still writing now, he's been up for another Hugo, and he is committed to science fiction and not some rival field.

I thought: I bet there are more good writers out there than Nick who have trouble *selling*. So it became my duty over the last twenty-five years to help them. Every time I find a good one, I collaborate with him or her to get them into print, I buy from them for my anthologies and now for my magazine, and at conventions I take them around and introduce them to editors and agents. I do everything I can to help them.

People ask why, and the answer is you can't pay back in this field. I'm seventy-four. Everybody who helped me at the beginning is dead or rich or both. I can't pay back, so I pay forward. It's very, very gratifying to see some of these kids go out and do wonderful things!

It means the field that I love, that I have devoted my life to, isn't going to lose ten or twelve or fifteen really talented writers every decade.

These are people who deserve to be in print. This field, like almost any other field, is limited. It can't publish an unlimited number of books. It doesn't have an unlimited number of dollars. It's like movies or anything else: once you're in you fight to maintain your turf. If that means being a little tougher on the guy coming up behind you, you do it. And my helping them is a way to even the playing field, because to be honest most people won't even define the playing field for them. You get an awful lot of platitudes out of how-to books on writing, many of which are quite good—but there aren't any how-to books on selling.

It makes me feel that I've helped pay the field back for being so good for me. For the last thirty or forty or fifty years I've been living a dream. When I was six years old I wanted to write a book called *Masters of the Galaxy*. Now, the subject matter has changed appreciably—but four years ago I did a book called *Masters of the Galaxy*. It happened to be about a hardboiled futuristic detective called Jake Masters, but for sixty-five years I wanted to write that book. This field has been phenomenal to me. It's given me everything I ever wanted. My spare time is spent going to conventions, associating with friends. The only people I tend to talk to now that we are out of dogs, on the computer or just about anywhere else, are science fiction fans and writers. And I am as much a fan as I am a writer. How do you thank a field for giving you a lifetime? This is my way.

Copyright © 2017 by Joy Ward.

AN APPRECIATION OF MIKE RESNICK

by Eric Flint

I first met Mike Resnick long before I met him in person. In my days as an aspiring but unpublished author, I followed his "Ask Bwana" column in Speculations *magazine. I invariably found the advice and guidance he gave wannabe writers like me to be more cogent and level-headed that anything I found elsewhere.*

Years later, after I'd not only gotten published but had started editing Jim Baen's Universe *magazine, I finally met Mike in person. Well...virtually speaking, anyway. I got an email from him accompanied by a story he wanted to sell to JBU.*

In the email, Mike said he was pretty sure the story had a real shot at getting a Hugo nomina-

tion. Given his track record—he'd gotten more Hugo nominations than any author in the history of the award—I took his estimate for good coin. But I sent him back an email telling him that while I'd be glad to buy the story, if he really thought it had a chance for a Hugo nomination he'd improve his chances if he published it in a more Hugo-prestigious magazine. (Yes, there's a pecking order in such things. If this comes as a shock to you, you've been living on another planet.)

Mike's response was: "Screw that. You guys pay better than anyone else."

Thus was born a friendship that lasted for more than a decade, and would still be going on if Mike hadn't had the ill-grace to shuffle off this mortal coil before he should have. (He didn't check with me first, either, which I'm still grumpy about.)

Our friendship transcended the many differences we had on non-literary issues like politics, where to buy gasoline and which was the best Greek restaurant in Chicago. What always struck both of us was how closely aligned we were when it came to our professional judgment. Mike wound up co-editing Jim Baen's Universe *and I can't recall a single instance when our opinions on a given story didn't either match or at least come very close to matching.*

And we had the same experience later, when we both wound up being judges on the Writers of the Future contest. Mike and I usually wound up judging the four quarterly first place stories which were competing for the annual Grand Prize. We never discussed the stories until we'd sent in our votes, which would have been inappropriate. But once the decisions had been made, we'd compare notes and invariably found that our opinions had either been identical or very close. There was only one instance in which we disagreed sharply—he gave a story first place out of four and I ranked it last—but the dispute wasn't over the quality of the story itself. The author had tried an unusual narrative device which Mike thought worked and I didn't.

I loved kicking around stories with Mike. I always learned something from him, and I like to think he gained at least a few insights from me. Whether he did or not, though, we always had a friendship that never wavered a bit.

Richard Chwedyk sold his first story in 1990, won a Nebula in 2002, and has been active in the field for the past twenty-nine years.

RECOMMENDED BOOKS

by Richard Chwedyk

At The Corner of Popular and Personal

It's funny that I've never seriously asked myself why I am, and always have been, drawn to science fiction and fantasy as my choice of literary (in the widest sense) reading. Call me lucky.

But it occurs to me, after reading a *lot* of books for almost a year, that among the many attributes of SFF is the apparent fact that the field has found the fulcrum point between the popular and the personal: a point of balance that sometimes carries the reader to one end of the implicit agreement between readers and writers (what the reader wants), or to the other end (what the authors want to share with readers).

Mysteries, thrillers, romances, etc. have a "popular" face, and publishers provide the product that satisfies their audience: mostly novels, and novels of a certain size and shape. Short fiction gets short shrift; anything that strays from the formulas gets marketed as "mainstream," if at all.

But SFF is wide open. Granted, a majority of SFF readers may want the tried and true. Nevertheless, every year the field produces work that transcends the boundaries, and a significant number of readers welcome new worlds and sensations heretofore unanticipated. The publishers' "well-made product" is like comfort food—and there's nothing wrong with that. But within our field one can find much that will appeal to more adventurous tastes.

In science fiction and fantasy, we're not so much a readership as a multitude of readerships.

We are multitudes containing multitudes.

As the books discussed below well demonstrate.

All Worlds Are Real: Short Fictions
by Susan Palwick
Fairwood Press
November 2019
ISBN: 978-1-933846-84-2

There's an exercise I give to my students in fiction writing classes. I hand out a bunch of magazines or anthologies, anything with a lot of short stories, and I ask them to pick one story at random, read aloud the first sentence (or in some cases, the first two or three) and then ask the student, and the class: Is this something we want to keep reading? The exercise is useful for a number of reasons, but primarily we do it to demonstrate how important it is for a story to catch your attention, to make you ask the question, "What happens next?"

Every story in Susan Palwick's latest collection has our undivided attention from the very first words. And no two stories are alike, neither in style, nor in theme, nor in voice.

Several deceive you at first, like "Windows," starting with seemingly familiar details of a setting not too distant from our everyday reality:

> *The bus smells like plastic and urine, and the kid sitting next to Vangie has his music cranked up way too high. It's leaking out of his earbuds, giving her a headache. He's a big boy, sprawled out across his seat and into hers as if she's not there at all. She squeezes herself again the window, resting her head against the cool glass to try to ease the throbbing behind her eyes.*

Rest assured, where Vangie is going isn't where you first might guess.

"City of Enemies" leaves no question where you are initially, and it certainly isn't Kansas:

> Scanning for infrared signatures, the search-and-rescue robot found the young woman at dusk in a pile of smoking rubble outside the city. She was unconscious, cheek pillowed on one filthy hand, a tangle of long dark hair obscuring her face. The robot, a tower of twinkling lights and sensors atop sturdy treads, used its wonderful machinery to scan her for pathogens, for implanted weapons and surveillance tech, and found none.

"Sanctuary" tries to picture the world after the Rapture:

> I'd just finished putting new eyebolts in the St. Andrew's cross in the Red Room—I hadn't installed the old ones, and they'd turned into pipe cleaners—when the angels came fluttering in, mewling and bumping into things.

"Lucite" catches you with a vision of Hell you might find at once unique and amazingly obvious:

> The Tenth Circle of Hell is a gift shop.

These openings not only demonstrate Palwick's ability to engage us from the get-go, but the immense variety of her vision and imagination. Some of these stories are solidly science fictional. Some are decidedly in fantasy territory. And some occupy that in-between area that drives critics, scholars, and itinerant categorizers crazy and makes them want to invent new names and new categories.

What unites these stories is their deep humanity—or hers, really. I was at a loss to find a comparison (and that may be just as well, since comparisons are rarely fair to either party, but indulge me this once) until I got to the stories "Hodge" and "Recoveries." You can't start reading them without thinking of Theodore Sturgeon. On a storytelling level, Palwick and Sturgeon do different things, but they speak the same language. Sturgeon wrote that as he matured as an author, he found in himself "...an increasing preoccupation with humanity not only as the subject of science, but as its source. It has

become my joy to find out what makes it tick, especially when it ticks unevenly."

It's not bad company to be in. Palwick's stories are always compelling and always beautifully crafted, but it's her insistence in finding the uneven ticks of humanity in even the slightest of her tales that make her work a pleasure to read.

◆ ◆ ◆

Interference
by Sue Burke
Tor (hardcover)
October 2019
ISBN: 978-1250317841

When I finally got my copy of Sue Burke's first novel, *Semiosis*, signed, she inscribed it: "Never trust plants. They always want something."

That is perhaps the best key to understanding that novel, as well as this, the second volume in her "duology." We don't often think of plants "wanting" anything, though obviously they do. Just try not watering your houseplants. The difference on the planet Pax, where colonists flee to once they believe their home is effectively done for, is that the indigenous life forms make their needs known in far more direct ways. As we learned in *Semiosis*, on Pax the plants run the show.

Interference takes places two centuries after *Semiosis*. The story is told from several points of view, which I'm glad to say includes the plants (call me a traitor, but if I had to choose a favorite character it would be Stevland), and in a more relaxed fashion than in the first volume. There is enough background information here that if you missed

Semiosis (for shame!) you'll have no trouble figuring out where you are or where you're going. This novel poses new challenges and new threats to both the humans and the indigenous residents of Pax, from another alien culture that has distinct plans for this world. Not only are we not alone, we're in grave danger.

Interference is science fiction at its best. It challenges our assumptions about how we define intelligence and what forms of life are capable of possessing it. It also addresses the importance of communication as a necessary survival skill. It also dismisses that Campbellian dictum that humans can/must/will end up at the top of the heap when alien cultures interact. Though the dominance of one species over another may be a likelihood, it is not an inevitability, and for humans not necessarily the end of the game. That aspect of this novel reminds me a little of the world in Octavia Butler's "Blood Child," though the circumstances and outcomes are quite different.

In some ways, this and the preceding novel owe a debt to the great-but-much-neglected Hal Clement—not in style or structure or characterization, but in placing at the heart of its story a scientific problem or concept. From there, Burke applies her considerable skills to raising the stakes on her drama, sharpening the emotional edges until even her sentient plants convey (dare I say it?) a "human" touch.

It doesn't hurt that it is also tightly written and paced.

This may be the conclusion of a duology, but I feel it's far from being the end of the story.

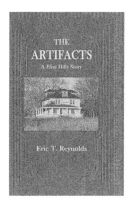

The Artifacts
by Eric T. Reynolds
Hadley Rille Books (trade paperback)
May 2019
ISBN: 978-0997118896

The author calls this a "spec historical" novel. It involves "timeshifting" that takes place mostly in an old farmhouse on the property purchased by Kayla Ramsey in the Kansas town of Flint Hills. There are two houses on the property, the other being a nicely kept Victorian, itself steeped in history. But the two homes represent a conversation of sorts, on many levels. Kayla finds herself immersed in the past, and in a very literal way.

The fantastic elements of the story are introduced and sustained by subtle means. We are asked not to be concerned with how the time travel works, but to measure the totality of history through the changes in a modest Kansas house over the course of a century and a half, much as the title suggests: through the discovery and consideration of "artifacts," some of which might be considered the detritus of rural life, but in their unique ways illuminate our perspective of human behavior, be it rural or otherwise.

Reynolds's writing is simple and direct, and his story doesn't contain any highly dramatic crescendos. The tone is deliberately meditative and personal—so much so that I understand why it's published by his own small press. However, I believe this novel deserves a wider audience, especially in an era when history is perceived by many, if perceived at all, as some sort of train wreck much in need of correction.

Reynolds has found an almost visceral, and emotional, way to view history that appreciates the specificity of objects and moments, while encompassing the inevitability of change.

❖ ❖ ❖

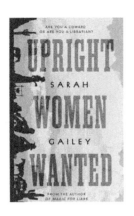

Upright Women Wanted
by Sarah Gailey
Tor
February 2020
ISBN: 978-1250213587

SFF writers are reinventing the western, so it seems. Perhaps it's time someone did. Those little sections of bookstores and libraries marked "Westerns" have either been shrinking or disappearing altogether. Westerns, to some degree, have always been more creations of myth and imagination. Recent works have tended to de-mythologize the category and rely more on historical accuracy. That's not the only way to go, however, as Sarah Gailey's novella ably demonstrates.

Esther is a young woman who stows away in a librarian's book wagon to escape a horrendous arranged marriage. What she discovers is that librarians are the secret do-gooders and fighters of injustice in a Southwest ruled by cruel fascists and overrun with bandits.

Instead of a Lone Ranger, imagine a *league* of Lone Rangers who are lesbian librarians and you have a rough idea of the world Gailey is giving us.

Esther is quite effective as a point-of-view character who helps introduce us to what, at its core, is a very dark vision. The bad guys are *really* bad, and the heroes have no easy time subverting a world gone terribly wrong. What mediates this grim milieu is Gailey's wit and expeditious pacing. Some readers might even find this good-versus-evil theme slightly—or even greatly—clichéd, that the author herself seems unable to take it seriously. Not me. On the contrary, I found Gailey's approach highly reminis-

cent of the sort of novellas one would find in the pages of *Galaxy* in its heyday, were that magazine upgraded to twenty-first century sensibilities.

Its novella length is perfect for its subject and voice. Its nimble prose disguises the seriousness of its themes. One cannot help but root for Esther and her allies in spite of the, at times, insurmountable perils they face. Paradoxically, this is a fun book to read, more so than many other dystopian mythologies publishers have shipped me recently.

◆ ◆ ◆

The Mother Code
by Carole Stivers
Berkley
May 2020
ISBN: 978-1984806925

Echoes abound here of science fiction novels of the past. Biological warfare threatens the end of humanity. Scientists genetically engineer children to survive the carnage. These children are raised in cocoons within AI robots. Unanticipated consequences. We've been here before.

The marketing material from Berkley is leaning heavily on phrases like "original and mind-bending." That kind of salesmanship may work in some corners, but hey, we're science fiction readers. It takes a hell of a lot to impress us on that front. Besides, it ain't how original you are, it's how well you execute your ideas and tell your story.

Stivers's novel is tough going at the beginning—a little too static and determined to legitimize its premise—but once it gets going, you'll be drawn into it. What impresses me most about this novel is how Stivers portrays the growth of intelligence and maturity in the AIs, specifically through our main protagonist robot, Rho-Z (or Rosie), whose job it is to nurture and educate the human, Kai. It questions much of the conventional wisdom not only about artificial intelligence, but about motherhood, society, education, and "instinct." It does what science fiction does best and does it with efficiency and aplomb.

Get past those first chapters. It's worth the effort.

◆ ◆ ◆

In closing...

Kirinyaga: A Fable of Utopia
by Mike Resnick
Del Rey (hardcover)
March 1998
ISBN: 978-0345417015

The Dark Lady: A Romance of the Far Future
by Mike Resnick
WordFire (paperback)
January 2019
ISBN: 987-1614752387

My practice of choosing an older book of note to end the column has become, unintentionally, a sort of means to mark the passing of some great authors in the field. Vonda N. McIntyre first; after that, Gene Wolfe. I can barely keep up.

It is difficult to express my sorrow now at confronting the passing of our editor, Mike Resnick. Words always fall short of the task. The best for which I can hope is to remind readers here of two of his finest works, which go some small way in explaining what made Mike Resnick so significant as both an author and as a human being.

The basis for the book *Kirinyaga* was a short story of the same name written for an anthology that never saw print. The theme of the anthology was to be Utopia in its various imaginings and permutations. Fortunately, when the anthology got canceled, he sold the story to *Fantasy and Science Fiction* magazine. It has since become a classic in the field.

I heard Mike say at a con many years ago that the field as a whole hadn't yielded many truly great novels, but he could think of dozens of science fiction short stories that could be counted among the greatest works of fiction ever written. If I recall, he also stated that, of necessity, most novels were written for remuneration, but anyone writing short fiction is doing so out of sheer love of the form.

"Kirinyaga," and all the other stories in this volume, are works of love. Some of them are heartwrenching and difficult, but not difficult to read. Mike insisted on a clarity and precision to his prose that is evident throughout this novel in stories—a tragedy about how the best of intentions can go awry, how subjective "best intentions" can be, and how it takes more than such to make a Utopia.

The short story "Kirinyaga" represents science fiction at its best. The "science" as such is a means, not an end. At its heart is one of SF's most important—maybe *the* most important—theme: the conflict between tradition and change. In its subtle way, the story argues the inevitability of the latter while respecting the ingenuity and determination of the former, in the role of Koriba, the tale's narrator who, on a terraformed planet, wishes to restore the culture of his Kikuyu ancestors from the time before the arrival of Europeans and Western Culture. Like many great literary characters, Koriba is part hero, part villain. Though he scores a victory (as he sees it) at the end of the story, tragedy is waiting in the wings, brilliantly communicated through Mike's subtle prose. And the rest of the stories in this volume also beautifully illustrate.

I'd also like to mention a novel of Mike's that's a personal favorite, one that I believe has been neglected and undervalued.

The Dark Lady is a sort of quest tale, told from the voice of an alien improbably named Leonardo—a quest for the source of mystery, of inspiration, of desire. Leonardo believes that the subject of a number of artworks, some separated by centuries, cultures, maybe even species, is in fact the same being, the beckoning "Dark Lady" of legend and lore. His search brings him in contact with many kinds of humans, and many aspects of human folly and frailty. The episodic structure resembles the approach Mike utilized in the better-known *Santiago*, but this novel is shorter, tighter, and leaves us at a very different terminus. At its heart, this story embraces another of the great themes of science fiction: the nature of what makes us human.

Critics at the time faulted the novel for what they saw as its ambiguous finale—that somehow Mike should have wrapped up the mystery in some nice, profound bundle. Their reading, I believe, is another case of critics looking through the wrong end of the telescope. The clarity and simplicity of Mike's prose veils the depth of his subjects.

The mystery behind the Dark Lady can't be solved because she is mystery incarnate. She is an answer that is always out of reach. But the pursuit of that mystery, especially (though not exclusively) through art, is as close as we can get to a definition of humanity. To tie up the ending of the novel in a neat bundle would have been a betrayal. Science, art, and intellect search for answers, and more often than not come up with deeper mysteries.

To understand humanity is to embrace the mystery.

Mike Resnick understood that. He worked the grind of popular fiction, but at his core was the personal touch that marks so many of our best storytellers. We have lost him, but we haven't really lost him.

And the Dark Lady beckons on.

I'LL NEVER BEAT MIKE

by Martin L. Shoemaker

I'll never beat Mike Resnick.

I'll never beat him on the fencing strip. He challenged me to a duel once, and I hoped we could've met on the strip sometime; but it never happened. And if it had, I wouldn't have bet on me. Sure, I was a couple decades younger; but Mike was a national class fencer in his youth, and I...wasn't. He knew tricks I didn't, and he was wily.

I'll never beat him at handicapping the horses. Even though he never bet a dime, he knew the ins and outs of every major race and contender in the country, and he understood. Whereas I... don't. My knowledge of horses mostly consists of how to haul hay bales and muck out stalls. Still, I have a lot of horse friends with horse opinions, and I used to love to maneuver him into those discussions and watch the fur fly. He wasn't always right; but when a different horse won, he had always predicted "...unless these conditions, then everything changes."

I'll never beat him at humor, though I do try. He had a natural gift for anecdotes and Borscht Belt classics, and he knew when to underplay and when to hit the joke hard.

I'll never beat him at heart (though again I try). For all that he came across as a canny business man, a crusty comedian, or a tough Chicago street kid, he could turn around and with just a few words make you weep for a character on a page.

I'll never beat his output. Not only did I start too late in life, but I lack his idiosyncratic but determined work habits: waking at the crack of noon, handling business and family until late in the evening, and then writing all night long. I used to get messages from him at all hours of the night, and I was only one of countless insomnia correspondents. He followed this routine day in and day out for decades, leading to an impressive and steady output. I have a day job; writing was Mike's full-time job, and his love.

I'll never beat his awards record. I have a belief that awards aren't something you can strive for, they just happen when you do good work. They happened to Mike. A lot.

I'll never beat his count of friends in the field. Mike knew everybody. He collaborated with many of my favorite writers.

I'll never beat his count of writers he helped in the field, new writers especially, because he had so many years and so many friends and such a gigantic, generous heart.

But I'm going to try. Because I promised Mike I would pay it forward, just like he taught us, and I'm not going to let him down.

APPRECIATION

by Marina J. Lostetter

Writing a tribute, appreciation, obit, or eulogy for someone is never easy. It's not just emotionally difficult. The words, they don't seem to want to flow. Which is counter-intuitive, given my line of work—the line of work I shared with Mike. It seems like this should be simple. Whether any of us knew Mike as a mentor, friend, family member, or even foe, it feels like whatever was special about him—whatever reasons we have for writing an appreciation—should simply fall from our fingertips. But for me, certainly, the words are fighting back.

Because how do you sum-up what someone meant to you in a few measly sentences? How that person changed or enhanced your life? These lines are too few to reflect the depth, breadth, and complications of Mike's existence, and what he meant to me as a mentor.

Mike gave me professional support when he didn't have to. Opportunities I wouldn't have found or had access to on my own. And he did it for no other reason than he wanted to see new writers like myself succeed. He was a fantastic cheerleader, never asking for anything in return, simply happy to help cultivate new authors in the field.

He and I co-wrote a story for the Aliens franchise, and he would have been the first to tell you that he knew nothing about said franchise going

in. But he'd been invited to write a story for an anthology, and he could have turned it down, or he could have done what he did: give a young author an opportunity. That was his modus-operandi, using his experience and his name to help the next generation, leveraging it in favor of those of us who, at this early stage in our careers, could only otherwise fantasize about working with some of our favorite authors, editors, and IPs.

Afterwards, there was a panel at DragonCon devoted to the anthology. The con put him on the panel, but not me. That didn't bother me. But it bothered him. He insisted I be on the panel with him, and announced to everyone in attendance, "She wrote the story, I just put my name on it."

He was always willing to give me, and other writers he mentored, our due—even, teasingly, at his own expense.

He was stubborn, often stuck in his ways, but open to pushback. Unless it was pushback about how many exclamations points a short story needed. He was always sure there should be more! So! Many! More! (Those are for you, Resnick.) He came from an old-school way of doing things, and having access to that history of the profession was enriching.

Thank you, Mike, for thinking of me as one of your "Writer Children." Thank you for all of the support, encouragement, and advice you've given me over these last few years. Thank you for the last thing you ever said to me—even when I knew your editing days were winding down—because it was so very, very like you:

"Send me a story."

Gregory Benford is a Nebula winner and a former Worldcon Guest of Honor. He is the author of more than thirty novels, six books of non-fiction, and has edited ten anthologies.

A SCIENTIST'S NOTEBOOK

by Gregory Benford

TIME: THE WINGED CHARIOT

**For the Royal Society
commemorating its 460th anniversary**

*But at my back I always hear
Time's winged chariot hurrying near:
And yonder all before us lie
Deserts of vast eternity*

—ANDREW MARVELL, 1600s

When the Royal Society began in 1660, time seemed a simple, obvious subject, understood since ages long past. To Isaac Newton and his colleagues, two longstanding traditions pervaded the idea of time.

The Greeks, like most ancient cultures, saw their world as not completely chaotic, though it could be capricious. This faith in a definite order in nature promised that it could be understood by human reasoning. To them, at least some physical processes had a hidden mathematical basis, and they sought to build a model of reality based on arithmetical and geometrical principles.

Adding to this was the Judaic worldview, which had a timeline. God created the universe at some definite moment, a cosmos arriving fresh and with a fixed set of laws. The Jews thought that the universe unfolds in a sequence running forward, which we now call linear time. Creation enabled evolution, which led forward in linear time to a future we could quite possibly change. This differed greatly from most other ancient cultures, which favored cosmic cycles, probably by generalizing from the march of the year's seasons. In cyclic time everything ends, but there is an eternal return.

These two ideas, linear vs. cyclic, persist today in physics and also emerge in our art, music and literature. Physics has constrained time, ordering the music of events, but the dance between these linear vs. cyclic views continues.

Four hundred years ago, Europeans assumed a God-created universe that unfolded in orderly ways, in linear time. Not that the universe always had to be as we see it now. Change was possible, but constrained by physical law. Einstein once remarked that what most interested him is whether God had any choice in his creation. The Judaeo-Islamic-Christian tradition answered with a resounding *yes*. Further, it insisted on nature's rationality, aided by mathematical principles. These were the only cultures to do so. This driving idea altered the concept of time itself, as the cultural agenda played out in modern science.

Evolving Time

Time has two faces.

First, our sense of it passing seems inevitable, an automatic intuition. Unlike space, in which we can move back and forth, time hammers on relentlessly. This is Intuitive Time.

Second, we frame our position in time, our historical era, by looking at our slowly changing landscapes, and our societies. These alter on the scale that we ourselves see as we age. This is Deep Time.

Both these faces appeal, but they deceive us.

In the 1700s, the philosopher Immanuel Kant saw space and time as elements of a systematic mental framework, structuring our experiences. Spatial measurements tell us how far apart objects are, and temporal measurements measure how far apart events occur. This eventually intersected Charles Darwin's idea that many abilities of organisms emerge from evolution by natural selection. Then it follows that time and space are the concepts we and other animals evolved to make the best use of the natural world. In this sense, they emerged from the primordial world where our minds evolved.

But that was not enough. Modern science reveals that time is supple, changeable, and even enigmatic. Further, we stand in a small slice of it, anchored in a moving moment that is an infinitesimal wedge compared with what has gone before, or will come after us. Our telescopes tell us of immensities of space, but other sciences—geology, biology, cosmology—speak of even grander scales of time.

Space and time are so familiar that we forget that they underlie the entire intricate and beautiful structure of scientific theory and philosophy. Perhaps it is not surprising that our first powerful theories built on assumed bedrock intuitions, to be questioned only later. Clocks in Newton's universe ran everywhere the same. He invoked "absolute, true and mathematical time" saying that it "of itself, and from its own nature, flows equably without relation to anything external, and by another name is called duration." Of the immense expanse of past time Newton had no true idea, for he took as gospel the Genesis story. Space was similarly absolute. Newton avoided the colossal scale of space by supposing that God had fixed up the cosmos so that gravity, the force he first quantified, had not made it collapse—at least, so far.

This view held up well until the nineteenth century. By then even atheist scientists accepted as an act of faith that nature had a lawlike order—not from philosophy, but because it worked. Though this assumption springs from an essentially theological worldview, it gave useful predictions without a god attached. Still, few saw the full implications of regarding time as a subject of study, not belief.

The first collision between religious views and the study of the far past, which we now call Deep Time, came with the newborn science of geology. In 1830, the geologist Charles Lyell proposed that the features of Earth perpetually changed, eroding and reforming continuously, at a roughly constant rate. This challenged traditional views of a static Earth with rare, intermittent catastrophes. In the eighteenth and nineteenth centuries the vast depth of the eras before humans arose became apparent through development in geology and evolution's grand perspective. These still had to be licensed by physics, the more secure and quantitative science. Historically, physics sets the stage for the events and processes probed by the other sciences.

When William Smith and Sir Charles Lyell first recognized that rock strata represented successive long eras, they could estimate time scales only very imprecisely, since rates of geologic change varied greatly. Even these early attempts got the sciences into trouble. Creationists, reasoning from the Bible, had been proposing dates of around six or seven thousand years for the age of the Earth based on the Bible. Early geologists suggested millions of years for geologic periods, with some even suggesting a virtually infinite age for the Earth.

Geologists and paleontologists constructed geologic history based on the relative positions of different strata and fossils, estimating the time scales based on studying rates of various kinds of weathering, erosion, sedimentation, and lithification. The ages of various rock strata and the age of the Earth were hotly debated. In 1862, the physicist William Thomson set the age of Earth at between 24 million and 400 million years, assuming that Earth began as a completely molten ball of rock, then calculating how long it took to cool to its present temperature. He did not know of the ongoing heat source from radioactive decay.

Physicists had more prestige, but even then, geologists doubted such a short age for Earth. Biologists could accept that Earth might have a finite age, but even 100 million years seemed much too short for evolution to have yielded such complex plenty. Charles Darwin argued that even 400 million years did not seem long enough.

Until the discovery of radioactivity in 1896, and the development of its geological applications through radiometric dating during the first half of the twentieth century (pioneered by geologists), there were no precise absolute datings of rocks.

Radioactivity introduced another measuring clock. Geologists quickly realized this upset the assumptions used before. They reexamined their estimates. This moved the age into the billions (thousands of millions) of years, sweeping away Bishop Ussher's dating of creation to 4004 BC. Ussher supposed that the Old Testament was the prelude to the New, and that the Biblical chronology therefore prefigured Christ. Matching Biblical events to historical ones, he found his 4004 BC date.

Much public ferment paralleled this scientific research and its clash with religion. By the early twentieth century, opinion settled on an Earth older than a billion years.

Physics, meanwhile, was making hash of the simple view of time that underlay the other sciences. Geology, biology and astronomy would have been happy with Newtonian time, giving them a simple marker of change. The physicists, though, worried about more basic matters.

Relative Time

In physics, time is, like length, mass, and charge, a fundamental quantity—intuitive, given by our basic perceptions. Newton used this view, holding that "I do not define time, space, place and motion, as being well known to all."—that is, obvious. But Einstein showed that it was not.

Nineteenth century physicists felt that space was the most basic and irreducible of all things. It persisted while time changed, and points made up space—infinitesimal grains close-packed. Einstein's fundamental insight was that space and time, which appear so different to us, are in fact linked. He argued this using *gedanken* (thought) experiments involving rulers and clocks. These were not just instruments to Einstein; he took them to generate space and time, since they represent it.

He took two basic assumptions. First, the speed of light seems the same to everyone in the universe, whether moving or buried deep in a gravitational well. This may strike us as odd, but an earlier experiment had found it to be so. Not that Einstein cared; his intuition led him to the conclusion. He proved it valid by using the even deeper second assumption: that the laws of physics had to treat all states of motion on the same footing.

Combining these two assumptions generates the equations of his special theory of relativity. It has astonishing consequences. Moving objects experience a slower passage of time. This is known as time dilation. These transformations are only valid for two frames at *constant* relative velocity. Naively applying them to other situations gives rise to such puzzles as the famous twin paradox. (As an identical twin, I found this a fascinating entry into physics, and thus my career.)

This is a thought experiment in special relativity, in which a twin makes a journey into space in a fast rocket, returning home to find he has aged less than his identical twin, who stayed on Earth. This result appears puzzling because the laws of physics should exhibit symmetry. Since either twin sees the other twin as traveling, each should see the other aging more slowly. How can an absolute effect (one twin really does age less) come from a relative motion? Hence it is called a "paradox."

But there is no paradox, because there is no symmetry. Only one twin accelerates and decelerates, so this differentiates the two cases. Since we each experience minor accelerations, whether on horseback or in a jet plane, we each carry around our own personal scale of time. These are undetectable in ordinary life, but real.

When time stretches, space shrinks. When you rush to catch an airplane, the wall clock you see runs a tiny bit slower than your wristwatch. Compensating, the distance to the airplane's gate looks closer to you. Time is pricey, though—a second time distance translates to 300,000 kilometers.

The stretching of space and time occurs because they are wired together. More fundamentally, Einstein's work implied that time runs slower the stronger the gravitational field (and hence the observer's local acceleration). His general relativity theory sees gravity not as a force but as a distortion of space-time.

The rates of clocks on Earth then depend on whether they are on a mountain or in a valley; the valley clock runs slower. This is somewhat like the slowing of clocks as they move past us at high velocity. This gravitational effect is unlike that of the smoothly moving observers on, say, two trains moving by each other, each of whom thinks the other's clock runs slowly. In a gravitational field, the clocks experience different accelerations if they are not at the same altitude. But observers both in the valley and on the mountain agree that the mountain clock runs faster. Experiments checked these results and found complete agreement. Further, particle acceleration experiments and cosmic ray evidence confirmed the predictions of time dilation, where moving particles decay slower than their less energetic counterparts. Gravitational time changes give rise to the phenomenon of gravitational redshift, which means that light loses energy as it rises against gravity. There are also well documented delays in signal travel time near massive objects like the sun. Today, the Global Positioning System must adjust signals to account for this effect, so the theory has even practical effects.

In empty space, the shortest distance between two points is a straight line. In space-time, this is called a "world line" that forms the shortest curve between two events. If gravitation curves a space-time, then the straight line becomes a curve, which is the shortest space-time distance between two points. That curvature we see as the curve of a ball when thrown into the distance, a parabola.

This linked with a radical view, pushed by Hermann Minkowski, that neither space nor time are truly fundamental. In relativity, both are mere shadows, and only a union of the two exists in the underlying reality. Minkowski had called Einstein a "lazy dog" when Einstein was his student. But while reading Einstein's first paper on relativity, he had a brilliant idea, and so laid the foundations for the next great insight. Minkowski's invention was space-time, a joint entity. Einstein later used his intuition to propose that mass curves space-time, and we sense this curvature as gravity.

The fundamental idea of space-time played out in many ways. Time runs faster in space than on a star, because gravity warps space-time. This leads to timewarps that can become severe, when a star implodes and time grinds to a halt. Any star a few times larger than our own can do this, capturing its own light and plunging into an infinitesimal speck we call a black hole. Its gravitation remains with us, though, a timewarp imprinted on empty space. Anyone falling along with the star will see the external world pass through all of eternity, while gravity pulls him into a spaghetti strand. The singularity where all ends up is a "nowhen" and "nowhere," signifying that the physical universe as we understand it ceases.

Einstein's singular geometric and kinematic intuition motivated his theory. He assumed that every point in the universe can be treated as a "center," whether it is deep in a gravitational well (such as where we live) or in empty space, far from curvatures in space-time induced by gravity. Correspondingly, he reasoned, physics must act the same in all reference frames. This simple and elegant assumption led, after much labor, to a theory showing that time is relative to both where you are and how you are moving. Newton's laws hold well enough in a particular local geometry. They work in different circumstances, though they must be modified for the environment. Still, this fact can be expressed in the theory itself.

This leads to the principle that there is no "universal clock." To get things right, we must perform some act of synchronization between two systems, at the very least.

There is another victim of his intuition. Not only is there not a universal present moment, but also there is no simple division between past, present and future in general—that is, everywhere in the universe. Locally they do mean something, but not necessarily to those far from us, in a universe that continually expands.

Though you and I on Earth may agree about what "now" means on the nearest star, Proxima Centauri, an astronaut moving quickly through the solar system who asks this same question when we do will refer to a different moment on Proxima Centauri.

Does this mean that only the present moment "really" exists? But one person's past can be another's future, so past, present and future must exist in a physical sense, and so be equally real.

Einstein said of the death of an old friend, within months of his own death, "Now he has departed from this strange world a little ahead of me. That means nothing. People like us, who believe in physics, know that the distinction between past, present, and future is only a stubbornly persistent illusion."

In physics, time is not a sequence of happenings, but a chain that is just there, embedded in space-time. Our lives move along that chain, like a train on a track. Observers differ over whether a given event occurs at a particular time, but there is no universal "now." Instead, an event belongs to a multitude of "nows," depending on others' states of motion or position. Time stretches away into past and future, as we see them, just as space extends away from any place. This is the interwoven thing we call space-time, and it is more fundamental than our particular sense of our local world.

Even more odd possibilities come from these ideas. General relativity allows time travel of a sort, in special circumstances. These may be disallowed by a more fundamental theory, but for now, some puzzling paradoxes emerge from our understanding of time. Presumably events may not happen before their cause, but proving this in general has so far eluded us.

Time's Mmentum

Time goes, you say? Ah no!
Alas, time stays, we go.
—HENRY DOBSON

Why do we think that time moves, instead of the fixed, eternal space-time that theory suggests? Because evolution has not selected us to see it that way. Time's flow is a simple way to order the world effectively; that does not mean it is fundamental. Space-time is simple and elegant, but that does not mean it plays well in the rough scramble of life. During a seminar at Princeton University, Einstein remarked that the laws of physics should be simple. Someone asked, "What if they aren't?" Einstein replied that if so, he was not interested in them.

Yet simplicity may not be the best way to regard time. Time seems to flow because that flow is a holistic concept, not reducible to simple systems like a collision of atoms. In this sense, the paradox of time's flow is an aspect of our minds. We can see time as moving, bringing events to us, or the reverse: we flow through time, sensing a moving moment.

This interlaces with the findings of Sadi Carnot in 1824, when he carefully analyzed the steam engines with his Carnot cycle, an abstract model of how an engine works. He and Rudolf Clausius noted that disorder, or entropy, steadily increases as machines operate. This means the amount of "free energy'" available continually decreases.

This is the second law of thermodynamics. The continual march of time then defines an arrow of time, defined by the growth of entropy. It is easy enough to observe the arrow by mixing a little milk into your coffee. Try as you might, you can't reverse it. In the nineteenth century, entropy's increase took its place beside other definitions of time's momentum. Another definition is the psychological arrow of time, whereby we see an inexorable flow, dominating our intuitions. The third view, a cosmological arrow of time, emerged when we discovered the expansion of the universe in the twentieth century.

This dramatic time asymmetry seems to offer a clue to something deeper, hinting at the ultimate workings of space-time. For example, suppose gravity acts on matter—what is the maximum entropy nature can pack into a volume? There is a

clean answer: a black hole. In the 1970s Stephen Hawking of Cambridge University, holding the chair Newton had, showed that black holes fit neatly into the second law. Originally the second law described hot objects like steam engines. Applied to black holes, that can also emit radiation and have entropy, the second law shows that a three-million-solar-mass black hole, such as the one at the center of our galaxy, has a hundred times the entropy of all the ordinary particles in the observable universe. This is astonishing. Collapsed objects are giant repositories of disorder, and thus sinks of the productions of time itself.

These ideas spread throughout science, with varying results. Entropy inevitably increases in thermodynamics, but that seems to fly in the face of our own world, which flourishes with new life forms and increasing order. In contrast to the physical view of time, biologists pointed out that life depends on a "negative entropy flow" which is local, driven by a larger decrease elsewhere. For us, this "elsewhere" is the sun, which supports our entire natural world. The sun will expand and engulf the Earth in about 5 billion years. By then we may have a fix for that problem, if we are still around as humans. But eventually all stars will themselves die out, having burned their core fuels. This will take several tens of billions of years more, and thereafter the universe will indeed cool and entropy will rise throughout.

Increasing entropy implies a "heat death" as our universe expands. This means the end of time will be cold and dark.

So biological systems do not refute the arrow of time; they define it well during our present, early state of the universe. These realizations ran in parallel through the nineteenth and twentieth century, promoting fruitful scientific dialogue.

Deep Time Revisited

The human perception of time has ramified through many sciences. Such fundamental changes in a basic view always echo through culture.

The enormous expansion of our perceptions of time has altered the way we think of ourselves, framed in nature. Paleontologists track the extinction of whole genera, and in the random progressions of evolution feel the pace of change that looks beyond the level of mere species such as ours. Geologists had told them of vast spans of time, but even that did not seem to be enough to generate the order we see on Earth.

The Darwin-Wallace theory explains our Earthly order as arising from evolution through natural selection. As perhaps the greatest intellectual event of the nineteenth century, it invokes cumulative changes that add up. The fossil record showed that mammals, for example, take millions of decades to alter. Our own evolution has tuned our sense of probabilities to work within a narrow lifetime, blinding us to the slow sway of long biological time. (And to the fundamental physical space-time, as we discussed.)

This may well be why the theory of evolution came so recently, in an era when our horizons were already quickly expanding; it conjures up spans of time far beyond our intuition. On the creative scale of the great, slow, and blunt Darwinnowings such as we see in the fossil record, no human monument can sustain. But our neophyte primate species can now bring extinction to many, and no matter what the clock, extinction is forever. We live in hurrying times.

Yet we dwell among contrasts between our intuitions and the timescape of the sciences. In their careers, astronomers discern the grand gyre of worlds. But planning, building, flying and analyzing a single mission to the outer solar system commands the better part of a professional life. Future technologies beyond the chemical rocket may change this, but there are vaster spaces beckoning beyond which can still consume a career. A mission scientist invests the kernel of his most productive life in a single gesture toward the infinite.

Those who study stars blithely discuss stellar lifetimes encompassing billions of years. In measuring the phases of stellar mortality they employ the many examples, young and old, that hang in the sky. We see suns in snapshot, a tiny sliver of their grand and gravid lives caught in our telescopes. Cosmologists peer at distant galaxies whose light is reddened by the universal expansion, and see them as they were before Earth existed. Observers measure the microwave emission that is relic radiation from the earliest detectable signal of the universe's hot birth. Studying this energetic emergence of all that we can know surely imbues (and perhaps afflicts) astronomers with a perception of how like mayflies we are.

No human enterprise can stand well in the glare of such wild perspectives. Perhaps this is why for some, science comes freighted with coldness, a foreboding implication that we are truly tiny and insignificant on the scale of such eternities. Yet as a species we are young, and promise much. We may yet come to be true denizens of deep time.

Cosmological Time

Through the twentieth century's developing understanding of stellar evolution, astronomy outpaced even the growing expanses of biological time by dating the age of stars. These lifetimes were several billion years, a fact some found alarming. In the mid-twentieth century, some globular clusters of stars even seemed to be older than the universe, a puzzle that better measurement resolved.

But a still grander canvas awaited. Perhaps the most fundamental aspect of time lies in our description of how it all began, along with the universe itself: cosmology.

There were many "origin stories" of earlier cultures, but these gave little thought to how the universe came to be, beyond simple stories. Ancient times, until the nineteenth century, preferred eternity to process. As the Bhagavad Gita says, "There never was a time when I was not…there will never be a time when I will cease to be." Since time and space began together—as both St. Augustine and the Big Bang attest—the Bhagavad Gita has a point. The chicken and the egg arrived at the same time.

Yet Newton thought that the universe had to be eternally tuned by God's hand, or else gravitation would cause it to collapse. This view held fairly well until a new theory of gravity and time arrived.

When Einstein developed his theory of general relativity in 1915, physicists believed in a perfectly static universe without beginning or end, like Newton. Though he had a theory of curved space-time, and so could consider all the universe, Einstein inherited this bias. He attempted the first true cosmology—that is, a complete description of the universe's lifetime, from simple assumptions—under the influence of the ancients.

To make his early equations describe a universe unchanging in time, he added a cosmological constant to his theory to enforce a static universe. It had matter in it, which he knew meant that gravitation favored collapse—but he demanded that it be a time-independent, eternal universe. Analysis soon showed that Einstein's static universe is unstable. A small ripple in space-time or in the mass it contained would make the universe either expand or contract. Einstein had brought his own concepts of time to the issue, and so missed predicting the expanding universe. Soon enough, astronomers' observations showed that our universe is expanding from an earlier, smaller event. After this era, cosmological ideas of time moved beyond him.

Modern cosmology developed along parallel observational and theoretical tracks in the twentieth century. Correct cosmological solutions of general relativity emerged, and astronomers found that distant galaxies were apparently moving away from us. This comes from the expansion of space-time itself, not because we are uniquely abhorrent. Tracking this expansion backward gave a time when space-time approached zero. St. Augustine had proposed that God made both space and time, and the Big Bang told us when that was.

Through the twentieth century, observations of how fast distant galaxies seemed to rush away from us have pushed the age of the universe back to the currently accepted number of 13.7 billion years. By then relativity had altered and even negated our understanding of Intuitive Time, so cosmology's enormous extension of Deep Time only added to the startling changes.

Now astronomers observe that the universal expansion is accelerating, perhaps because of the unknown effects represented by Einstein's added cosmological constant. We now seem to occupy an unusual niche in the long history of this universe, living beyond the early, hot era, yet well before the accelerating expansion will isolate galaxies from each other, then stars, and finally may wrench apart all of matter as space-time stretches ever-faster. Time seems then like a judge, not a mere clock.

The essential dilemmas of being human—the contrast between the stellar near-immortalities we see in our night sky, and our own all-too-soon, solitary extinctions—are now even more dramatically the stuff of everyday experience. We now know what a small sliver we inhabit in the long parade of our universe. Who can glimpse these perspectives and not reflect on our mortality? We are mayflies. Yet we now know enough of time and our place in it to reflect upon truly immense issues.

Time is a fundamental, its nature slowly glimpsed. After all this time, we do not fully understand it.

Here on the level sand
Between the sea and land,
What shall I build or write
Against the fall of night?

—A.E. HOUSMAN

APPRECIATION

by Andrea Stewart

I first met Mike at the Writers of the Future workshop. He would hang out at the bar late at night, entertaining questions from us baby writers, telling us stories about his peers and the history of science fiction. I was honestly a little terrified, so I didn't say much. I still didn't feel like I belonged. He was a little out-of-touch (I say this fondly as I suspect aging does this to us all), but kind, genial, and blustery. I'd not known my grandparents well, and Mike felt like what I imagined a grandfather to be.

I got to know him better after I started submitting stories to Galaxy's Edge. *He published everything I sent, and I always did my best to only send things I thought were top quality. Through our chats, I learned about his love of musicals, yet his disdain for* Les Misérables. *When I told him about the musicals I liked, he was kind enough to send me copies of recordings he'd collected of various stage productions. He teased me often about my missing ears since my hairstyle covered them. I* laughed with other writers about Mike's penchant for adding exclamation marks to the stories he edited (though I feel a few of those were definitely warranted!).

I remember when my first book on submission failed to sell. As a newly agented writer with a book I believed in, it was a hard blow. I wasn't quite sure what to do with it or myself. I asked Mike for advice, and he gave me the best advice: to set it aside for now, to focus on something else. I could always possibly sell it later. I didn't, but I was later glad I put it aside.

And that's how Mike was: quick with advice, welcoming, a little bit silly, discerning, opinionated, eager to pay it forward. I know I wasn't the only new writer he bolstered, supported, and helped. And when you're still learning the ropes, when you're wobbly and unsure, that sort of thing means the world. It certainly meant so to me. When you're new to the industry, you feel like you're not a real writer yet, like your stories don't yet matter. Mike made so many people feel like they mattered, like their stories mattered.

I wish I'd known how sick he was. I wish I'd dropped one last line to him. I suppose that's the way that grief is: there is never enough time to say the things you want to.

So I'll say this: thank you, Writer Dad, for being a listening ear. Thank you for being so generous with your time and advice. I hope I've made you proud, and I hope I can continue to live up to your belief in me.

And I swear, for the last time, I really do have ears.

APPRECIATION

by Alex Shvartsman

Mike was a larger-than-life character, someone seemingly more likely to inhabit the pages of a book than to be writing one. Over the course of his life he bred dogs and edited men's magazines for a living; traveled numerous times to Kenya on safari and attended several lifetimes' worth of science fiction conventions.

Enormously generous with his time, advice, and praise, he was the embodiment of pay-it-forward. Dozens of us younger writers unironically and proudly call ourselves his Writer Children. Mike advocated for newer writers by sharing his wisdom and opportunities, mentoring, judging awards and teaching at workshops. He published so many new voices right here, on the pages of Galaxy's Edge. He was equally helpful to new editors and anthologists, always happy to contribute a reprint from his enormous back catalog to a fledgling project, or even write a brand-new tale.

Mike was a natural-born storyteller. Not only in his books, but also in person, always surrounded by eager listeners at conventions. He knew and met just about everyone and had a story to tell about that person—and those stories were never mean-spirited or negative. He had a way of humanizing the people he spoke about, just like his fictional characters. On social media he would write about his passions, making those of us who have never attended a derby care about which horse was going to be the favorite; convincing those who are disinterested in football to share his joy at the occasional victory by his beloved Cincinnati Bengals.

He didn't watch much TV except for an occasional sporting event, but was an avid reader. Due to his poor eyesight he became an early adopter of ebooks, and even went as far as to have a service scan in and convert titles that weren't available in electronic format.

All his numerous interests were superseded by writing. When not traveling to conventions, he kept unorthodox hours, sleeping during the day and writing all night long, when the world around him was quiet. There was a certain type of mechanical keyboard he especially liked. When they were discontinued, he bought a box full and kept them in his closet so he would never have to risk running out.

To me he was a friend and a mentor, and I'm still processing his loss. Somehow, the mental image of those keyboards he never got the chance to wear out really punches me in the gut.

But then I remember his easy-going personality and his wit, and I feel better. I'm convinced that Mike wouldn't want us to be sad. Instead, he'd like for us to share stories about him, to smile remembering the moments of humor and camaraderie we've shared with him and—through him—with each other.

Robert J. Sawyer's twenty-fourth novel, The Oppenheimer Alternative, *will be published in June 2020 by CAEZIK Books, the new imprint of the company that also publishes this magazine. Rob holds two honorary doctorates and is a Member of the Order of Canada, the highest civilian honor bestowed by the Canadian government. Find him online at sfwriter.com.*

DECOHERENCE

by Robert J. Sawyer

THE PROBLEM WITH THREE BODIES

My friend Cixin Liu made honest-to-God front-page newspaper headlines in China in 2015 when the English translation of his 2006 novel *The Three-Body Problem* won the Hugo Award. During one of my six (so far!) visits to China, I was asked on stage about the notion of "the dark forest," which is central to *Three Body* and its sequels.

The idea is simple: given the likely vast differences in technology and psychology between any two previously unacquainted planetary civilizations, the best thing any world can do for its own survival is stay hidden. As far as SETI is concerned, neither a listener nor a sender be; keep quiet and hope no one ever discovers that you exist.

I can't remember if Cixin was present at that particular event, or whether he's simply been relying on a second-hand account, but he's repeatedly said the following, including on Tor.com:

Not long ago, Canadian writer Robert Sawyer came to China, and when he discussed Three Body, *he attributed my choice of the worst of all possible universes to the historical experience of China and the Chinese people. As a Canadian, he argued that he had an optimistic view of the future relationship between humans and extraterrestrials. I don't agree with this analysis.*

Well, that's not actually what I said—something got lost in the translation, I'm sure. I opined that a view of the universe in which alien beings are best avoided was derived from what happened in the Ming Dynasty during the 1400s, when China had, by far, the world's greatest fleet of sailing vessels. But in 1433, the Yongle Emperor decided to destroy his Treasure Fleet, either—depending on which source you believe—by setting fire to the boats in the harbor or by allowing them to rot there. China turned its back on the world and left the seas wide open for European explorations and depredations.

Cixin went on to say:

But if one were to evaluate the place of Earth civilization in this universe, humanity seems far closer to the indigenous peoples of the Canadian territories before the arrival of European colonists than the Canada of the present. More than five hundred years ago, hundreds of distinct peoples speaking languages representing more than ten language families populated the land from Newfoundland to Vancouver Island. Their experience with contact with an alien civilization seems far closer to the portrayal in Three Body.

It's an interesting comment, and I don't deny the parallel. But my positive Canadian approach to aliens is rooted in our *present* reality of being physically bigger than the People's Republic and yet having only thirty-five million people. (The entire population of Canada is lost within a five-percent margin-of-error in the Chinese census figure of 1.4 billion residents.)

Canada's openness to outsiders comes in part from the fact that our government's economic studies have shown that we have to pretty much double our population this century if we have any hope of maintaining our social safety net and high standard of living, and since Canadians are breeding at less than replacement rate, almost all of that growth will have to come from immigration. We welcome newcomers from all over with open arms—but we do it, in part and in stark contrast to Liu's contention, as a matter of our own survival.

To make my point another way, one could also compare a country, like China, that historically built the longest wall in human history (and still has among the harshest and most-difficult visa requirements of any nation) to a country, like mine, which shares the longest undefended border in the world with a much more powerful neighbor.

Although in his comments quoted above, Cixin denied the influence Chinese history had on his perspective, he actually embraces the notion in his afterward to the English edition of *The Three-Body Problem*:

"But I cannot escape and leave behind reality, just like I cannot leave behind my shadow. Reality brands each of us with its indelible mark. Every era puts invisible shackles on those who have lived through it, and I can only dance in my chains."

Yes, indeed—for him, me, and everyone else. As I've often said, no matter when it's putatively set, all science fiction is really about the present in which it was written—and, of course, that present is shaped by its past.

However, in that same afterword, Cixin also wrote:

"I do not use my fiction as a disguised way to criticize the reality of the present. I feel that the greatest appeal of science fiction is the creation of numerous imaginary worlds outside of reality."

If this were true, it would put him at odds with the tradition of Mary Shelley and H.G. Wells and so much of the work that turned western science fiction from just pulp entertainment into literature. But, with all due respect to my friend, I don't think it *is* true. *The Three-Body Problem* brims with ruminations on China's Cultural Revolution, on its legacy, on the moral responsibility of the scientist, and on the virtues and weaknesses of various modes of government. I quote from Ken Liu's English translation of the novel, as a "Trisolaran" native of Alpha Centauri is speaking to his leader:

"To permit the survival of the civilization as a whole [on Trisolaris], there is almost no respect for the individual. Someone who can no longer work is put to death. Trisolaran society exists under a state of extreme authoritarianism. The law has only two outcomes: The guilty are put to death, and the not guilty are released."

The leader, known as the Princeps, replies:

"The kind of civilization you yearn for once existed on Trisolaris, too. They had free, democratic societies, and they left behind rich cultural legacies. You know barely anything about them. Most details have been sealed away and forbidden from view. But in all the cycles of Trisolaran civilization, this type of civilization was the weakest and most short-lived."

To which one might quip, in the vernacular of Western youth, "China much?" Indeed, as if to drive the earthly parallels home, at no point in his entire *Remembrance of Earth's Past* series, of which *Three Body* is the first volume, does Cixin Liu tell us what the Trisolarans look like; the narrator actively invites us to fill in mental images of human beings instead.

But it's all good: science fiction is history extrapolated into the future and, as we broaden our horizons and seek diversity, we all gain from those who draw on their own history to tell their futuristic tales—whether they realize they're doing that or not.

Copyright © 2020 by Robert J. Sawyer.

119

APPRECIATION

by Kay Kenyon

I first met Mike in 1997 at LoneStarCon. We were at a terrific outdoor publisher's party (back when they went all-out for such things) and we ended up eating barbecue at the same picnic table. A few months earlier he'd given me a great blurb for my first book and I could hardly wait to engage him in a long, meaningful discussion of its merits. Mike said, "Yup, I liked it a lot. I read every other page." I was taken aback. He hadn't read the whole thing? He was just giving me a boost?

You can see where this is going. New author, full of herself and leading with her chin, wishes to dine on praise. I managed to enjoy the party anyway, but I wasn't sure about Mike. Little did I know, he had at that moment embarked on a small project to help me navigate the world of publishing. So maybe he didn't see me as a project. Maybe he was just responding with his usual contagious, and always respectful, humor.

It turned out that Mike did like my writing. He'd said as much at that con in Texas, and what I didn't understand at the time was that he meant it. That was the opening volley of a couple of decades of Mike coaching me on the general theme of: it's never as good or as bad as you think it's going to be. He taught me to hang in there. My fellow writers, you know that is a key to the universe.

I wasn't the only writer for whom he was a mentor and champion. But at first hand I knew his generosity of spirit, to lend a hand, put in a good word, take a panicked phone call, and steer me to a chair in the con hotel lobby to find out what I was working on and if I was going to stay up late enough to go to the parties where he would introduce me to people who could buy my work.

He could never figure out why I traveled to cons regularly and then went to bed early. Being a morning person, I never took advantage of the self-evident fact that most business is done after 10:00 PM in the bar. And that the last thing before sleep, there is always time to write a short story.

I never met anyone like him, nor anyone who could better deliver emotional impact in a story. Thinking back to that picnic table encounter, I hear myself responding to him: "Right, so which page was your favorite?"

You know someone has deeply touched your life when, after they're gone, you keep talking to them.

Serialization of Chalker's *Midnight at the Well of Souls* will continue with issue 44

CLOSING NOTE

by Carol Resnick

The love of my life is dead but remember him not in sorrow but with joy. It was the way he lived. Nothing pleased or entertained him more than science fiction—the community, the literature, the fans, the conventions—the whole SF world. He was a happy and fulfilled man and an extraordinary human being. What more is there to say.

Printed in Great Britain
by Amazon

36367313R00072